D1260825

This book is for my dad and for everyone who helped bring him home safely to his grandchildren.

To my husband and my brother-in-law, for the last minute flights, the late night messages, and the shoulders to lean on.

To my family in India and the US, for their attentive care and guidance.

To the doctors and staff at HCG Hospital, most especially to Dr. B.G. for her dedication and patience.

Also By Shail Rajan

The Summer Breeze Bed & Breakfast
(book 1 in The Summer Breeze Series)

The Recipient

Contents

A Spring Wedding

Callie awoke with a start, worried she had overslept her alarm. But the early morning spring sunlight gently peeking around her curtains offered her reassurance that she was ahead of schedule, just as she preferred it. Turning towards the beautiful dress hanging on the back of her closet door, she smiled with anticipation at the reaction it would draw from Nick. He had never seen it before, but she was certain it would become his new favorite.

Taking a deep breath, Callie sat up in bed and did her morning stretching routine, a series of flowing yoga movements meant to get her body ready for the day and improve her mood. Not that her mood needed improving, Callie acknowledged, but her body certainly did. The combination of delicious meals and decadent desserts served by the bed and breakfast's chef extraordinaire Tiny and the often-harsh upstate New York winter weather which kept her inside, had left her feeling sluggish and unhealthy. When she couldn't button her favorite pair of jeans by late February, Callie had been forced to make some serious fitness decisions. After a few lengthy conversations with her family, Callie had decided to convert a portion of the garage which was not being used for The Summer Breeze spa into a small gym her guests could also use. Kirsten, one of her dearest friends and the massage therapist turned co-owner of the spa, had readily agreed to the plan.

The decision had ended up being a good marketing move and helped Callie slowly get back into shape. She was certainly not as painfully thin as she had been back when she lived in New York City, but that had never been her goal. No, Callie thought to herself as she looked at the dress one more time. Her goal had been to fill out that dress perfectly. And to sweep Nick off *his* feet for a change.

Swinging her legs over the edge of her bed and sliding her feet into her soft, fuzzy slippers, Callie stood up and shuffled to the window of her private first floor suite. Pulling open the curtains, she heard the distant sounds of a truck slowly making its way up the long, winding driveway lined with oak trees to The Summer Breeze Bed and Breakfast. As it came into view, Callie was pleased to see that it was the party rental company.

Right on schedule, just as she liked. It would take several hours to set up the tent, which would give Tiny, Grace, and her dad, a veritable food lover's dream team, enough time to prep the elaborate menu they had planned.

As if on cue, Grace's brand new eco-friendly compact car pulled into the driveway and the passenger side door flew open before the car had even come to a complete stop. Callie laughed aloud when she realized Grace had finally convinced Tiny to take a ride with her. The car seemed to heave a sigh of relief as the gentle giant slowly extricated himself from its confines. As she watched her friend walk over to open the driver side door, Callie could almost picture the slow blush spreading across Grace's cheeks when she took the hand being held out to her. The porcelain skinned petite redhead, who looked even smaller when standing next to one of the largest men in Seneca Springs, tilted her head back to look up at Tiny and said something which made him smile. As they walked towards the back entrance, Callie wondered for the hundredth time if they would ever become more than just friends.

The sudden buzzing of her old-fashioned alarm clock jarred Callie out of her contemplative mood and into action. It would be no good, she thought to herself, if she was late to a celebration in her own backyard.

"About time," Tiny snapped as Callie walked into The Summer Breeze kitchen wearing her favorite pair of grey sweatpants and an oversized sweatshirt emblazoned with the name of her alma mater. "Nice outfit," he added sarcastically.

"Good morning to you, too. Coffee ready?"

"Yes, ma'am. And we picked up some pastries from my mom's bakery on our way over."

"What would I do without you," Callie asked as she poured herself a steaming cup of coffee and looked through the box of flakey, buttery goodness sitting on the large, rustic kitchen table. The early morning sunlight that poured into the kitchen danced off the glassware stacked along the open shelves and shone off the spotless professional grade stainless steel appliances, without a doubt the jewel in the crown of The Summer Breeze kitchen.

"I ask myself that same question every day."

Callie took a sip of her coffee and chose, against her better judgement, an apple fritter that was the size of her outstretched hand. "Where's Grace?"

"Across the street at Lynette's. Something about looking at each other's dresses. Who knows." Tiny shrugged his enormous shoulders.

"Wow, you're in a pleasant mood," Callie mumbled.

"I just don't understand why weddings make women so crazy. And you know what else I don't understand?"

"Enlighten me," Callie managed through a mouthful of the warm apple cinnamon goodness that she so relished.

"Why did she have to buy that ridiculously small car and then guilt me into riding in it?"

Callie rolled her eyes and took another bite of her fritter.

"Are you going to sit there all day eating fritters or are you planning on actually doing anything useful?"

"Stop yelling at your boss, Tiny," Lynette, the no-nonsense manager of the inn and one of Callie's best friends, said as she walked into the kitchen followed by Grace.

"He's just in a bad mood because I made him ride in my car."

"Well, he'd better get himself in a good mood or he's going to ruin the food. You know everything he makes tastes better when he's happy."

"You know what puts me in a good mood?" Grace asked.

"Weddings," the three women said in unison.

Which, unfortunately, did nothing to improve Tiny's mood.

Tiny wiped the sweat off his face with the end of his apron and sat down dejectedly as Callie handed him a glass of cold water.

"You have got to calm down," she commanded.

"I cannot believe that I let the bechamel break. I have literally made it a hundred times, and it's never broken."

"What is that smell? Is something burning?" Callie's younger sister Nica asked as she walked into the kitchen. The two siblings were so similar, they were often mistaken for twins. These days, though, there was one big difference between the two. A difference that was due to arrive in a few months.

"Tiny broke the bechamel sauce. Where's everyone else?"

Ignoring her sister's question, Nica sat down and began examining the contents of the pastry box. She practically squealed with childish delight when she found her favorite, an oversized blueberry muffin.

"I can't even tell you how much I would pay to drink an entire cup of coffee with this muffin," she said before taking a huge bite and closing her eyes in ecstasy.

"Did you skip breakfast this morning?" Callie asked, mildly alarmed, and simultaneously entertained by her sister's obvious culinary pleasure.

"That was almost two hours ago!" Nica said, feigning offence as she took another bite. "This baby is always hungry!"

Callie laughed and gently patted Nica's baby bump.

"Mom, Dad, and Jack are unloading the car. They should be here any minute." Nica said, answering Callie's earlier question. She took another bite of her muffin, licked her fingers, and then scrunched up her nose in disgust. "That smell is awful. Can you open a window or something?"

Tiny groaned aloud and put his head in his hands. "Maybe someone else should make the bechamel, Callie."

Callie squinted her eyes at Tiny, wondering what had her usually unflappable chef in such a bad mood. She was about to ask him when Lynette walked into the kitchen with a strange expression on her face.

"Callie, can I speak to you for a moment? We've got a little problem. You'll have to come out to the front desk." Without any further explanation, she turned to leave but then stopped. Looking as though she was trying to suppress her laughter, she added, "What is that awful smell? Is something burning?" And then, she walked out as abruptly as she had entered.

Maybe Tiny was right, Callie thought. Weddings do make women crazy.

—ele—

Callie walked to the foyer and was surprised to find the front desk chair unoccupied. "What is going on?" she asked aloud to no one. The sleek, modern laptop sitting unopened on the small reception table and the waxy, green, heart shaped leaves of the potted pothos provided no hints.

Hearing the faint sound of giggling coming from the living room, Callie walked in to find both Lynette and Grace sitting on one of the sofas looking like they had just heard a very funny joke.

"What on earth is going on?" Callie asked again, unable to hide her frustration. First her chef was having a culinary crisis and now two women who were usually imperturbable were behaving like silly schoolgirls.

"Come sit down, Callie." Lynette, finally suppressing her laughter, patted the seat between her and Grace, and Callie reluctantly joined them.

"I heard Tiny burned the bechamel?" Grace asked, almost gleefully.

Callie just looked at her, dumbfounded.

Lynette started tittering again and clapped her hands. "It smells awful in there, Grace. And you should see Tiny. He's a mess!"

Grace beamed from ear to ear as if Lynette had just informed her that she had won the lottery.

"Have you both lost your minds?" Callie demanded.

"No! Listen, Callie, this is great news. Grace, you explain it to her."

Grace nodded and took a moment to compose herself. "Callie," she said reaching out and taking her friend's hand. "Do you know how I feel about Tiny?" A slow blush started to spread across Grace's cheeks. "About Dominick?"

Callie, feeling the beginnings of a smile spreading across her own face, nodded and grasped Grace's hand tighter in hers, hoping this was going where she wanted.

"I'm pretty sure he feels the same way about me, but I had to be certain. I wouldn't want to do anything to ruin our friendship or my relationship with Bertha and Hank. They're like family to me. So, I came up with a simple little plan."

Lynette started chuckling again and said, "Which is why Tiny burned the bechamel."

"When we were driving over here this morning, I told Dominick I was bringing a date to the wedding. I know how much his mood effects his cooking, and I wanted to see how he would react. If he cooked as beautifully as he always does, I'd know he only thought of me as a friend. But...."

"If he ruins the food, it's because he has feelings for you, too!" Callie finished Grace's sentence, now feeling strangely overjoyed that Tiny had indeed burned the bechamel.

"Exactly!"

"Oh, Grace! I'm so happy for you!" Callie gave Grace a hug and laughed. "I never thought I'd be so happy about a ruined main course!"

As this last sentence sank in, the laughter died down and the three friends looked at one another.

"I'd better go tell Dominick," Grace said hurrying out of the room.

—ell—

"Taste this," Tiny said holding out a small spoon.

Callie tasted the silky-smooth lemon garlic aioli and almost moaned aloud. "As perfect as the bechamel."

"Right?" Tiny asked rhetorically.

Callie smiled, "I'm glad to see you got your swagger back. Is everything else ready? Dad?"

Callie's dad, who had been busy decorating a stunning three-tiered cake layered with a decadent chocolate sponge and a light, tangy raspberry jam looked up and nodded. "It is now."

"Should we run through the menu one last time?" Callie asked grabbing the handwritten menu that had been taped to the refrigerator.

"You're the boss."

"Lasagna?"

"Four large casserole dishes keeping warm in the oven. With perfect bechamel if I do say so myself."

"Salad?"

"Prepped and ready to be tossed with the dressing you made earlier today."

"The charcuterie boards?"

"Like works of art. We had to put them in the dining room to keep Nica from eating everything. I'll go grab one to show you."

"Where is she, by the way?"

"Taking a nap, thank goodness. Your father has been having a hard time keeping up with her appetite!" Callie's mom said as she put the finishing touches on a floral centerpiece. The soft white of the ranunculus and the multihued colors of the sweet pea flowers made for a bright, cheerful display perfect for the occasion.

"Voila!" Callie's dad proudly announced as he returned from the dining room balancing a huge charcuterie board with both hands. He placed it on the island, and everyone gathered around to appreciate the beautiful arrangement of assorted cheeses and crackers, and heaping piles of nuts, grapes, figs, and olives. Interspersed throughout were bowls of homemade hummus, tzatziki, and baba ganoush.

"No wonder Nica couldn't control herself. This looks delicious!" Callie ran through the items on the menu one last time and said, "Looks like the only thing that's left is the grilled asparagus."

Tiny nodded. "I want them to stay tender-crisp, so I'll grill them just after the ceremony is done. Speaking of which, what time is Nick getting here? He's cutting it awfully close, isn't he?"

"He's not the only one. We should all probably start getting ready," Grace said.

"You guys go ahead. I just want to check on the arrangements one last time."

"You already checked on them 'one last time'," Lynette said. "And so did I. Everything is ready. You really should get dressed."

"I know, but I just want everything to be perfect."

"Calliopi! That's enough now! Go get ready. Nick will be here any minute." Callie knew that whenever her mother went to the trouble of using her full name, she meant business. Without another word, she did as she was told and went straight to her room.

—ele—

Callie was standing at the entrance to the outdoor tent waiting for the ceremony to begin when she felt the light brush of someone's finger tracing its way from her bare shoulder down to the small of her back.

"Did you do something different to your hair?" Nick whispered into her ear. A shiver ran through Callie's entire body. His closeness and the tone of his voice left her feeling light-headed. Determined to be the one to leave him speechless for a change, Callie suppressed her urge to turn around and throw herself into his arms.

"You're late," she said without turning to face him.

"If I had known what you were going to be wearing, I would have gotten here a lot sooner."

Callie smiled, pleased with herself.

"Have I seen this dress before? What exactly is this color called?"

Slowly, Callie turned towards Nick and was about to say "Eggplant," but her breath caught in her throat, and the word evaporated from her mouth. Nick, dressed in a light grey suit with a dark blue button-down shirt that did amazing things for his eyes, looked nothing short of stunning. His hair had been combed back away from his face to expose his chiseled jawline, and, despite her best intentions, Callie's gaze drifted down to his perfect lips.

"You're staring again."

Hearing the teasing laughter in his voice, Callie forced herself to focus on his eyes, and said the line she had been practicing just in case he managed to get the upper hand.

"You should see what I'm wearing *under* this dress."

She watched as his eyes traveled down the length of her dress and back up to meet her now steady gaze.

"Why don't you show me right now."

Unfortunately for Nick, the bride chose that exact moment to make her appearance.

Cheatuh

"More oatmeal anyone?" Callie asked as she began clearing the table. Her family, all still in their pajamas, were seated at the kitchen table enjoying an unusually late start to their day. Kirsten and Chad's wedding had gone off without a hitch and everyone was savoring the success of the first ever wedding at The Summer Breeze. Her bed and breakfast guests weren't expected to arrive until later that afternoon, so no one was in any rush. They were all perfectly content to linger at the table.

"I couldn't eat another bite," Nica proclaimed, rubbing her belly.

"At least not for another hour," retorted her husband Jack, who was holding a glass of cold orange juice against his forehead. "I'm never drinking again," he groaned.

Callie's dad chuckled. "You didn't drink that much last night. I was surprised you even had a beer. I thought you and Nica had agreed you had to follow all the rules she has to follow because she's pregnant."

"It wasn't my fault. It was Tiny's. He told Nica he wouldn't let her have any lasagna unless she let me have a beer with him. What got into him last night, anyway?"

"Yeah," Nica added, "I never pegged him for a dancer, but he was tearing up that dance floor. He and Grace make a good couple, even with their size difference."

Jack cocked his eyebrow at his wife's bulging stomach but was smart enough to keep his observations to himself.

Callie smiled thinking about the reason for her friend's sudden mood change after the bechamel mishap.

Grace had gone back into the kitchen with Callie and Lynette and artlessly announced that her date for the wedding had cancelled on her at the last minute. And from that moment on, Tiny had practically skipped around the kitchen as he remade the bechamel perfectly and then cooked every other dish like a master. It was so obvious to everyone in the room, and Callie had hoped Tiny would recognize it himself.

"Jack, you look like how I feel," Nick said, coming in through the back door.

Callie had to disagree with Nick. In her opinion, he looked incredible. His combed hair and perfectly tailored suit from the night before had been traded out for a pair of old jeans and a plaid shirt. His hair was messy and tousled and an open invitation to Callie to run her fingers through it.

"Where are you coming from? I didn't hear your car pull in," Callie's mom asked, pouring him a cup of coffee and holding it out to him.

"Thank you," he beamed. "I had to stay at Lynette and James' place last night. Can you believe that? I was supposed to crash at Tiny's dinky little apartment, but he told me I couldn't. Just like that. No explanation. I don't know what's gotten into him."

Callie and her mom both squinted their eyes at Nick.

"Really, Nick? You have no idea what's gotten into him?"

"No. He just said he needed to get Grace home safely and there wasn't enough room in her car for me. Which doesn't make any sense because it's a four door. It would have been a tight fit, but I'm sure they could have fit three of us in there. I know they say two's company but three's a...."

Callie stared steadily at Nick and watched as the realization slowly dawned on him. His eyes widened, and a huge smile lit up his face. "Really? I had no idea. Go, Tiny!"

"You're all clueless," Nica said, annoyed, as she tried to heave herself out of her chair. "Anyone want to go for a short walk? I can't just sit here all day."

She didn't have to ask twice.

"Is that what you're going to be like when you're pregnant?" Nick asked as he and Callie stood on the front porch and waved goodbye to her family.

The unexpected question caught Callie completely off guard, and she turned to face Nick. "What is that supposed to mean?" She tried to keep her tone light and playful but failed miserably. Instead, she heard herself sounding peevish.

Nick looked at her, smiled, and held up his hands. "Easy there, tiger. Just asking a simple question. I think your sister is adorable, and I wanted to know if you're going to be the same way when you're pregnant."

Callie didn't know how to respond, didn't understand why Nick was suddenly asking her about being pregnant when they had only been together for a few months. Technically speaking, anyway. But if you added up the actual days they had spent together since that first night after the now infamous "ice storm of the decade," it would be less than a handful of weekends. It just wasn't feasible for them to spend much more time together than they already did. He was busy with a multimillion-dollar construction project in New York City, and she was busy with the bed and breakfast. While he would have been overjoyed to spend every weekend with her, it was out of the question because she refused to visit him in the city. A topic he had brought up only once before it had been completely shut down by Callie.

"I'm not sure what I'll be like," Callie snapped, feeling increasingly as though she was being backed into a corner. And for reasons she didn't quite understand, she added, "I'm not even sure I want kids." A statement she knew, without a doubt, to be false.

Callie noticed a flicker of hurt flash in Nick's eyes, and she immediately regretted what she had said. "Look, I'm sorry, I don't understand why we're even talking about this. You're only here for another couple of hours. I can think of better ways to spend our time."

"Yeah, you're right."

Grateful for the opportunity to move past the awkward conversation, Callie took Nick's hand and led him back inside the house.

"The Summer Breeze, how can I help you?" Callie asked as she answered the phone later that evening. She was sitting at the front desk trying to finish up some weekly accounting reports, but her mood just wasn't in it. There was a hollowness in her stomach and an unfamiliar feeling of loneliness. The short amount of time she and Nick had had alone after her family had left felt flat and forced. They had both tried to enjoy themselves, but the sting of her comment about not wanting children had left a sense of unease and awkwardness between them. Callie wished she could take it back, but then just as quickly, she wished he had never asked the question in the first place.

"Hello? Hello? I think we may have lost our connection."

"I'm sorry, I'm still here!" Callie forced her attention back to her caller.

"I said we're staying at your place tonight, and I need directions from the thruway," the male voice on the other end of the line asked with barely suppressed annoyance.

"Just take the exit for Seneca Springs and follow Main Street traveling west. If you keep the lake to your right, you'll be heading in the right direction. The fourth street on the right will be Oak Trail which winds up a small hill. We're the sixth house on the right, you'll know it by the barn-shaped mailbox at the end of our driveway."

"Right, right, and another right. Got it." Callie could almost visualize the man rolling his eyes. "Did you get all that," he asked of his travelling companion.

"I'm not deaf," snapped a female voice. "Anyway, at least I know how to follow simple directions, and we know we won't get lost with me driving."

The line suddenly went dead, and Callie stared at her phone dumbly for a moment before placing it on the desk. These were definitely not the kind of guests she was in the mood to deal with tonight.

Logging into her online reservations system, she quickly found two entries for that evening. The first belonged to a mother-daughter duo who had written a personal message in the comments section of their reservations form. They were visiting The Summer Breeze, it said, for a relaxing spa and wine tasting weekend. Thankfully, Kirsten had had the foresight to get a friend who was also a licensed masseuse and aesthetician to cover for her while she was on her honeymoon. Callie didn't think she'd be seeing much of these guests.

And she hoped she wouldn't have to see much of the guests who had just called. Their reservation only contained the required information, including their names. Mr. Badman and Mrs. Badman.

Callie would have found this very funny if she hadn't been in such a foul mood. A mood she didn't think would improve upon the arrival of the Badmans.

⁓

The Sunday night dinner service at The Terrace, the restaurant at the back of The Summer Breeze with spectacular views of Cayuga Lake, was usually in full swing on a beautiful spring evening. But Callie had decided to close the restaurant over the wedding weekend to give Tiny a chance to recover from his catering duties. It was a good thing she had, too, because she imagined he was too busy with Grace to be bothered with working tonight.

Normally, her dinner would consist of a little of whatever Tiny was cooking. But tonight, she was looking forward to leftover lasagna from the day before. She had just taken the piping hot casserole dish out of the oven and placed it on the dining table when the doorbell rang. Callie sighed and walked to the front door reminding herself to be polite to the Badmans.

She opened the door with a flourish and a loud, "Welcome to The Summer Breeze! I'm Callie!"

The couple standing on her doorstep stared at her as though she was from another planet. The man, who appeared to be in his mid-60s, had a receding hairline and a protruding paunch. He had the countenance of someone who had just unknowingly sucked on a lemon. The woman standing next to him had a similarly dour expression. She seemed to be about the same age as her husband and had her thinning hair pulled back in an excessively tight bun. There was something strangely similar about them. Callie had heard that married couples often take on each other's characteristics, but this seemed a little excessive.

Mr. Badman was the first to compose himself. "Good to meet you. We'd like to go straight up to our rooms please."

"Certainly!" Callie said, making way for them to walk into the front hallway. "I'll just get you checked in." She sat down at her desk and pulled up their reservation record on the laptop. "Here we go! I see that you'll be staying with us until Wednesday?" She looked up and smiled at the couple, hoping to elicit some goodwill. Unfortunately, their expressions didn't change at all. They simply stared back at her, clearly wanting to get the formality over so they could retire to their room.

Callie looked back at her computer and squinted at the monitor. "I'm sorry, there must be some mistake. It says here that you have booked two rooms?"

"Well, you don't expect me to sleep in the same bed as him, do you?" the woman snapped, making it sound like Callie had just asked her to curl up with an old, sweaty sock.

Callie, unsure of what to do or say, decided her best bet might be to simply continue staring at her computer. The woman's comment, however, brought an unexpected chuckle from Mr. Badman. Seemingly as surprised by the sound as Callie was, the woman cast a sideways glance at him and then a smile slowly spread across her face.

Grasping at this momentary détente as a chance to get the Badmans out of her hair, Callie grabbed two keys from a locked drawer in her desk and said, "Let me show you to your rooms."

Callie sat back and rested her head on the back of the dining table chair. She couldn't eat another bite. By the time she had rid herself of the Badmans, her lasagna wasn't as piping hot as she had wanted, but it was still indulgent and delicious. Reaching under her sweater, she discreetly unbuttoned the top button of her jeans to give her stomach some room to breathe and then she burst out laughing. This, she thought, is how Nica must feel every day.

As Callie was clearing the table, the doorbell rang again. Thankful that at least these guests were considerate enough not to interrupt her dinner, Callie retraced her steps to the front door and opened it with a genuine smile. "Welcome to The Summer Breeze!"

But the smile quickly evaporated from her face and was replaced by a gaping mouth. In the split second it took for Callie to recognize who one of the women standing in front of her was, she was transported back to that fateful morning in New York.

Callie had gone to her then fiancé David's apartment unannounced to break off their engagement. She had let herself in with the key he had given her only to hear the unexpected sound of conversation. Callie had only seen the woman for a brief moment before David, in his alarm at being caught with another woman, had spilled orange juice all over the beautiful silk robe she had been wearing. *Callie's* beautiful silk robe.

"Callie...I can explain," David had stammered guiltily.

"You ruined my robe!" the woman had whined as she got up from the table and ran toward the bathroom.

"That's *my* robe!" Callie had yelled after her, as if clarifying that point was what she had come to do in the first place.

"Ohhh emmm geeee. This is so aww-kward," squealed the younger of the two women standing on her doorstep, the one whom Callie had recognized. Her thick New York accent and loud, brassy voice sent a shiver down Callie's spine. She turned towards the woman standing next to her and said, "You're not going to buh-lieve this. You remembuh that fancy politician guy I was seeing couplah years ago? I met him at my awfice pahty?" Without waiting for an answer, she continued, "Well, remembuh I told you how he lied about being single? This is...or I guess I should say *was*, his fiancée."

In what seemed like a theme for her evening, Callie wasn't sure what to say or do. On the one hand, she wanted to slam the door in the woman's face for sleeping with her fiancé. On the other, she wanted to thank her for making what could have been a painful breakup a whole lot easier.

Thankfully, the mother-daughter duo was at no loss for words.

"You apawlogize to this lady right now. I want her to know that I did not raise a hussy."

"You don't have to tell me twice." Turning towards Callie, she looked steadily into her eyes, and said, "I am so sawwy for what I put you through. I want you to know that I broke up with that bah-stawd that same day. If I had known he was engaged, I nevuh woulda agreed to see him. And you know what? Maybe I did yous a favor. Once a cheatuh, always a cheatuh. Better you found out before you married him."

Hearing these words, spoken with certain sincerity, Callie felt a weight lift from her shoulders. A weight she hadn't even realized she had been carrying around. Her genuine smile came back unbidden, and she held out her hand. "I'm Callie," she said warmly. "It's a pleasure to meet you. Welcome to The Summer Breeze."

"I'm Michelle and this is my mahm, Lorna. What's that delicious smell? Are you baking lasagna?"

Cheater, Cheaterrrrr!

"Top of the morning to you, lass!" Tiny beamed, holding out a steaming hot cup of coffee for Callie.

"Good morning to you, too!" Callie blew gently on the cup and took a sip of the hot liquid. Smiling, she asked, "Looks like someone woke up on the right side of the bed, today." Taking another sip, Callie added, "I'm just not sure whose bed."

Tiny blushed fiercely and asked, "Is it that obvious?"

Callie laughed at her friend's cluelessness. "It's been that obvious almost since the first time I met you."

"I guess I was just a little slow to the party," Tiny admitted with a smile. "What's left in the fridge? I need to do some menu planning and ordering for the week." He walked over to the refrigerator, opened the door, and gasped aloud. "Callie! Did you eat all the lasagna? There was half a casserole dish left!"

"No!" Callie said, and then added guiltily, "Well, not all of it. Two of the guests who came in last night helped me."

"Were they my size?" Tiny asked incredulously.

"No one is your size."

Tiny rolled his eyes in response. "What time did Nick leave yesterday?" he asked, changing the subject. "I think he was mad at me for ditching him Saturday night. Where'd he end up staying?"

"At Lynette's. She's got plenty of space, so it was fine."

"Did he realize why I ditched him? He's never going to stop teasing me when he finds out. I don't even know what to tell him."

"Don't worry, he already knows. He couldn't figure it out on his own, so we helped explain it to him. We needed charts and graphs, but eventually he got there."

Tiny was about to laugh at Callie's sarcasm when a loud, brash voice called out, "Callie? Where awr you?"

"In the kitchen, Michelle."

"Hi! Good mawhning!" Michelle walked into the kitchen and stopped dead in her tracks as she noticed Tiny standing near the fridge. "Oh? What have we he-uh? Hi big boy. I'm Michelle." Dressed in skintight jeans, an even tighter neon pink sweater that flattered her curves, and matching neon pink heels, Michelle was a sight to behold. A sight Tiny didn't quite seem to know what to do with.

"This is Tiny, our chef de cuisine," Callie added by way of introduction.

Most people couldn't help but laugh when they heard the misnomer, but Michelle took it in her stride. "Are you the one who made that lasagna?"

Back on more familiar ground, Tiny managed a nod.

"It was puhrfection. Absolute puhrfection."

Tiny beamed from ear to ear. Next to Grace, nothing made him happier than a well-deserved compliment about his cooking.

⁓⁓⁓

"They are a hoot and a handful," Tiny observed and then added, "And very loud. You're not going to get a moment's peace while they're in the house."

"They liven up the place."

"That's one way to put it." Tiny paused and looked at his friend. "I gotta hand it to you, Callie. You've got a lot of class. Most women would have slammed the door on a woman who had had an affair with their fiancé."

"Ex-fiancé," Callie needlessly clarified. "It really wasn't Michelle's fault, and she apologized. Besides, I was going to end things with David anyway. Michelle just made things easier."

"Still...hat's off to you. How'd they find this place anyway? Seems like an unlikely getaway for...such a boisterous pair of ladies. I'd expect them to vacation in New Orleans or Miami."

"Don't judge a book by its neon pink cover, Tiny! Apparently, they do a mother-daughter trip a couple of times a year and prefer to stay in the...," Callie made quotation marks in the air and semi-groaned, "country."

"So, they're off to get massages now and then on a wine tasting tour all afternoon? What about the other couple? Which room did you put them in again?"

"Rooms. Plural."

"Wait, they're sleeping in different rooms?"

"Yup. There's definitely a story there."

"Callie...keep your nose out of it."

"I'm just saying."

"And I'm just saying mind your own business. I have to run to the store to pick up a few things. I'll be back in about an hour, then we can start prep for the lunch and dinner crowds."

As he walked out of the kitchen, Tiny paused and pointed a warning finger at Callie. A warning, he suspected, she would most likely ignore.

———

Callie was sitting at the front desk playing a game of solitaire on her laptop when the Badmans finally came downstairs within moments of one another. For two people who slept in different rooms, they certainly seemed to be on the same schedule.

"Is there any place nearby that we can get breakfast?" Mr. Badman asked in a much friendlier tone than Callie had heard from him so far.

"It's a bed and breakfast. Which means you can get breakfast here," Mrs. Badman snapped.

Before Mr. Badman could fire back a response, Callie stood up and said as pleasantly as she could, "I have fresh coffee, fruit, and breakfast pastries in the kitchen. Come on back, and I'll get you situated."

Once they were seated, each choosing a chair at opposite ends of the table, Callie tried to make small talk to learn something about them. But it was no use. For every innocent question she asked, the two of them found a reason to argue. After a few failed attempts, Callie politely excused herself and went back to her rousing game of solitaire. She didn't hear a sound out of them until they walked to the front desk about half an hour later.

"What is there to do around here?" Mr. Badman asked, in what sounded again like a friendlier tone.

Mrs. Badman was about to say something, when he silenced her with a nasty glance and a not-so-friendly, "I'm not asking you!"

Now, Callie thought to herself, would be a good time to have one of those whistles that referees blow on. "I guess it depends on what you enjoy doing. We have some wonderful hiking trails in the area."

As she was reaching into her drawer to pull out a trail map, Mrs. Badman said, "I have knee problems."

"Oh, I'm sorry to hear it. We have plenty of easy, flat trails near the lake. The views are amazin—"

"Pass. What else?"

"There's our spa. We offer relaxing aromatherapy massages that people rave about."

"I have a bad back. I don't want some masseuse to make it worse," Mr. Badman said.

"Okay...let's see, we have some fantastic wineri—"

Before she could finish, she was interrupted again. This time by both Badmans in unison. "We don't drink." For some unknown reason, this caused both of them to look at each other and start giggling.

Exasperated, Callie wracked her brain for ideas on ways to get these two grown adults out of her hair for the day. Grown adults who were acting like children. Suddenly, Callie had an idea, and she snapped her fingers on impulse. "How about some board games?"

"Board games?" Mrs. Badman asked with a hopeful tone.

"Board games." Mr. Badman stated with confidence.

They both looked at each other and smiled, almost timidly as if asking each other for permission to play.

Callie breathed a sigh of relief. "Come on, I'll show you where we keep them."

—·ℓℓ·—

"Have they stepped outdoors even once yet today?" Lynette asked about the Badmans. Thankfully, she had come in later that afternoon to help with the dinner service at The Terrace.

"Stepped outdoors?" Callie asked. "They haven't even come out of the basement ever since I showed them how to work the TV in the media room!"

"To each his own, I guess."

"First, they spent hours hunched over the game table in the living room playing one board game after another. I have never seen two people be so competitive. I swear I thought I was going to have to break up a couple of fights." Callie laughed out loud and did her best imitation of little snippets of the arguing she had heard. "'It was my turn!' 'You're cheating!' 'Hey, I saw you move that piece!' 'Cheater, cheaterrrrr!'"

"You know what you need?" Lynette answered her own question, "One of those referee whistles."

"My thoughts exactly. Maybe now they'll call a truce and want to sleep in the same room."

"Callie...do not get in the middle of it." Lynette warned, and she picked up the reservations log for The Terrace, attempting to put an end to Callie's musings about the Badmans.

"Do you know what they had for lunch? They both wanted peanut butter and jelly sandwiches. On white bread. With potato chips crushed inside. It was weird, but kinda cute at the same time. Maybe they'll rekindle their romance while they're here. That would be a great story, wouldn't it?"

Ignoring the question entirely, Lynette observed, "Wow, we're almost fully booked tonight. Not bad for a Monday."

"It's the weather. Everyone has been cooped up for so long, they're all itching to get out of the house."

"I don't blame them. Plus, I think word of Tiny's cooking is spreading. Mr. W and I were out with some friends who have a house on Seneca Lake, and they were asking us if we had heard of a restaurant that, and I quote," said Lynette, "'Serves great food on the back porch of some bed and breakfast.'"

"Lynette, can I make a suggestion?"

"Will I be able to stop you?"

"No."

Now it was Lynette's turn to laugh. "That's what I thought. Suggest away."

"You're living under the same roof. You eloped, without telling a soul, mind you. Maybe it's time to stop calling the love of your life Mr. W?"

"Oh, trust me, my friend. When we're at home together, I drop the 'Mr.'" Lynette wiggled her eyebrows mischievously, making Callie laugh out loud.

"But we digress. The point I was trying to make is that maybe we need to get some more help around here."

Callie knew Lynette was right. The bed and breakfast side of The Summer Breeze and the spa were well staffed. Between her, Lynette, and Kirsten, they were able to keep things running relatively smoothly. But it was the popularity of The Terrace that was putting a lot of pressure on everyone.

Fortunately for Callie, Lynette was as committed to the success of The Summer Breeze as she was. She had been her very first hire and had been with her since before the grand opening. Without Lynette's steady guidance and salt of the earth practicality, Callie knew her dream might not have become a reality. And, even though she no longer *needed* to work because of her marriage to a very successful financier, Lynette *wanted* to work.

Callie remembered the day Lynette had called her to share the news that Mr. W had asked her to marry him. Thrilled for her friend's newfound happiness, Callie had nonetheless been worried about finding a replacement. She hadn't mentioned anything about it to Lynette at first, even after Lynette had returned from her trip to New York City.

"What are you working on?" Lynette had asked her one afternoon a couple of weeks after she had gotten back from the city. Callie had been sitting at the kitchen table intently focused on her laptop. She hadn't heard Lynette come in and felt like she had just gotten caught with her hand in the cookie jar.

"You were doing it again, you know," Lynette said, seemingly unaware of Callie's feelings of guilt.

"Doing what?"

"Talking to yourself. What are you up to anyway?" When Callie didn't answer, Lynette took a closer look at her friend and asked with some concern, "Callie, are you okay?"

"I need your help," Callie asked in a serious tone, realizing she desperately needed Lynette's input to find her own replacement.

"Of course! Anything. How can I help you?" Lynette sat down at the table next to Callie, looking increasingly worried by her friend's attitude.

Without saying a word, Callie turned her laptop towards Lynette and waited.

"Facilities Manager, Job Description," Lynette read aloud. "The Facilities Manager will be primarily responsible for.... Wow, you didn't get very far. Are you trying to hire someone new?"

Callie nodded and felt the sting of tears threaten.

"Wait a second!" Lynette said as realization began to dawn. "I'm your Facilities Manager. Are you firing me? Is this your way of firing me? I mean, I know I've taken some time off recently, but you approved it! As a matter of fact, you're the one who encouraged me to take as much time as I needed!"

"What?" Callie asked dumbly. "I'm not firing you. What on earth would make you think that? And why are you getting so mad?"

Lynette squinted her eyes at Callie. "Gee, I don't know," she said sarcastically. "Maybe the fact that you're working on a job description for *my job*! Maybe the fact that I've been with you from practically the beginning, and The Summer Breeze is almost as much my baby as it is yours. Maybe the fact that I thought we were friends!"

It took Callie a moment to realize the misunderstanding, but once she did, she couldn't help but laugh with relief.

"Are you kidding me right now? Have you lost your mind?" Lynette stood up angrily.

"Take it easy, Lynette. I'm not firing you."

"You're not?"

"No."

"Then what's with the job description?"

"I thought you were going to quit!"

"Why on earth would I quit the best job I've ever had? With the best boss I've ever had?"

Callie had simply reached out and taken Lynette's left hand, adorned with a 2-carat emerald cut Tiffany's diamond engagement ring, and looked at it pointedly. "That's why."

———ele———

"I know one job I won't have to post an opening for."

"You got that right. So, let's do your favorite thing and make a list of what we do need help with. We have exactly fifteen minutes before Tiny starts barking orders at us about helping with dinner prep."

"Let me just get my laptop."

"No! There is no time for me to wait around while you format some spreadsheet with fancy colors and filters. Just grab a scrap of paper!"

Callie simply stared at her friend. "You're kidding me, right? I don't think so. You know I don't do scraps of paper. Besides, I was working earlier, and my laptop is at the front desk. And I promise I won't format anything until after we're done."

Lynette rolled her eyes in response and followed Callie to the front desk, where she watched her boss quickly shut down the game of solitaire she had been "working" on earlier.

Opening a new file, Callie started making a list of the things they needed assistance with. It was much easier than she had expected and within fifteen minutes, she and Lynette had a surprisingly comprehensive list. As they looked over it, they realized the biggest challenge was that none of the positions warranted full time employees. Instead, what they needed were flexible, multi-tasking people who could take on a variety of roles. Someone to help Tiny with kitchen prep during the meal service, but then help with clean up after the fact. Someone who could help with day-to-day cleaning of the bed and break-fast, but then help with the dinner service on busy evenings. Someone who could play the role of concierge to help guests plan their trips in advance or in real time.

"That's a tall order. It's a wonder we survived this long without more support."

"I know! Things feel like they're running smoothly, but it's because we're both working crazy hours, Lynette. And so is Tiny, especially now that The Terrace is growing at such a fast pace. We can't sustain it unless we get help."

"So, the next logical question is how do we find people to fill these positions."

Before Callie could answer, they heard Tiny's car pull into the driveway and knew they'd have to put the question on hold. It was time to switch hats and help with dinner prep.

Al Fresco

"Is it just me, or was that one of the busiest Monday nights we've had in months?"

Callie leaned back in her chair and stretched her legs out onto the opposite seat. "It's not you, Tiny. I wasn't expecting that many walk-ins. My feet are killing me."

"I hate to break this to you, boss, but I think we're going to need to get some help around here."

"Callie and I were talking about that earlier today," Lynette added, reluctantly getting up to grab a printout of the list she and Callie had made. "What do you think of this?"

Tiny read it over and said, "I think there's one thing you'll need to add. I know I'm a bit of a control freak in the kitchen, but I don't think I can avoid getting a sous chef. This whole limited menu idea was working great, but I think we'd be shortchanging ourselves if we didn't start expanding it to include more items. Besides, I think it's time I flexed my culinary muscles a bit."

Callie and Lynette looked at each other, relieved that Tiny had broached the subject on his own. Wanting to strike while the iron was hot, Lynette grabbed a pencil from what was a perennially messy kitchen drawer and added 'sous-chef' to the list.

"There's another thing we may want to consider." Callie said tentatively. She had been mulling over an idea ever since she had seen the outdoor tent setup for Kirsten's wedding. But it was an idea she wouldn't even consider acting on without Tiny and Lynette's input. "Maybe we should increase our capacity."

"There's no way we can fit more tables on The Terrace, boss. Besides, it would ruin the intimate vibe we have going out there. And unless we get help, I can't cook for that many more people."

"I'm not talking about more tables on The Terrace. Ever since the wedding, I've been thinking about creating a fully outdoor dining experience. We have enough of a flat expanse out back to setup at least a dozen tables. We could make it seasonal, from May to say...October? That way it would be an experience people could look forward to during the winter months. Maybe put up a bunch of those outdoor string lights and plant some fragrant flowers."

Lynette was about to put the brakes on Callie's musings and expecting Tiny's full support when she noticed a faraway look in his eyes.

Before she could say anything, he added dreamily, "Why just plant flowers? Maybe we could have some raised garden beds. We could grow some of our own food. Nothing fancy, maybe just some herbs and tomatoes."

"Slow down, you two. We really should think this thr—"

"Oooh, that's a great idea!" Callie added. "I can ask my parents to come down and help us get the garden started. You guys know what amazing vegetables they grow. And why limit ourselves to just herbs and tomatoes?"

"Listen, I really think we shou—"

"You're right, Callie!" Tiny interrupted Lynette and rubbed his hands together eagerly. "Why would we limit ourselves to just herbs and tomatoes? We can grow peppers and eggplant. Green beans...maybe even some berries for the dessert course."

"We need to make a list! I'll grab my laptop." Callie began walking towards the front desk but stopped and turned back. "Sorry, Lynette, what were you saying?"

Lynette knew a lost cause when she saw one. "Nothing. Absolutely nothing."

Callie stayed up later that night than she had in a long time. The adrenaline rush of a new venture combined with her natural enthusiasm for making to-do lists made her lose track of time. Talking aloud to herself while typing away on her laptop, she added to the notes she, Lynette, and Tiny had started. Adding the fine details she knew would mean the difference between a smooth, successful project and a doomed attempt, she spent several hours enumerating all the employees she needed to hire, the specific supplies she would need to purchase, a timeline to get the al fresco service up and running, and an outline of DIY projects, which included enough raised garden beds for all the vegetables Tiny hoped to grow.

"Six beds, each six feet by four feet. That gives us," she paused to do the calculations, "One hundred forty-four square feet of planting space. That doesn't sound like enough."

Closing her eyes, she recalled the sketches her father had drawn before starting work on his vegetable beds and knew she needed more space. But where?

Grabbing a pencil from her desk and a blank sheet of paper off her printer, Callie crept quietly out of her bedroom towards the kitchen. The small light over the stove, always left on in case one of her guests felt like having a late-night snack, gave off enough light for her to make her way to her messy kitchen drawer. Digging around, she searched for a flashlight but came up empty handed. Then she remembered the emergency kit Nick had put together for her after the ice storm.

Using her cell phone light to make her way to the coat closet in the front hallway, Callie found the two large bright red duffle bags. Grateful for his thoughtfulness, she reached into one of the bags and found a heavy-duty flashlight. She pressed the power button and said a silent thank you to Nick when the light flickered on and cast its bright glow on the floor.

Callie turned off her phone light and used the flashlight to guide her towards the back doors of The Terrace. She was about to step out into the cool, dark night to measure the backyard when she realized she needed measuring tape. Making her way back to the same kitchen drawer, she searched until she found it. "You're getting cleaned tomorrow," she whispered to the drawer, "And you're going to stay clean this time!"

Callie sat back and looked at her handiwork. The scaled sketch of her backyard was nowhere near as good as the one her father had made, but it was definitely passable. And it put a big smile on her face. She had carefully measured the area and drawn the outline on graph paper. Then she had added circles to represent the dining tables and chairs, rectangles for the raised garden beds, and a shaded rectangle at the far end to indicate where the in-ground garden would be. And then there was the pièce de résistance, the thing that would put a big grin on Tiny's face: a built-in, outdoor kitchen.

It was well past midnight when Callie turned off her laptop and crawled into bed, sighing with satisfaction.

———

"How can one drawer get so messy? Didn't I just clean and organize you a couple of months ago?"

"Who are you talking to?"

Startled, Callie turned to see Mrs. Badman enter the kitchen. "Oh, I was just talking to this messy kitchen drawer."

"Those are the worst. I have one at my house, too." To Callie's surprise, Mrs. Badman smiled and continued, "Sorry to have snuck up behind you."

Returning the smile, Callie said, "That's okay. I didn't hear you come downstairs."

Mrs. Badman, now looking a little guilty, but still smiling, offered an explanation. "Actually, we fell asleep watching movies downstairs."

"Those chairs are very comfortable," Callie agreed as diplomatically as possible, unsure of what else to say and hoping that sleep was the only thing that had taken place on the chairs.

"Can I ask you for a favor?" Mrs. Badman asked changing the subject. Without waiting for an answer, she asked, "Can you order a small cake for Harry? It's his birthday, and I want to surprise him."

That was unexpected, Callie thought to herself. Out loud, she said, "Oh that's so sweet...yes, of course. I'll ask Tiny to pick one up on his way into work."

"Thanks! I'm just going to go get ready. Harry's still sleeping downstairs. Please don't wake him."

As Mrs. Badman left the kitchen, Callie called Tiny and asked him to pick up a small cake from his mom's bakery. "It's Mr. Badman's birthday and his wife wants to surprise him."

"I guess they made up then. Okay, I'm on my way to the bakery now. I'll grab the cake and some fresh bread for the lunch crowd. See you in a bit."

Callie hung up the phone and turned her attention back to the messy drawer. "Now, where were we?"

"Who are you talking to?"

Startled once again, Callie turned to see Mr. Badman enter the kitchen. "Oh, I was just talking to this messy kitchen drawer."

"Those are the worst. I have one at my house, too." Callie got a strange feeling of déjà vu.

Mr. Badman smiled and continued, "Sorry to have snuck up behind you. We fell asleep downstairs watching movies."

"I heard." Callie smiled.

"Oh, did Carrie already go upstairs?"

Harry and Carrie? You have got to be kidding me, Callie thought to herself. "Yes, she just went up a few minutes ago."

"Great, can I ask you for a favor? Can you order a small cake for her? It's her birthday, and I want to surprise her."

Callie stared stupidly at Mr. Badman, as if she was trying to figure out a difficult math question.

"Callie?"

"Oh, sorry, yes. That's so sweet...yes, of course. I'll ask Tiny to pick one up on his way into work."

"Thanks!" And with that, Mr. Badman left the kitchen, leaving Callie standing there alone, scratching her head.

A few seconds passed before she realized she needed to call Tiny. Grabbing her cell phone, Callie redialed his number.

Tiny answered on the first ring. "What did you forget?"

"I need you to pick up a small cake."

"You already called me about that! Not 5 minutes ago!"

"I need you to pick up another one. It's Mrs. Badman's birthday and her husband wants to surprise her with a cake."

"Have you been drinking?"

"No! The first time I called you, it was for Carrie who wanted to order a cake for Harry. Now Harry wants to order a cake for Carrie."

Exasperated, Tiny hung up.

"I think I'm going to talk to some of the regulars about the outdoor dining idea," Callie said.

"Maybe you can start with Harry and Carrie," Tiny teased.

"Ha. Ha. Who else is here tonight, Lynette?" Callie asked, hoping for a serious response.

"Well, let's see, we have Jenny and Benny," Lynette laughed. "And also, Lark and Mark."

"You, too?" Callie chuckled.

"Didn't you also tell me Tate and Kate have reservations tonight?"

"You two keep going with your comedy routine, I'll be outside on The Terrace." Callie couldn't help but laugh as she walked out of the kitchen. She loved her friends and their sense of humor, even if it was at her expense.

"If you see Sam and Pa—"

Callie could easily guess the rest as she walked between the tables greeting her new customers and stopping to chat with the familiar ones. She spotted two of her favorite diners, Doug, and his wife of over fifty years, Susan, and almost burst out laughing with relief that their names didn't rhyme.

"Callie! What's so funny?" As she walked up to their table, Doug stood up like the old-fashioned gentleman that he was.

"Oh, it's nothing. Tiny was just cracking some silly jokes in the kitchen." Changing the subject, she asked, "Sit, please. How's your dinner tonight?"

"You know it's my favorite. Ravioli night at The Terrace is a big deal around here."

"And you, Susan?"

"It's absolutely delicious. You know, Callie, I'm so glad you opened this place. Doug always used to complain that there was no place a man could take his wife out for a special occasion dinner in Seneca Springs. And now that we have this beautiful restaurant, instead of coming here only for special occasions, we're here at least once or twice a week!"

Callie beamed at the kind words. "I remember he said exactly those words to me over lunch one afternoon at Paolina's. It was his comment that set me down this path. Which is why I'm so glad you're here tonight. I have an important question to ask you."

⁓

As soon as Callie had mentioned that she was thinking about expanding The Terrace to include an outdoor dining area, Doug had insisted she join them for dessert. A slice of apple and ginger upside-down cake and a cup of coffee later, Callie felt almost certain the idea would be a success. As she was getting ready to stand up, one of the servers, Alicia, who also doubled as a housekeeper, stopped by to clear the table. Which reminded Callie to ask the Lenardsons one more question. "If you know of anyone who is looking for work, let me know. I have a feeling I'll be hiring!"

"We don't, but we'll be sure to ask around."

"Dessert is on the house by the way!" Before Doug could protest, Callie added, "Alicia, can you make sure to take it off their bill? See you next week?"

"If not sooner!"

Callie took her leave and stopped by to greet a few more diners before she spotted the Badmans at a corner table. Both of them were staring at her, and both of them were making strange twitching motions with their eyes like little kids who were trying to wink but didn't know how. When they realized they had her attention, each of them started gesturing towards the other. It took a painful second before Callie realized they were signaling for her to bring out the cake. Or cakes in this case.

Callie smiled, nodded at them in acknowledgement and walked quickly back to the kitchen where Tiny and Lynette were relaxing at the table after the rush of the dinner service.

"Hey, did you see the Badmans? I was out there a couple of minutes ago, and it looked like they were having some sort of facial spasms. I think they were trying to get your attention."

"Oh, they got my attention all right. I think they want me to bring out the cakes. Should I just take both out at the same time?"

"Yes, unless you want them to start fighting like children again!"

Callie took two light pink pastry boxes, emblazoned with two elaborately swirled large letter B's for Bertha's Bakery, out of the refrigerator and placed the cakes on a serving tray.

"I think we still have some birthday candles left in the messy drawer." Lynette said as she walked over and opened the drawer. "Correction. Looks like Callie has made another attempt at organizing the drawer."

"And it's going to stay that way this time."

"Mmm hmmm, if you say so." Lynette placed a birthday candle in each cake and lit them. "Off you go. Be sure to wish Harry and Carrie a happy birthday from us."

Rolling her eyes, Callie made her way to the Badmans' table with both cakes. As soon as they saw her, they both beamed from ear to ear and started clapping. Callie couldn't help smiling back at their childlike enthusiasm.

"Happy birthday to both of you! I've never met a couple with the same birthday!"

For a moment, their smiles fell abruptly from their faces, and Callie worried she had said something to offend them. But then, much to her surprise, they burst into laughter.

"A couple? She thinks we're a couple!"

"Oh, I...I'm sorry, I just assumed," Callie stammered.

"We're not married, dummy! We're twins!"

As Callie was getting ready for bed that night, she laughed out loud thinking about the Badmans and her misunderstanding. It was so obvious now that they were twins. Fortunately, they had taken her faux pas with good humor. The trip to the bed and breakfast, they explained, had been forced on them by their children as a last-ditch effort to save their sibling bond. A disagreement between the twins from several years earlier had turned into an argument. The argument had turned into an epic fight which had put a wedge in their otherwise unique bond. Their kids, distraught by the family feud, had concocted a plan to force them to spend their birthday week together.

"And we're so glad they did. We've had so much fun today. It was almost like our birthdays together when we were younger," Carrie had said as she cut into her birthday cake.

Harry cut a piece of his cake, and together, they had both taken a bite, happy and reunited. "We used to play board games together all the time and watch movies. I'm so glad they forced us to do this. Honestly, we can't even remember what we were arguing about."

Callie sighed as she thought about Harry's words, and how small misunderstandings can ruin a relationship. Feeling suddenly pensive, she picked up her cell phone and called the one person she wanted to talk to the most. He answered in a sleepy voice.

"Hey gorgeous. Still mad at me?"

Callie smiled at his tired but still sexy voice. "No." Even as she said it, Callie realized it was the truth. She wasn't mad at him. "I woke you. I'm sorry, go back to bed."

"No. I'd rather talk to you. How was your day? What's this I hear about outdoor dining?"

"News travels fast."

"Tiny's got a big mouth."

Callie laughed and filled Nick in on her idea, leaving out most of the details despite his requests for more information. "It's late, and you need to sleep. I'll tell you everything tomorrow."

"Are your lists made?"

"You know they are."

"You should think about doing a rough sketch of the area. Try to draw it to scale."

"Already done."

"Why am I not surprised?"

"Because you know what an amazing woman I am?" Callie could sense the smile spreading across his face. Closing her eyes, she imagined him lying next to her. Unfortunately, his next words ruined her mood.

"Listen, Callie, I need to tell you something. And you're not going to like it."

"Sounds ominous."

"You know that hotel down on the south end of the lake that's been on the market for the past year or so?"

"Yes."

"A European boutique hotel chain bought it a couple of months ago, and they're planning a major renovation and re-opening."

Callie swallowed hard. She knew her small, four-bedroom bed and breakfast had been a success in large part because there was very little competition in the area. "When?"

"Timeline is aggressive. Six months."

"How many rooms?"

"Twenty-five."

"I changed my mind."

"About?"

"Being mad at you."

Nick laughed. "How about I come up there next weekend and try to change your mind? You can show me all your lists, and I promise to listen to every word that comes out of that sexy mouth of yours."

A Hot Bath

"Have you seen Alicia today?" Lynette asked walking down the stairs towards Callie who was sitting at the front desk going over trip planning requests from guests who would be arriving later that day.

Callie nodded, "She came in a little late today. She must be upstairs cleaning one of the rooms."

"I was just up there checking on our inventory for toiletries, and I didn't see her. What I did see was a poorly made bed and some dusty windowsills in one of the suites, which is not like her." Lynette paused, not wanting to add to Callie's growing list of worries. But then thought better of it and added, "Has her work seemed a little off to you lately?"

Now that Lynette pointed it out, Callie had to begrudgingly agree. She had noticed Alicia hadn't been doing her job with as much attention to detail as she normally did. It was Callie's habit to check every room before a new guest arrived, and there had been more than a couple of occasions in the past few weeks when she had had to tidy up a room herself or add missing toiletries to the spa-quality bathrooms. Giving her employee, who she also considered a friend, the benefit of the doubt, Callie had chalked it up to simple oversight. But maybe Lynette was right. "It's not just her work that's been off, Lynette. Now that I think about it, Alicia has been dragging a bit. She looks tired. I wonder if she's fighting something off?"

"That's one way to put it," said Alicia as she unexpectedly came out of the powder room on the main floor.

"Hey! I didn't know you were in there." Hoping her friend hadn't heard the entire conversation, Callie asked awkwardly, "Is everything okay?"

"I don't know how to tell you this, Callie. I'm so sorry to have to do this to you. Especially since I know you're thinking of expanding the restaurant and need to hire more people."

A hollow feeling began to grow in Callie's stomach as she watched Alicia fiddle with her wedding ring. There was something familiar about the look on her face. And suddenly, it all made sense. Callie recalled seeing a similar nauseous, early morning look on Nica's face many months earlier, and guessed what Alicia was about to tell her.

"I'm pregnant, Callie."

And there it was. Another hit to The Summer Breeze. But, Callie reminded herself, a piece of wonderful news for her friend.

"Alicia, I'm so happy for you!"

"*We're* so happy for you," Lynette corrected. She gave Alicia a warm hug, and Callie immediately followed suit.

"There's more."

Callie knew that many working women continued with their jobs throughout a pregnancy, but she wondered about women with physically demanding jobs. Granted, she only purchased organic cleaning products for The Summer Breeze, but still, there was a lot of bending and hard work involved with cleaning a hotel room. Selfishly, Callie wondered if keeping a pregnant woman on her cleaning staff would be a liability.

Taking a deep breath, Alicia nervously plowed ahead. "I don't think I need to work anymore. Caleb is working full time now for Mr. Blake, so money isn't as tight as it used to be. Plus, you know how I've been dabbling a little in online graphic design? I've actually started bringing in some extra money doing a side hustle with it."

"Alicia," Callie said gently, "You don't have to explain yourself to us."

"It's the least I can do, Callie. You took a chance on Caleb and me when we were just starting out. If it hadn't been for the work he did for you on The Summer Breeze, he never would have landed the job with Blake's Construction. And if I hadn't started cleaning for you, we would have been in a really tough position that first year." Tears collected in Alicia's eyes and slowly rolled down her face. "I feel so bad about doing this to you. I've loved working for you so much."

"And we've loved having you here. You're a big part of why The Summer Breeze has been so successful." Callie fought back tears of her own and gave Alicia another hug.

Lynette, never one to get overly emotional, especially when it came to the operations of the bed and breakfast, decided she had to be the voice of reason. "Needless to say, Alicia, you're always welcome here. If you decide you want to continue working at the restaurant, we'd love to have you. If you want to come back to work after you have the baby, we'd love that, too. It's absolutely up to you. We can figure all that out later." Thinking ahead, Lynette added, "You know, there is one thing we could use your help with...."

"Finding my replacement?" Alicia asked before Lynette could finish. "As a matter of fact, I think I know of someone who is looking for work. I was at Grace's store yesterday, and I overheard a young woman asking if Grace was hiring. I'm pretty sure Grace got her contact information."

Lynette dialed Grace's number before Callie even had a chance to respond.

Later that week, as Callie was reviewing her online reservations system, the doorbell rang. Callie looked at her watch. It was a few minutes before four. "Early," Callie mumbled to herself as she got up to open the door. "I like that."

"Hi. Callie?" The young woman standing on the front porch smiled. She had big blue eyes, almost blindingly white teeth, and deep dimples. She was dressed in what looked to be a rather expensive outfit. She had on trendy jeans and a lovely cream-colored silk blouse with tasteful jewelry. Her hands were manicured, and her hair was nicely styled. For someone who had mentioned several times during their brief phone interview earlier in the week, that she was desperate for a job to make ends meet, this young lady seemed awfully fashionable. Callie reminded herself not to jump to conclusions. Maybe, she told herself, she had wanted to make a good first impression. Another promising sign.

"I'm Evie, here for my interview." There was something eager about her expression, which *should* have pleased Callie even further.

"Hi Evie. It's a pleasure to meet you, come on in." Callie led Evie into the dining room and motioned for her to sit.

"Thank you so much for this opportunity. I can't tell you how much this means to me."

Callie smiled in response. "Since I don't have your resume, why don't you tell me a little bit about yourself?" She had asked Evie to email it to her, but apparently, Evie's laptop hadn't been working properly.

"Well, there's really not much to tell. I grew up on the lake, about twenty minutes from here. Graduated from high school two years ago and went to college down South, but that didn't really work out for me. The kids at my school were a little too snobby for my taste. So, I dropped out and moved back to my parent's house. But that's not really working out either. They still treat me like I'm a little kid. I'm desperate to get my own place, which is why I was at that grocery store asking for a second job."

"A second job?" This was news to Callie.

"Oh, didn't I mention that? I work part time as a nanny for one of the families over on the north side of the lake. They live in this big fancy house, which I absolutely love, but their kids are not very well behaved. I can quit that job and start working for you full time any time you like."

A little red flag had gone up in Callie's mind as she listened to what Evie said. College didn't work out, living at home didn't work out, her current job wasn't working out. Evie either had very bad luck or was not good at adapting and making the best of a situation. Callie's concern must have been reflected in her expression because Evie started talking again.

"And now, here I am. This place is absolutely beautiful! I can't believe you own all of this yourself! You must be really successful! And smart! I would love the opportunity to learn from you! I can really see myself growing and taking on more responsibilities here."

Callie was in a tough spot. She knew she had to find someone to take over Alicia's job. She and Lynette had split the cleaning duties for the past few days, and it was exhausting work. But, regardless of how desperate she was, she was smart enough to know she should never ignore a red flag.

"Thank you. I just want to be clear that the job you're applying for is to help with the day-to-day cleaning of the bed and breakfast. Also, if we're short staffed at the restaurant, you might be called on from time to time to help with clearing tables and doing the dishes. Do you have any related work experience?"

Evie nodded eagerly. "During the two years I was in college, I worked a couple of different jobs doing odds and ends on campus through a work study program to help me pay for school, including some cleaning and cafeteria duties."

"Great, can you get me some references?"

"Oh, that might be tough. Each job was very short term, a couple of months here, a couple of months there. And there were tons of other students moving in and out of the jobs.

I doubt anyone there would remember me. That won't be a problem, will it?"

"What about the family you're working for now? Will they be able to provide a reference?"

"I don't really want to tip them off that I'm thinking about leaving, plus I'm not sure it would be relevant. Being a nanny really has nothing to do with what you'd like me to do here."

Not being able to talk to any previous employers was another red flag. Maybe, Callie wondered, she should bend her own rules this one time. What was the worst that could happen? At least she would have a warm body to help with the cleaning. She and Lynette were already spread thin with planning for the outdoor restaurant. If things didn't work out, she could always find someone else. The Summer Breeze was booked solid for the next six months, and no one wanted to stay at a dirty bed and breakfast. Callie knew that one bad online review could set off an avalanche of canceled reservations.

"When can you start?" Callie asked, deciding for the moment to ignore her intuition.

Evie pulled out her phone to check her calendar. Callie was surprised to see it was an even newer model of smartphone than the one she herself owned.

"Would next week be okay? I would start sooner, but I need to find a place to live first. Besides, I need to go shopping and buy some casual outfits. I don't want my nice things to get dirty."

<center>~~~</center>

Callie turned off the water faucet and lowered herself into the soaker tub in her bathroom. She was hoping that a hot bath would help her relax. Resting her head back on the bath pillow, she wondered why she was feeling so overwhelmed.

For the first time in a long time, she found herself feeling the kind of stress she had chosen to leave behind almost two years earlier when she quit her job in New York City. The frantic feeling of never being able to find enough hours in the day to finish everything that needed to get done was beginning to rear its ugly head. It was a feeling she hadn't had since, even when she took on the daunting renovation of the O'Connor place and turned it into her dream business.

"And this restaurant project isn't even as close to as much work as the renovation," Callie mumbled to herself as the hot water eased her muscles and helped relieve some of the physical tension.

She closed her eyes and thought back to the day when the idea of opening her own bed and breakfast had presented itself. She had been gently swaying back and forth on the garden swing in her parents' backyard under a lush green canopy of leaves, one of her favorite places in the entire world. It had been months since she had left her job and moved back into her childhood bedroom. Her days had passed in a happy cycle of spending time with her family. She had spent hours gardening with her mom, cooking with her dad, and learning woodworking skills with Nica and Jack. The only lists she had made during those first few months had been for Nica's wedding.

But after that day on the garden swing, when a soft summer breeze had whispered the idea of opening her own bed and breakfast into existence, Callie had immersed herself in her new project. Excited by the opportunity, she had approached everything as a chance to learn something new. The months of relaxation had replenished her motivation, giving her a seemingly endless source of energy. And her family had been in lock step with her throughout the process. Taking on projects, helping with decision making, and always, always encouraging her to chase her dream.

Callie wondered if that was the difference this time. She had been running on all cylinders from that day. First with the renovation, then with taking care of her guests and opening The Terrace. There had been no time for a proper vacation. No time for a refueling period.

Callie sighed, feeling sorry for herself. Almost immediately, she reminded herself to focus on the things that were going well.

"At least Evie is working out better than I had expected." While Evie wasn't as detail oriented as Alicia, Callie appreciated the fact that if she or Lynette pointed out something for Evie to improve, they never had to tell her a second time. She may not have been the hardest worker, but at least she was a quick learner.

The water had started to turn tepid, and if there was one thing Callie hated, it was sitting in a lukewarm bathtub. Pulling the drain plug, she stood up and wrapped herself in the plush robe that had been hanging next to the tub, the same luxuriant kind placed in each guest suite. The decision to use these particular robes had been a pricey one, but Callie was certain they had been worth every penny. When her guests wrapped themselves in the soft, cushy fabric, they felt special and pampered. Many of them had specifically mentioned them in their reviews, and on a few occasions, some had even asked Callie to charge the cost of a new robe to their room so they could take it home.

Callie sat on the edge of her bed and sighed. The temporary stress relief from the bath began to dissipate as her to-do's wrestled their way, unbidden, back to the forefront of her mind. Although she could picture each numbered item on her spreadsheet clearly, and each sub-item along with its respective due date equally as clearly, what Callie couldn't imagine was where she was going to find the time to get it all done.

"You're doing it again." Callie reminded herself to dispense of the self-pity, changed into her favorite slightly worn, red flannel pajamas, and smiled as she put them on. They had been a gift from her parents, five matching sets of pajamas for everyone in the family to wear while they were sleeping in the garage, which had been converted into a makeshift dormitory in the early days of the renovation.

And that's when the antidote to her anxiety became obvious. The only way she would be able to get through the next couple of weeks was with her family by her side. And she knew they would come happily. It wasn't even a question in her mind.

She'd give her room to Nica and Jack. Her parents could sleep on her pullout sofa, and she'd make do on an inflatable mattress on the floor. It would be like those early days but with more creature comforts. Including Tiny's cooking. The thought of food made Callie think of her pregnant sister who, by all accounts, had recently developed a need for numerous small meals throughout the day. Callie laughed aloud. She'd have to be sure to give Tiny advance notice that Nica was coming.

Mimosas and Bellinis

"Looks like you two had a good weekend," Lynette teased as Callie walked in through the front door.

"Is it that obvious?" Callie tried not to smile. She felt like a young girl in the throes of first love. Her weekend with Nick had been absolute perfection: equal parts romantic and productive. It was a strange combination but one that made her ridiculously happy. As promised, Nick had listened to "every word that comes out of that sexy mouth." And Callie had shared all her ideas about expanding the restaurant and adding the vegetable garden, leaving absolutely nothing out. She had painstakingly walked him through her extensive planning list. The only time she wasn't talking was when Nick was kissing her. Which was just fine with her.

Lynette rolled her eyes in response. "'Is it that obvious?'" she mocked. "Have you seen that silly grin on your face?"

"What? I'm smiling because he really helped me work through a lot of things."

"I bet he did."

"Oh, and what? You think I don't notice when Mr. W has helped you 'work things out'?"

"Touché," Lynette laughed, trying to cover the blush that was spreading across her cheeks.

"Now that we have that settled, let's go over this week. I think all the suites are booked for the entire week, right? Anyone interesting?"

Lynette nodded and glanced at her computer screen. "Three suites are booked for a group of women who used to be sorority sisters in college. Best friends, it seems from the message they wrote when they did their booking."

"Have we booked any wine tastings or spa visits for them?"

"Nope, it says here that this is the first time in more than thirty years they've managed to find a time and place that works for all of them. They're planning to stay at the b and b pretty much the whole time."

Callie sighed, hoping she would be able to get at least a few of the things on her to do list accomplished. But with guests underfoot every moment of every day, it would be tough. "And the other suite?"

Looking back at her computer, Lynette burst out laughing.

"What?"

Lynette just pointed at her screen. "You won't believe me if I tell you."

Callie leaned over the front desk to see what Lynette was pointing at and started laughing, too. "Wow, you can't make this stuff up! What time do they get here?"

The Goodmans, Lynette informed Callie, would arrive within the hour.

—ele—

Callie rubbed the back of her neck and rolled her shoulders. A hot bath and a good book were her only priorities for later that night. She smiled in anticipation as she sat down at the kitchen table, surrounded by the murmur of conversation and laughter from The Terrace. Despite how much work they required, her restaurant and The Summer Breeze were filled with happy people this evening, and Callie felt truly grateful. She took a deep breath and settled into the feeling of gratitude for a moment. Sometimes, her obsession with the minutiae of planning and operations got the better of her, and she had to remind herself of everything she had accomplished in just two years. The life she had built for herself.

She wondered where she would be right now if her sister hadn't shown up on her SoHo doorstep just over two years ago and dragged her to a B&B on Long Island. Wondered what her life would be like if she hadn't walked in on David and Michelle. Would she have married David, or would she have listened to her inner voice, the one that had been whispering to her for months that something wasn't right? That she wasn't happy. That she deserved better. The thought of being stuck in an endless cycle of wearing the "right clothes" and meeting the "right people," would have exhausted and drained her.

But, Callie reminded herself, Nica *had* shown up. And Callie *had* left David. And now, here she was sitting in the kitchen of the beautiful bed and breakfast she had created. The smile slowly returned to her face and a gentle warmth flowed through her.

"What are you smiling about? And why are you just sitting there? Do we still have the Calabrian red chili flakes?"

"Huh?" Callie asked dreamily.

"Have you been making lists in your head again?" Lynette asked, clearly annoyed as she walked to the spice cabinet and searched for the chili flakes.

"No."

"Thinking about Nick?"

"No."

Lynette looked over at the expression on Callie's face and surmised that her friend was being honest. "Then what? Aha, here it is!" She triumphantly held up a clear jar filled with small, ruby colored flakes of crushed chilis.

"Let me guess, Dr. Joshi is here?"

"Yup. That man likes his food spicy."

"He likes his women even spicier."

Lynette giggled. Dr. Joshi wasn't exactly a regular at The Terrace, but he made it a point to eat at the restaurant at least once every couple of months, sometimes alone but oftentimes with a very beautiful woman on his arm. A different one almost every time. Slightly balding and slightly out of shape, he was a prominent surgeon with a penchant for much younger women. Tiny never understood how a man like him attracted the type of women he came in with, even going so far as to question whether they were paid companions. But Callie and Lynette knew. There was something incredibly sexy about Dr. Joshi that was almost impossible to describe. He oozed with confidence and intelligence, and once you found yourself in a conversation with him, it was hard to tear yourself away.

"I don't know what it is about that man. I swear I could talk to him for hours."

"Agreed."

Both women sighed, feeling slightly guilty for daydreaming about another man.

"Did you find the chili flakes?" Alicia, who still came in to help out with the restaurant from time to time, asked with a glassy look in her eyes.

Lynette nodded and held up the jar as proof.

"Can you please take it to him?" Alicia asked, sounding a little desperate. "I swear if I get into another conversation with him...I feel like I'm being unfaithful to Caleb every time I talk to that man! How is he able to make me feel like the only woman on the planet?"

"Agreed," Callie and Lynette said in unison.

Tiny walked in at that exact moment, and without saying a word, Lynette handed him the bottle of chili flakes.

"Are you kidding me?" Tiny looked at the expression on all three of the women's faces, sighed, and promptly exited the kitchen to deliver the seasoning to Dr. Joshi himself.

—⁓—

"Was that Grace who just left? Is today pancake day? Did the delivery guys drop off the wood?" Callie asked in rapid succession as she joined Tiny in the kitchen.

Tiny turned towards his boss, and Callie was taken aback by the look on his face. His usual happy-go-lucky expression was nowhere to be found. Immediately concerned, Callie walked towards him and was about to ask what had happened when the voices of several women could be heard coming towards the kitchen. Tiny shook his head as if to let Callie know not to ask any questions.

After four straight days spent in their rooms, Callie couldn't believe her guests had picked this exact moment to come downstairs.

"Good morning," one of them announced happily. "I think we've finally managed to get caught up on every single detail of every single one of our lives, and we're ready to leave our little cocoons! Thought we'd come downstairs for breakfast today!"

Callie took a quick glance at Tiny who had turned his back and was busy stirring something in a large bowl. Not wanting to embarrass him, Callie plastered a smile on her face and said, "Good morning. Of course! It's a beautiful morning, why don't we get you set up at a table on The Terrace. Can I start you off with some mimosas?"

Thankfully, the bit about the mimosas distracted the women's attention away from Tiny, and they fell into a heated discussion about which breakfast cocktail was better, a traditional mimosa or a peach bellini. Their votes fell evenly divided between the two drinks, and in the end, Callie offered to make both, mostly as an excuse to get back into the kitchen to talk to Tiny.

"You're in for a treat today! Lemon ricotta pancakes with blueberry compote! I'll be back with your drinks, and breakfast should be ready in a few minutes."

As Callie walked to the kitchen, she tried to guess what could possibly have made Tiny so upset. She wondered if he and Grace had had an argument. But what couple didn't? And even if they had, Callie doubted Tiny would tell her any details. If that was the case, she'd know soon enough by checking on how the pancakes were coming along.

"I think I've got them settled for a few minutes." Callie walked over to the stove where she was relieved to find Tiny flipping perfect, fluffy, golden pancakes. "Those look great."

Casting a sideways glance at Tiny, Callie placed her hand gently on his shoulder and asked, "Want to talk about it?"

Tiny took a deep breath and nodded as he took the first batch of pancakes off the griddle and placed them on a serving platter. "Mom and dad are retiring. Closing down the bakery." As he said the word 'bakery,' it stuck in his throat, and his lower lip quivered.

For a brief second, Tiny reminded Callie of a young child who had lost his favorite toy. She almost burst out laughing imagining the behemoth of a man standing next to her as the biggest child she had ever seen.

Much to her chagrin, Tiny noticed the strained expression on her face. "Are you laughing at me, too?"

Callie noted the word 'too' at the end of his question and guessed Grace must have had a similar reaction. Poor Tiny.

"No! No! I would never laugh at you! But I thought you'd be happy for your parents. They've worked so hard for so many years. They deserve a chance to relax and enjoy themselves."

"You're both being mean to me!" Tiny pouted as he added six pats of butter to the sizzling griddle. He poured a heaping scoop of batter onto each pool of melted butter as he whined, "Grace said the same thing, and I don't think it's fair that you're both trying to make me feel guilty."

"I'm not trying to make you feel guilty! I'm just pointing out that when most people get to be your parents' age, they retire. Look at my parents! They're retired, and they've never been happier!"

Tiny lifted one corner of a pancake that had begun to turn golden brown on the edges and had small bubbles erupting on top. Deciding it needed a few more seconds, he put down his spatula, and looked Callie in the eye.

"It's not that I don't want them to be happy. It's just that it feels like the end of an era. I practically grew up in that bakery. And the thought of it sitting empty just breaks my heart." With tears threatening again, Tiny turned back to the griddle and flipped the first pancake.

"Oh, I'm sure it won't sit empty. That's prime real estate on Main Street. Someone will grab it up as soon as it hits the market. Turn it into some trendy hipster clothing store or artisan cafe." As soon as the words were out of her mouth, Callie knew she had made a mistake.

"Out."

"Wait, that didn't come out right!"

"Out of my kitchen. Now!"

Callie didn't think it was the right time to point out that, technically, it was her kitchen. "I, I uh, I have to make mimosas and bellinis for the ladies," she stuttered.

"Your cocktails are awful. I'll make them. Get. Out. Now!"

Bakery Blues

C allie stared at the pile of neatly stacked cedar wood feeling slightly overwhelmed. While she was confident that she could build the raised planter boxes herself given enough time, the pile was more intimidating than she had expected, and she was grateful her family would be arriving the following morning to help. The beds needed to be built and filled and planted in time for the soft opening of Al Fresco at The Terrace. Six empty planter boxes wouldn't exactly add to the ambiance she was hoping to create.

"Hey Callie! What's with the wood?"

Callie turned towards the voice and smiled as Eric and David, the appropriately named Goodmans, joined her.

"Hi guys! You're up early!"

"We were going to go on a hike. Want to join?" David asked. He was dressed in a t-shirt, shorts, and rugged hiking boots with a backpack slung over his shoulders. There was not a single ounce of flab anywhere on his body. It was all lean, sinewy muscle, and everything about him screamed outdoorsman.

"Sorry, can't today. Besides, I'm still sore from that hike you took me on two days ago."

"That was a tough one. But the gorges around here are spectacular. I can't believe you'd never been there with your guests."

Callie laughed. "Yes, well, most of my guests come here to relax, a concept I don't think you're familiar with!" From the moment the young couple had arrived at The Summer Breeze, they had been on the go. Hiking, canoeing, ziplining, and even some aerial adventuring. They had convinced her to join them on what they promised was a "moderately" difficult hike just a "short" drive from the bed and breakfast. Desperate for a break from her to-do lists, Callie had agreed without asking any questions.

She was still paying the price for the grueling eight-mile hike over an hour's drive away from The Summer Breeze. But the gorges and waterfalls they had seen had been spectacular and the company had been wonderful. Both Eric and David were easygoing, intelligent men with joie de vivre that was unparalleled and contagious. Callie had simultaneously felt physically exhausted and emotionally uplifted by the time her head had hit the pillow that night.

"I know what that wood is for! Are you working on those planter boxes?" Eric was similarly dressed and equally well built. But there was a kindness and intelligence in his expression, a softness that made her drawn to him.

"Yup." Callie smiled, "This pile of wood is bigger than I expected."

"I'll let that one go." David quipped mischievously. "Need some help?"

"I was thinking I'd do some prep work before my family comes out tomorrow to help me, but I think I'll just wait until they get here. You guys go ahead. It's your last day here!"

The two men exchanged a look and simultaneously took off their backpacks. "We're staying. What's the plan?"

<hr />

Four hours later, Callie sat down on the back porch steps, utterly exhausted. She was covered in sweat, sawdust, and soil, and absolutely thrilled by how everything had turned out.

By the time she had finished going over her plans and sketches with David and Eric, Tiny had arrived with the bed of his pickup truck filled with rich, dark soil. Although his mood had marginally improved since the day he found out his parents were closing down the bakery, Callie had hoped spending time with the Goodmans and doing some physical labor might improve it further.

She had been right. Although Tiny had been quieter than usual, Callie had been happy to hear his easy laughter on a few occasions. And he had poured himself into the work with gusto. Callie had been in charge of cutting the wood, the three men had carried it to the exact locations indicated on Callie's sketches, and then they had all worked together to assemble the boxes in situ. After Tiny had backed his pickup truck onto the yard, the foursome had taken turns painstakingly unloading the soil, shovel by shovel, into a wheelbarrow which was then dumped into the raised boxes. It had been hard, physical labor.

At one point, the Kappas, as the college roommates had come to be known, had come outside to watch them work and entertained them with plenty of unsolicited, and often downright inappropriate, observations about strong men and tools. All in all, it had turned out to be a fun and productive morning.

"I could use a cold glass of lemonade," Eric said as he lounged on the grass near Callie.

"Same. And some lunch. I'm starving." David sat down next to Eric. Both men looked at Tiny, expectantly.

"You're kidding me, right? I worked just as hard as you did." Tiny turned pointedly towards Callie, and added, "I could use some lemonade and lunch, too!"

Holding up her soiled hands in surrender, Callie laughed. "All right, all right. After all your hard work, the least I can do is make lemonade!" She dragged herself up and slowly climbed the steps to The Terrace. She smiled as she added almost as an afterthought, "Oh, and good thing I called Grace a little while ago. She should be here any minute with sandwiches."

———

"David and Eric are good people," Grace observed as she stretched out in the grass with her head in Tiny's lap.

"And these were some great sandwiches. Nothing beats your mom's sourdough, Tin—" Again, Callie regretted the words as soon as they were out of her mouth. The return of the forlorn, puppy dog expression on Tiny's face made her feel guilty.

Grace noticed it, too, because she unexpectedly sat up and shouted, "Arrgh, that is enough, Dominick!"

Shocked by her response, both Tiny and Callie stared at Grace.

"I cannot stand your pouting anymore! They are your parents! They deserve to be able to retire and enjoy their lives without worrying about how sad you'll be because you can't get fresh baked bread and pastries every day! How. Can. You. Be. So. Selfish." Grace accentuated each word of her question with a futile punch at Tiny's massive arms.

"Ow! Cut it out, Grace! What's gotten into you? I'm not being selfish! I'm just sad that the bakery is going to stand empty."

"Well, technically, it probably won't sit empty because it is prime real—"

"You stay out of this," Tiny pointed his finger at Callie and glared. "I don't want to hear any more of your thoughts on real estate and trendy stores."

"I'm sorry to break it to you Dominick, but Callie is right. The bakery isn't going to stay empty. In fact, it's already been purchased."

"Wha...no it hasn't! I was just there this morning, and my parents didn't say anything about it to me."

"I'm telling you it has."

"And how do you know that?"

"Because I signed the paperwork when I went to pick up the sandwiches."

Callie could swear she heard the chirping of crickets during the silence following Grace's unexpected announcement. She watched as Tiny's face went through a series of emotions starting with disbelief, then incredulity, and finally a calm curiosity.

"You bought the bakery?"

Grace nodded.

"Why?"

"I didn't do it for you, if that's what you're thinking."

"Why, Grace?" Tiny asked gently, as he reached out and took Grace's hand in his.

"I love my grocery store. You know I do. And I'm not planning on giving that up, but I've been wanting to try my hand at something else, something new, for a while now. And when Bertha and Hank said they were going to sell the bakery, I realized it was the perfect opportunity for me."

"How come no one told me any of this?"

"Because we wanted to be certain before we got your hopes up."

"You're not going to turn the bakery into a trendy, hipster clothing store, are you?" Callie asked jokingly.

"No," Grace laughed, "I'm definitely not."

"What then?" Tiny asked, not able to take his eyes off Grace.

"I'm going to keep it as a bakery."

"You are?"

"Yes, with some new items on the menu."

"And you signed the paperwork already? It's a done deal?"

"It's a done deal."

"Why?"

"I already told you why. Because I wanted to do something different."

"And this had nothing to do with me?"

"Maybe it had a little to do with you."

"Just a little?"

"Yes! Just a little!"

"Grace?"

"Yes?"

"Will you marry me?"

Bakery Bliss

"I can't believe he proposed to her just like that! With you sitting there watching like some nosey neighbor."

"They were in my backyard!"

"But still, you should have known what was coming and made yourself scarce."

"How could I have known what was coming, Lynette? I don't even think Tiny knew what he was going to do! One minute we were talking about bakeries and the next minute he's proposing to Grace."

"I think it's all so romantic. I guess when you know, you know."

"Oh, now you're a philosopher, too?"

"Yup, I'm going to add it to my list of skills," Lynette called out as she walked to the front door. "I'll see you tomorrow."

Callie chuckled and shut the door. She was looking forward to a quiet night before her family arrived the following morning. She hoped they wouldn't be too disappointed she had started the garden project without them, but she felt fairly certain it was for the best. Her parents, while in excellent shape, weren't as young as they used to be, and Nica was in no condition to do any physically demanding work. The Goodmans and Tiny, on the other hand, had been up to the challenge and eager to get their hands dirty. Besides, Callie reminded herself, her family would be just as happy spending hours planning out where to plant all the vegetable seedlings they were going to pick up from a nursery on their drive down to The Summer Breeze.

Callie knew it was probably the last time Nica would be comfortable enough to make the drive, and she wanted to spend some quality time with her little sister before she had her baby. Unbidden, an image of Nica as a chubby, squirming infant with her toothless smile popped into Callie's mind and brought a smile to her face. She couldn't believe her baby sister was going to be a mother. The thought suddenly brought on a rush of emotion, and Callie felt the sting of tears in her eyes and a lump in her throat. Life would never be the same again, and there was an unexpected bitter sweetness that came with the realization.

Taking a deep breath, Callie made her way to her bedroom and changed into her pajamas. As she crawled into bed, the toll of the physical labor she had done that day overtook her, and she fell asleep almost as soon as her head hit the pillow.

—⁘—

"I can't believe Tiny proposed to Grace just like that! With you sitting there watching like some nosey neighbor."

"That's exactly what Lynette said! Need I remind you that they were in *my* backyard?"

"You should have known what was coming."

Callie rolled her eyes at her sister who didn't even notice because she was so intent on getting every last crumb of maple syrup-soaked pancake off her plate, onto her fork, and into her waiting mouth.

"I couldn't eat another bite."

"Good thing, because there's literally nothing left for you to eat."

"Ha. Ha."

"Are we going to sit around all day or we actually going to do some gardening?" Callie's dad asked as he pushed his chair away from the table.

"You and Jack go on and unload the truck. Callie can help me clean up."

"Why do I always have to clean up? Why can't Nica help?" Callie laughed as she repeated a phrase that was practically her mantra growing up.

Callie thought she heard Nica mumble something under her breath. Assuming it was one of the many excuses she always managed to come up with as a child, Callie joked, "Let me guess. You have to go finish your homework."

Nica looked up at her sister with wide eyes and said just loud enough to be heard, "No. It's because my water just broke."

———

"You're sure it's okay to drive all that way with a new baby?"

"Callie, stop fussing, we'll be fine."

"Why don't you stay here for a few more days?"

"Because a crying newborn isn't exactly the relaxing bed and breakfast vibe people come here for. Besides, you'll come up in a couple of weeks, and I promise you can monopolize little Aidan all you want."

Callie sighed and lowered her face to the tightly swaddled bundle in her hands. She nuzzled his soft skin and breathed in his baby smell. "Love you, Li'l Bug. See you in a couple of weeks."

"Hello? Callie? Dominick? Where are you?" Not hearing an answer, Grace guessed correctly that they were both probably out in the backyard tending to the garden. Carefully balancing a small tray she was carrying, Grace opened the back door and climbed down the stairs.

"Hey, you two! Have you started any dinner prep, or have you been out here puttering around all day?"

Tiny laughed in response. "Puttering. But it's not my fault. I got here a couple of hours ago to prep and found Callie moping around the kitchen looking like a forlorn puppy."

"Oh please, if that isn't the pot calling the kettle black," Callie said in defense.

"What's that supposed to mean?"

"At least I'm productive when I'm in an off mood." For added emphasis, Callie raised an eyebrow at her giant friend.

"Huh?"

Grace and Callie exchanged knowing smiles and promptly changed the subject.

"What's on the tray?" Callie asked just as Grace said, "You got all the plants in!"

Tiny looked from one woman to the other and felt certain a joke had just been shared at his expense.

"You can give me a tour of the garden, but first, I'm in need of some taste testers." And with a slight flourish, Grace lifted the cover off the tray to reveal three beautifully decorated cupcakes.

"Those are beautiful, Grace! Is this what you've been working on the past couple of days?"

Grace nodded, "I've been testing some different recipes, trying some new flavor combinations. Dominick, come hold this for me."

Doing as he was told, Dominick took the tray from Grace and beamed from ear to ear. "These look spectacular."

"They need to taste good, too!" Picking up a small knife that had been lying in the tray, Grace cut one of the cupcakes in half. "This one is cranberry and candied orange with cream cheese frosting."

Callie picked up a piece with anticipation and took a small nibble, knowing she should pace herself. While the frosting and the cake practically melted in her mouth, it was the unexpected tang and the punch of flavor from the candied orange peel that made her abandon her resolve. Finishing the rest of the cupcake in two bites, she said through her mouthful of food, "That is one of the best cupcakes I have ever had."

Tiny just nodded and waited eagerly for Grace's next offering.

"Maybe I'd better cut the rest into smaller pieces," Grace laughed as she split another cupcake. "This one is cardamom with an espresso frosting and cardamom cream filling."

"Cardamom and espresso?" Callie asked, her mouth already watering in anticipation of the unexpected flavor combination.

"Yup, it turned out even better than I expected," Grace said proudly as she handed Callie a piece and popped another bite into Tiny's open mouth.

Closing her eyes, Callie savored the delicately spiced cupcake and then moaned aloud as the cool cardamom cream combined with the espresso frosting to create an explosion of flavor unlike any she had ever had before.

"Delicious. Just absolutely sublime."

Grace smiled and cut the last cupcake in half. "This one is my favorite. Mango, with mango and coconut buttercream frosting and a passionfruit curd."

Without waiting to be served, Callie reached into the tray and picked up what appeared to be the bigger half and ate it whole.

"Oh, Grace...you have outdone yourself! This makes me feel like I'm on a tropical beach somewhere. It's like summertime in my mouth. I had no idea you were this good!"

"I did." Tiny beamed from ear to ear.

Déjà Vu

"You've got a real green thumb, you know that?"

"I have a lot of talents."

"Mmmm, I can attest to that. But those talents are reserved for me." Nick kissed the top of Callie's head and ran his fingers through her disheveled hair.

Callie propped herself up on his bare chest and smiled. "I'm glad you came up this weekend."

"Me, too. And I'm glad we drove up to see your family yesterday. It was nice to see them and meet your nephew. I never knew a baby could sleep so much. You were fantastic with him. A natural."

For a split second, Callie felt the stirring of annoyance at Nick's comment. She looked up at him to retort, but then saw the earnest look in his eyes, and knew he meant nothing more by his words. They were simply meant as a compliment. She quickly quashed her irritation, not wanting to ruin a wonderful weekend by overreacting to an innocent remark.

"He's an easy baby," she said noncommittally and laid her head back down.

With an almost imperceptible sigh of relief that Callie hadn't misinterpreted his words, Nick stroked her hair again and promptly changed the subject. "When do you think you'll be able to start serving some of the stuff you've grown here?" He shouldn't have been so relieved.

"You know what? That's a great question! Let's go look." Callie sat up, swung her legs off the bed, and grabbed her robe.

"Whoa, where are you going? Come back here."

"Out to the garden!"

"Now?"

"Yes, now! We've already wasted half the day in bed! Come on, get up!"

"Half the day? It's not even 8:30." Callie heard him mumble.

—ele—

"It could be anything. Deer, rabbits, moles, chipmunks. We've seen all of those around here. We should have listened to your dad when he told us to put up a fence around the vegetable beds." Lynette, always the pragmatist, pointed out the obvious without sparing Callie's feelings.

Callie replied without lifting her head from the kitchen table. "You mean me. *I* should have listened. I'm the one who wanted to preserve the aesthetics of the backyard, the views of the lake. I'm the one who wanted to create the 'restaurant in a garden' feel. I'm the one who refused to listen to reason."

"Well, when you put it that way...."

Callie groaned. "When Nick and I went out there yesterday morning, I thought I was overreacting, but there's definitely something making its way through the vegetables."

"My guess is that there's more than one something at work out there."

"What about a scarecrow? Would that work?"

"Oh, yeah, great idea. That would really add to the ambiance you want to create," Lynette said sarcastically. "Besides, birds aren't your problem. It's something or several somethings with four legs." Pausing for a moment to think whether it was even worth mentioning what she would do, Lynette decided to go all in. "What about hiring an exterminator? Or putting down some poison?"

At this, Callie raised her head off the table and pointed her index finger at Lynette. "No. Absolutely not."

"I figured that would be your answer."

Callie groaned again. "There's gotta be something we can do."

"There is. Build a fence."

"Besides that."

Sighing with frustration at the pointlessness of this conversation, Lynette got up from the table. "While you sit here and try to figure that out, I'll be at the front desk making sure your b and b is running smoothly." And for good measure and in good fun, she chuckled and threw in, "Well, at least more smoothly than your garden."

Fortunately, she didn't see the other finger Callie pointed at her retreating back.

elle

"Hey, Cal. I don't know if you've noticed but it looks like something is eating at your vegetable beds," Kirsten said as she walked in through the back door of the kitchen dressed in one of her perennial floral, ankle length dresses and adorned with an assortment of beaded bracelets and rings. Her naturally blond hair, bleached to an even lighter shade during her honeymoon in Tahiti, fell in soft waves down her back.

Despite her comment, which did nothing to relieve Callie's stress level, there was something about Kirsten's presence that always managed to soothe Callie. "Yeah, I've noticed."

Hearing the dejected tone in Callie's voice, Kirsten asked, "Want to talk about it? I have a few minutes before my next client. I was just going to grab a Kombucha and head back to the spa to prep, but I'd rather hang out with you for a bit."

Without waiting for an answer, Kirsten grabbed a bottle out of the fridge and sat down across from her friend.

Callie tried to muster up a smile, and Kirsten burst into laughter.

"What? What's so funny?"

"Have you been eating chocolate ice cream?"

"No," Callie said guiltily.

"Callie! It's not even noon."

"Well, this situation called for it!" Callie wiped her mouth and licked her lips in an attempt to erase the damning evidence from her face.

"You still missed a spot. Let me guess, straight out of the container?"

"Is there any other way?"

—ele—

Callie, feeling much calmer after her conversation with Kirsten, decided that the best way to tackle her garden pest problem was to get informed. She had grabbed her laptop and made her way to the back porch steps to do some online research while keeping her eye out for any culprits that decided to make an appearance.

She was hunched over her laptop reading intently when the sound of Lynette's voice startled her.

"Humane ways to get rid of garden pests," Lynette read aloud the phrase in Callie's search bar. "Still stuck on that, I see. I thought when I saw you with your laptop, maybe you were actually doing some work."

"You're a real comedian today. And, I'll have you know, this is work. I'm researching ways to make our business more successful."

"Indeed." Callie's use of the word "our" was not lost on Lynette, and she was reminded again why she loved working for her. Changing her tone, she added gently, "My parents used to do a lot of gardening when they were younger. I can ask what worked for them."

Callie looked at Lynette, wondering if another quip was coming her way. But the earnest expression on Lynette's face let her know that she was just trying to be helpful.

"That would be great, thank you."

"Have you found any good ideas?" Lynette asked.

"Yes. One." Dejectedly, Callie concluded, "Build a fence."

———

"What time are our new guests arriving?"

"Should be any minute now. I hope they're more interesting than the folks we have here right now."

"Lynette! Shhh, they'll hear you!"

"How? They're out on a vineyard tour."

"Oh, well, still. It's not nice to talk about our guests."

"But it's okay to meddle in their lives?"

"Touché. So, who do we have joining us today?"

"Father and son duo."

"That's a first."

"Says here," Lynette gestured towards her laptop, "that they're visiting the university. The dad's an alum."

"He put that in the comments?"

"No," Lynette said sheepishly. "I Googled him."

"Lynette! Why?"

"He's got a really unique last name, and I thought I'd heard it before. Turns out, I was right. One of the buildings on campus is named after him."

Callie whistled. "That's a pretty big deal. What's his name?"

"Jansen Smith."

"Smith? That's the unique last name?" Callie asked incredulously.

"Oh, fine. I was bored one day when you were busy in the garden and started doing some...'work-related research.'"

"Is that what we're calling it? I think maybe I need to add a clause prohibiting the invasion of guest privacy to your employment contract."

"We don't have a contract."

"Maybe I'd better draft one."

Lynette laughed and opened a new browser window on her laptop, "Check this out."

—ele—

By the time Jansen Smith and his son arrived, Callie felt like she knew almost everything there was to know about him. He had started his own software company straight out of college, taken it public and now had a net worth that ended with more zeros than any one person could ever need. Like many of the wealthy elite, he had signed a pledge to give away half of his wealth during his lifetime and was living up to his promise by being a prolific philanthropist. The building on the university campus that Lynette had mentioned was a state-of-the-art cancer research facility, built in honor of his wife whom he had lost to cancer several years earlier.

"And they only have the one son?"

"Looks like it."

"I'm surprised he's staying here. I would think the university would put him up somewhere nice."

"*This* place is nice, Callie!"

"You know what I mean."

"Does it say whether he was referred by anyone?"

"I never checked. Hold on." Lynette scrolled to the bottom of the screen and added, "Nope."

"I wonder how he found out about us."

At that moment, the doorbell rang. "I guess we're about to find out."

***

"He seemed like such a regular guy," Callie observed.

"Right? Friendly, easy-going."

"I thought his son was going to be with him."

"Guess they're arriving separately?"

"Hopefully he's like his father. Being born into that kind of money can't be an easy way to grow up."

"Oh, please. Play me a violin."

"I'm serious, Lynette. Jansen earned his money. His son has never had to lift a finger his whole life. That can really mess a person up."

"Yeah, it can turn him into a snobby, entitled little—"

Before Lynette could finish, a flashy sports car with music blaring from the open windows pulled up the driveway and came to a stop.

Lynette gave Callie an 'I told you so' expression and decided it was the perfect time to go find a snack in the kitchen.

Sighing, Callie walked out to the front porch to welcome her newest guest. As she squinted in the bright sunlight to get a look at the young man now walking towards her, Callie thought her eyes were playing tricks on her. There was something about his build and the way he walked that was oddly familiar to her. It gave her a strange, uneasy feeling of déjà vu. And when he bounded up the stairs two at a time and stopped in front of her, Callie felt like she had seen a ghost.

"Hi there! I'm Jansen Smith's son, Jansen Junior. But everyone just calls me JR. Is my dad here yet?"

Before Callie could regroup enough to answer, a voice behind her asked, "What did I tell you about that loud music?"

"It was just that one song." JR smiled at his father and held up his right hand, as if to say, 'I swear.'

"Don't make me regret buying you that car."

"Promise."

The two men gave each other a warm hug and turned towards Callie, who was staring at them with her mouth open.

Mistaking her expression for disapproval, Jansen clarified. "Don't worry, Callie. I promise he won't be playing any loud music and disturbing your other guests. Callie? Callie are you okay?"

"Oh, yes. Yes, I'm fine." Callie shook her head as if to clear it and continued lamely. "The sun was just in my eyes."

"Great place you've got here. We were here a few years ago when they inaugurated my mom's research building on campus, but I can't remember where we stayed. I don't think it was around here, was it, Dad?"

"No, they put us up at that upscale hotel down on the other end of the lake."

"Now I remember it. Less upscale and more uptight, if you ask me. Glad we're not staying there again."

Realizing which property they were talking about, Callie pulled herself together and joined the conversation. "That hotel went out of business about a year, year and a half ago. Some boutique hotel chain just bought it, and they're planning to remodel and reopen later this year."

Callie hadn't meant to inject any of her worry about the impending competition into her comment, but it must have come through anyway.

"Well, I don't think it's anything you need to be concerned about. Looks like what you have here is something completely different. As soon as I walked in the front door, I felt a warmth and homey-ness about this place that I think a lot of people are looking for and will be drawn to. I already feel like I can let my guard down and relax here. Something you definitely can't get at a hotel."

"Thank you...we strive to give people a place they'll want to come to over and over again. May I ask how you found us?"

"Give me one second, and I'll tell you." At this, Jansen pulled his phone out of his pocket and tapped in a few words. A split second later, the incoming message notification came through. "Looks like my assistant is part of an online network of personal assistants who share inside tips on travel, and someone named..." Here, he looked down at his phone and back up at Callie. "Rita Pearson recommended your place. Name ring a bell?"

Callie smiled broadly, pleasantly surprised that the very exacting Rita Pearson had been satisfied with the experience her A-list celebrity clients had had at The Summer Breeze and nodded her head. "It does. Two of her clients stayed with us."

Callie fondly recalled the week Sean and Rina Weston, the Hollywood 'it' couple, had spent at the B&B just a few months earlier. They had desperately needed time out of the limelight, and they had found it in the warm embrace of The Summer Breeze.

And then, to allay any questions, she quickly added, "But I'm not at liberty to tell you their names."

"As it should be," Jansen replied, with newfound respect for Callie, who could have easily name-dropped Rita's clients to impress him.

"Will you be joining us for dinner?" Callie asked hopefully, changing the subject. Apart from wanting them to try Tiny's cooking, Callie had her own reasons for inviting the two men to join them at The Terrace.

Jansen looked at JR, "Up to you."

"Love to." JR smiled at Callie, and the feeling of déjà vu returned and sent a shiver down her spine.

Doppelgänger

"What'd I tell you?"

Lynette sat down across from Callie at the kitchen table, her eyes wide. "The similarities are uncanny."

"Well?" Callie prompted and waited patiently to hear the words she had been expecting.

"You were right. There, I said it. Happy now?"

"As a matter of fact, I am."

"This can't just be a fluke or a doppeldanger or whatever that word is."

"Doppelgänger."

"Right."

"This is something way more than that."

"Right. Have you said anything to Kirsten, yet?"

"No! If I recall, I was expressly forbidden *by you* to stick my nose in other people's business!"

"I think this time we need to make an exception to that rule. But we have to handle things carefully."

"I'm all ears."

———

"Good morning, Callie."

"Hi Jansen, heading out so early? Have you had breakfast?"

Jansen shook his head. "We're running late. This guy overslept."

JR, looking like he was still half asleep, mumbled "We'll just grab something on the way to campus."

"Why don't I pack a to-go box for you? We've got the best coffee around and Tiny just made some blueberry scones that are to die for."

"If that's the same chef from last night, then I'm in."

"Great! Come on back to the kitchen with me, and I'll get everything ready for you."

As they were walking to the kitchen, Jansen commented, "You know, Callie, you're doing a great thing here. Creating jobs and opportunities for so many people. I even love that you've got your intern starting with the fundamentals by rotating through every job at the bed and breakfast."

"My intern?" Callie asked, confused.

"Yeah, that young lady named Ellie."

"Oh, you must mean Evie. Right. Yes, well, we all have to start somewhere."

Intern? Callie thought to herself.

"And kudos to you for making it a paid internship."

Callie smiled noncommittally and wondered why Evie would tell a white lie about something so innocuous.

＿ℓℓ＿

"I still can't get enough of that car," Evie announced as she walked into the kitchen for her evening shift at The Terrace.

"What car?" Callie looked up and was surprised to see that Evie, who usually dressed in black trousers and a white button-down shirt like the other servers, was instead dressed in a body-hugging, short black skirt with a very form fitting white t-shirt. Her hair was styled in soft waves that framed her face instead of in a more practical up-do, and her make-up looked as though it had been professionally done. There was no denying how pretty she looked, but it all seemed very inappropriate for dinner service at the restaurant.

"What do you mean, 'what car?' *That* car. The one that must have cost at least, *at least,* $100,000."

As Evie spoke, Callie noticed an odd, almost rapacious glimmer in her eyes.

"You're kidding, right?" Tiny turned from the stove and Callie watched as he took in Evie's appearance. Callie thought she noticed a subtle transition in Tiny's expression from surprise to disapproval, but thankfully, he was tactful enough not to linger on Evie's bare legs. Instead, he turned back to the stove and added, "That's a Lamborghini Huracan. It *starts* at $200,000."

Evie's eyes grew wide, "Wow, these people are legitimately loaded. How old is the son?"

Maybe, Callie thought to herself, she'd have to add a fraternization policy to the non-existent contract she had with her employees.

"I'm not sure. Anyway, it's none of our business."

"I can just Google it and find out."

"Why would you want to do that?" Callie asked, more indignantly than she had meant to. She found herself feeling protective of the Smiths and very put off by Evie.

"Just curious," Evie replied, sounding annoyed herself.

Callie cocked her eyebrow at Evie, "You'd better put your stuff away. It's going to be a busy night."

As Evie walked off, Callie could have sworn she heard her mumble something about why someone so rich would want to stay at a "dinky little bed and breakfast."

———ele———

"Are you going to say something to her, or do you want me to?"

"Which 'her' are we talking about?"

"Both, I guess. First, Evie. She cannot wear clothes like that again. It was distracting for the customers and just all around inappropriate. Every time she bent over a table to clear something, I thought we were going to see her—"

"Lynette!" Callie interrupted.

"What? It's true. You need to say something. Who was she trying to impress anyway?"

"I think she was hoping the Smiths would come in for dinner, but they had some big reception to attend at the university."

"Why would she want to impress the Smiths?"

Callie filled Lynette in on her conversation with Jansen earlier that day about Evie being a paid intern.

"'Intern?' Why on earth would she lie about something like that?"

"At first, I thought maybe she had a little crush on JR. I thought maybe that's why she was dressed up."

"Barely dressed, you mean," Lynette clarified mercilessly.

"And then she was going on about JR's car and how rich the Smith's must be. It was all a little over the top."

"That girl's a climber. The more I know her, the less I like her."

"There's not much we can do about it right now. We need the help."

Lynette, also feeling oddly protective of the Smiths, added, "Maybe we can shift her schedule around? Have her work hours that we know the Smiths won't be here."

"That's a good idea. Speaking of the Smiths...."

"Yeah, we need to talk to Kirsten. You're closer to her, maybe you should be the one to do it."

———

Callie made the short walk to the spa the next morning, her heart beating loudly in her chest and her hands clammy. She had spent an uneasy night wondering what she should say to Kirsten. Should she tell her outright? Try to get some background information first? Lynette had been no help whatsoever beyond telling Callie that she had to be the one to handle it.

"Kirsten?" It took Callie's eyes a moment to adjust to the dim, soothing mood lighting in the spa after coming in from the bright morning sunshine. She looked around with pride at how beautiful the small waiting area was. A cream-colored velvet sofa with plush throw pillows and a small antique coffee table with a selection of tasteful magazines made up the bulk of the furniture. The walls were painted a soft, warm grey and adorned with several paintings, Callie's favorite of which was a large watercolor of the sun setting over Cayuga Lake. A small desk and chair sat across from the main entrance and just off to the side was a short hallway which led to the two treatment rooms.

Kirsten, wearing what looked like a white lab coat over her dress, came out of one of the rooms, wiping her hands on a white towel.

"Hi! I thought I heard you! This is a nice surprise, you hardly ever come out to the spa. Do you want to schedule a massage? Facial? I have an opening later today, or I can get you in first thing tomorrow morning if that's easier."

Feeling utterly unprepared, Callie decided her best course of action would be to get straight to the point. "Actually, I was hoping to talk to you about Chad." As soon as the words were out of Callie's mouth, she regretted it. Her serious tone didn't help matters either and came across as foreboding.

"Chad? Is he okay? Did something happen?" There was no mistaking the panic in Kirsten's voice.

"No, no. I'm sorry, I didn't mean to make that sound so ominous. Look, why don't we sit down for a minute."

"Callie! You are making me very nervous. Spill. Now."

"Is Chad an only child?"

Squinting her eyes at Callie as if she was having a hard time making sense of her question, Kirsten slowly nodded her head. "Yes, you know this. Only his parents and a couple of cousins came out for our wedding. You remember I introduced you to them? His dad gave that emotional toast that got everyone teary eyed?"

"Of course, I remember."

"Then why are you asking me if Chad is an only child?"

Callie thought she noticed a slight shift in Kirsten's voice. The panic had been replaced by a cautious, concerned tone.

"Callie? Why are you asking me that question?"

"There's someone here I think you should meet."

Kirsten raised her hand to her mouth, "Oh no. How did they find him?"

"Who?"

"What?"

"How did who find him?" Callie asked.

"His parents."

"I am so confused. Why would his parents need to find him? They were just here."

"Not his adoptive parents! His biological parents!"

"Chad is adopted?"

Kirsten sighed with frustration, and Callie realized that her friend had shared more than she had wanted to.

"Yes, he almost never talks about it, because he's never known any parents other than the ones who have raised him. Look, Callie, I don't know why I just told you that. It's really not my story to share. It's Chad's."

Callie reached over and took Kirsten's hand in hers. "I'm never going to say a word about this."

"I know, I know. But I shouldn't have said it. It just kind of came out, you know? I've always had this deep-seated fear of his life being turned upside down by the unexpected appearance of his biological parents."

"It's not them." Callie wanted desperately to reassure Kirsten that her husband's life wasn't about to be upended but knew there was nothing she could do but plow ahead. "I'm so sorry, Kirsten. I didn't mean to upset you or put you in this position. But there's a young man staying at the bed and breakfast who I think you need to see."

Holding tightly to Callie's hand, Kirsten nodded her head just once.

A Heart Shaped Mark

"**I** feel like I've seen a ghost."

"Now you understand why we wanted you to see him."

Kirsten, her face ashen, looked up at Lynette and nodded, "I do."

Callie, who was sitting next to Kirsten on the back porch steps, asked gently, "Do you know what you're going to do?"

"I have to tell him. This can't possibly be a fluke."

"But what if it is? Doppledangers are a real thing, you know."

"Doppelgängers," Callie corrected.

"Whatever," Lynette snapped. "Before you cause the same sort of panic that Callie caused for you this morning, maybe you should do some research. Try to get more information."

"How? I can't just Google 'who are Chad's biological parents?'"

"You'd be surprised how much Google knows," Lynette mumbled.

"Maybe you can talk to Jansen first?" Callie asked. "See if you can find out anything from him about JR."

"I don't know...I wouldn't even know how to start the conversation. What if I find out something that Chad doesn't even want to know?"

"Lynette, when are they scheduled to leave?" Callie asked, trying to buy her friend some time to figure out what to do next.

"They were supposed to leave tomorrow, but they asked me to extend their stay by a few days. Said they'd been so busy ever since they got here, that they didn't feel like they'd had much time to explore the area and spend quality time together."

"Okay, so that gives us a little breathing room." But Callie knew the breathing room would be short lived, and Kirsten would still have an inevitably difficult decision to make.

—— *eee* ——

"Is Evie scheduled to work tonight? I thought we were going to switch out her hours so that she's not working when Jansen and JR are around," Callie asked as she walked in the front door carrying a handful of freshly cut flowers. While her vegetable garden may have been struggling, the flower beds in her front yard were thriving, and she beamed with pride as she breathed in the heady fragrance of light pink lilacs.

Lynette, who had been sitting at the front desk responding to customer inquiries, answered without looking up from her computer. "I did. She's not scheduled to work tonight. Why?"

"I just saw her car pull in behind JR's Tornado."

Lynette chuckled, happy to be correcting Callie for a change. "His car is called a Huracan. Not a Tornado."

"Whatever. I wonder why she's here if she's not working."

Before Lynette could venture a guess, the front door opened and Jansen and his son entered, both looking very handsome in dark tailored suits, crisp button-down shirts, and silk ties.

And through the open door, Lynette saw Evie's car pull out of the driveway and speed away. Almost as if she didn't want to be seen.

"You two look very nice! How was the press conference and the tour?" Jansen had mentioned to Callie earlier that morning that he and JR would be out for most of the afternoon attending events at the university.

"It was fantastic. The university's President was incredibly supportive of our vision to expand the medical school program."

"Dad! Of course he was supportive. Fifty million dollars would make anyone supportive."

Callie glanced at Lynette who was staring wide-eyed at JRs announcement.

"I thought you agreed with me on the amount," Jansen replied, sounding surprised and a little hurt.

"I do. It's not that." JR softened his tone and added, "It's just that I don't want you to forget how much money changes people. You've told me that my whole life. And I've seen it with my own eyes. People treat me one way when they first meet me, and then the moment they find out who I am, everything changes."

Then maybe don't drive around in a flashy sports car, Callie thought to herself.

"I mean, I get it. I'm not naïve. I'm grateful for everything we have. But I can smell avarice from a mile away. You taught me that, too. And that man? He was practically licking your boots."

"Fair enough. But he's getting no personal financial benefit out of my donation. His ego has been inflated, yes. But I'm willing to allow that as long as he gets the job done. At the end of the day, he and I have the same goal. We both want to make the university research program and medical school the best there is. You and I know what your mother went through those last few months. What we went through. If we can spare another person, another family, that pain, I will have accomplished something worthwhile with my life."

As Jansen spoke the last few words, his voice cracked. Softening, JR place his arm gently around his dad's shoulder and gave it a squeeze.

"Mom would be incredibly proud of you."

Jansen nodded and whispered, "There's not a day that goes by that I don't miss her."

"Same."

The two men looked at each other and smiled sadly.

Callie, aware that their presence was intruding on a very private moment, tried to think of a way for her and Lynette to discreetly leave the room. Lynette must have had the same thought because she tried to slowly get up from her chair. Unfortunately, the chair decided to make a very awkward squeaking sound at just that moment.

Jansen turned towards the sound, suddenly reminded that he and JR weren't alone in the room and cleared his throat loudly. "Sorry about that, ladies. It's been a very emotional couple of days for me. Exactly two years today since we lost JR's mom."

"Please don't apologize. You're doing incredible work here in her honor, Jansen. Truly inspiring."

"Thank you. And as I said before, so are you. Giving Evie the day off today so that she could attend the press conference was incredibly generous."

"Evie was at the press conference?" Lynette asked, unable to keep the incredulity out of her voice.

"Yes, she even stayed for the tour. Said she wanted to learn as much as she could about the school and the medical program. It's incredible really, her interest in learning about business from you while wanting to pursue a career in medicine. You don't see that kind of ambition in a young person very often these days."

"I'm not sure 'ambition' is the right word for it," JR said, sounding annoyed. "If you ask me, that girl is only interested in one thing."

"Oh? I thought you two were getting on pretty well. Every time I looked over, she was chatting away with you. I think she's taken quite a fancy to you."

"The feeling isn't mutual, Dad. Sorry, Callie, I don't mean to be rude. I just get the feeling Evie is only interested in one thing, and it's not business or medicine. I hope I haven't offended you."

"No, not at all," Callie answered politely, unsure of what else to say. But she privately questioned how Evie had found out about the press conference. It had only been announced in the local newspaper the day before, and Callie was almost certain Evie was not a newspaper reader. For a moment, the thought crossed her mind that maybe Evie had simply followed JR's car.

—еее—

Callie changed into her preferred sleeping attire for warm months, a pair of shorts and a tank top, both emblazoned with her alma mater's logo, a caricature of a fierce looking yellow-jacket. She crawled into bed knowing that sleep would not come easily. The conversation between Jansen and JR weighed heavily on her, and she said a silent prayer of gratitude again for the health of her family. With everything the Smiths had, their wealth, fancy cars, multiple houses, they didn't have the one thing they both wanted the most. Callie knew they would give everything up in a heartbeat for more time with JR's mom.

Maybe, she thought, finding out that he had a brother would fill a small part of the hole left in JR's heart when he lost his mom. But then again, maybe the hole would just grow bigger if this all turned out to be an uncanny coincidence.

JR walked into the kitchen, unsure of whether there would be anything available for breakfast given that it was almost noon. The giant man everyone incongruously referred to as 'Tiny' was busy cutting a large mound of mushrooms and whistling happily to himself while Callie and Lynette sat at the kitchen table, both huddled around a laptop.

"Hey there, sorry, didn't mean to interrupt. Is there any way I can grab a banana or some cereal? I'm starving and my dad is stuck on calls for the next couple of hours."

JR noticed all three of them exchange a look and wondered if he had committed some sort of faux pas by walking into the kitchen uninvited. He had been immediately relieved by Tiny's response.

"We don't do 'grab a banana or some cereal' around here. You like pancakes?"

"Love 'em."

"What flavor?"

"Oh, I don't want to trouble you."

"Sit. Don't talk back," Tiny commanded pointing the knife he had been using to cut the mushrooms first at JR and then at the kitchen table. "What flavor? Blueberry? Banana? Chocolate chip?"

Doing as he was told, JR sat down at the table and said, "Blueberry, please." At the thought of freshly made blueberry pancakes, his stomach made an audibly loud rumble.

"One order of blueberry pancakes coming up," Tiny said with a chuckle and then added, "A double stack."

JR sat quietly and watched as Tiny set aside the mushrooms and went about making the pancakes in short order. A sense of bonhomie pervaded the kitchen. No one was talking much, but the three coworkers and friends were quietly going about their business, clearly relaxed and perfectly content to be exactly where they were.

When Tiny set the heaping stack of pancakes and maple syrup in front of him, JR's sense of happiness intensified, and he dug in without a word.

"Those are some of the best pancakes I've ever had. And pouring the syrup on the plate *before* adding the pancakes and then again *on top* of the pancakes is genius."

"I'll take credit for that," Callie chimed in.

"Are there any good trails close by? If I can pry my dad away from his phone, I'd love to go on a hike. And after this meal, I need it!"

"He seems like a good kid. Clearly comes from a lot of money but doesn't seem to treat people differently because of it."

"You just like him because he loves your cooking."

"That's the sign of a good human."

Callie smiled distractedly. "I wonder how Kirsten's doing right now. I wish we could have given her a head's up."

"How? We didn't know she was going to come out of the spa when we were outside with JR showing him the hiking trails, and we certainly couldn't have known that he would decide in that moment to ask for a massage."

Callie knew Lynette was right, but she still wished she could have spared her friend an uncomfortable situation. "True. At least she handled it well."

"It's been ages since I've gotten a massage." JR said, his voice slightly muffled by the massage table.

Kirsten worked the warm aromatherapy lotion into JR's youthful, supple skin and wondered why someone as young as JR would even need a massage. But it wasn't her job to ask questions or to judge. Her job was to make a person feel like the hour they spent with her was all about them. She knew that that intangible benefit from a massage was really what kept people coming back. The physical comfort was fleeting, while the emotional rejuvenation lasted much longer.

"That sounded like I used to get massages all the time, didn't it?" Without waiting for an answer, JR continued, "I just meant that the last time I got a massage was when I hurt my back after a lacrosse game. I had to go to a physical therapist for a couple of months, and part of the therapy included a massage."

"It's always good to get back problems taken care of...I take it you're fully recovered?"

"I am. It was years ago. When I was in high school. We were playing a team much better and rougher than ours. I got hit pretty badly and sprained my lower back. Needless to say, that was the end of my lacrosse career. My mom was very protective."

"Only child?" Kirsten hadn't meant to ask such a personal question, but she had just blurted it out. Partly because she enjoyed learning about her clients, but mostly, she admitted to herself, because she needed to know how JR would answer.

"Mmmm," JR confirmed, his voice taking on the slow, relaxed, faraway tone which signaled to Kirsten that she was doing her job well.

JR turned his head to the other side and sighed. "Although when I was younger, I was convinced I had an older brother. When I used to get scared or have a hard time sleeping, my mom would tell me a story about how my older brother was always watching over me and would never let anything bad happen to me. She said I'd know who he was because he was marked with a little heart on his right shoulder. I always believed her and felt better afterwards."

Kirsten's voice caught in her throat, and she didn't trust herself to say anything. Fortunately, JR kept talking.

"It was kind of a weird thing, actually. After she'd tell me the story, I'd feel better, but she'd always seem sadder. And then one day, I must have been five or six, I asked to meet him. She seemed shocked because I had never asked before. And when she told me he was just an imaginary big brother, a story she had made up to make me feel better, I had a full-on little kid tantrum. I went to my dad and demanded that he find the boy with the heart on his shoulder."

JR stopped talking, and after a few moments, Kirsten wondered if he had fallen asleep, but then he started talking again, in an even more faraway voice than before.

"It was one of the strangest feelings I've ever had. Hearing my mom telling my dad that she had made up an imaginary brother for me, when for all those years, she had made it sound so real. I can still remember the feeling because it feels like the only time in my life when my mom lied to me. Sounds crazy, right? Obsessing over something that happened almost fifteen years ago."

JR's voice trailed off, and Kirsten knew there was no need for her to talk.

Forgotten and Found

Callie's relief over having a plan to talk to Jansen was dampened by her nervousness at how he would react. She could only imagine how Kirsten, who was sitting next to her at the kitchen table, must be feeling.

When Kirsten had first filled them in on everything JR had told her, tears had filled her eyes. "When JR told me the part about the heart shaped mark on his 'big brother's' shoulder, I knew I had to do something. I've always said that I knew Chad was the man I was meant to marry because he came stamped with a heart just for me. And now I know, he came stamped with a heart so that he could find his little brother."

"Let's not get ahead of ourselves," Lynette, always the voice of reason, had cautioned. After talking things through a little further, Lynette's restraint prevailed, and they had all agreed the best course of action, the one that would cause the least amount of trauma if they were wrong, would be to talk to Jansen before saying anything to JR and Chad.

As Jansen walked into the kitchen, thankfully alone, he smiled to see both Callie and Kirsten sitting at the table. Unbeknownst to him, Kirsten had reached under the table and taken Callie's hand tightly in hers.

"Good morning, ladies! Is Tiny around? I hear he makes a mean blueberry pancake."

"He just ran out to grab something from the store. Jansen, can you join us for a minute? We'd like to talk to you about something important."

The serious tone in Callie's voice immediately put Jansen on his guard, and he wondered what was going on. Without sitting down, he asked, "Is everything okay?" Knowing it was unlikely but also knowing what twenty-year-olds could be like, he asked, "Did JR do something?"

"No, it's nothing like that." Kirsten got up from the table and walked to where Jansen was standing. "I'm so sorry to ask you this, but there's no easy way to do it." Taking a deep breath but not managing to keep her voice steady, Kirsten asked, "Is there any chance that JR has an older brother?"

Jansen took an almost imperceptible step back, as if a wave of emotions had pushed him. "What makes you ask that?"

Feeling an inexplicable need to connect with Jansen physically, Kirsten reached out and took his hand in hers. Jansen didn't resist and instead repeated his question, "Why do you ask?"

Kirsten looked over her shoulder at Callie and nodded once. Callie took her phone, walked to Jansen and handed it to him. With his free hand, he took the phone, and sensing there was no turning back from what he was about to see, Jansen looked down at the photo on the screen. What he saw there took his breath away. It was a slightly older version of his son staring back at him. The man in the picture was sitting on the edge of a pool, smiling at the camera and shirtless. And on his right shoulder was a small heart shaped mark.

For a brief instant, Jansen wondered if this was some twisted ploy to get his money. But he dismissed the notion, knowing that the man in the photo had no legal claim to his estate. And when he looked up at Kirsten who was quietly crying, tears rolling unheeded down her cheeks, he knew for certain that this had nothing whatsoever to do with money.

"Tell me everything, Kirsten. Don't leave anything out."

"JR has already been through so much. I just want to be one hundred percent positive that we're doing the right thing. We need proof."

"The only way to get proof is to do a DNA analysis. And that would require either a blood sample or a buccal cells test."

Lynette, who had joined Jansen, Callie, and Kirsten in the kitchen, turned towards Callie. "A what?"

"Buccal cells. Those are what you collect when you swab the inside of a person's cheek." As if wanting to validate her claim, Callie pointed at her laptop and added, "I Googled it."

"There's no way you can get either of those things without them asking questions," said Kirsten, giving voice to everyone's concerns.

"Not necessarily," said Jansen, thinking aloud. "We can always make it sound like curiosity about family trees. Everyone is doing those these days, I see commercials all the time. In fact, I think I may have invested in one of the companies that makes the at-home kits. Maybe I can tell JR that's why we're doing it."

"It just feels too deceptive, and there's no way I can convince Chad to do it. He always says that his adoptive family is the only family he needs to know about. I think he feels like he would be betraying them in some way if he tries to find out anything about his biological family. But I think he would want to know about JR." Kirsten shook her head as if to emphasize her point, "No, we need to find another way."

Chad took the front stairs two at a time. He had stopped by the spa first, but when he didn't find Kirsten there, he figured she was in the main house. Finding the front door unlocked as always, he walked in and bumped into a man who seemed to be in a rush to get outside.

"Sorry about that! Didn't see you coming!"

"No worries, my bad! I should watch where I'm going. I forgot my phone in my car!"

They both looked up as they passed each other and smiled politely.

As JR stepped outside, his pace slowed almost without him knowing it. He paused at the top of the stairs, his heart suddenly pounding in his chest.

Chad, feeling an intense emotion he couldn't name stood rooted to the spot where he had bumped into the man, whose image felt burned into his brain. Slowly, he turned around and stood at the open door looking out at the man who had stopped at the top of the stairs.

JR turned too, knowing his life was about to change forever.

—ell—

"Just like that, huh?" Nick asked, amazed by the story Callie had just shared with him.

"Yup, just like that."

"And you had nothing to do with them bumping into each other?"

"Nick! I already told you I was in the kitchen talking to Jansen and the others. And besides, how on earth could I orchestrate two men bumping into each other? I had no idea Kirsten had forgotten her purse. Or that Chad would stop by The Summer Breeze to bring it to her. And there's no way I could have known that JR had forgotten his phone. Or that he would pick that moment to go out to his car to get it."

Nick chuckled on the other end of the line, "Fair enough. So how are they taking things?"

"Pretty good, considering. At the end of the day, it's a joyful thing, and they're both thrilled to have found one another. I think they'll still do a DNA test just to have proof on paper, but really, there's no doubt in my mind that they are brothers. When Chad rolled up his sleeve to show JR the heart shaped mark on his shoulder, JR broke down in tears."

"I can imagine."

"I think the only really sad part about all of this is that it has tarnished JR's memory of his mom, and I'm sure it's brought back some feelings of abandonment for Chad. Neither of them said anything, but that's just my opinion."

"It'll take some time, but hopefully they learn to forgive her and move on."

"I think Jansen might buy a place up here, just so the boys can visit each other and spend some time together."

"That's another new resident in Seneca Springs because of The Summer Breeze."

Callie smiled, "I can't take all of the credit."

"But you will," Nick replied. And Callie could just imagine the mischievous smile tugging at his perfect lips.

Grand Opening

"**I**'m glad you were able to come up for Grace's big day."

"Didn't have much choice really."

Callie glanced over at Nick who was sitting on the edge of her bed rubbing the back of his neck. He looked tired, and, judging from the tone of his voice, he was annoyed.

"What time do we need to be there?"

"Noon."

Nick brought his wrist up and glanced at his watch. "I'm going to take a quick shower."

"Nick! It's already 11:40. Didn't you shower before you drove up here? We're going to be late."

Without responding, Nick got up from the bed and walked towards the bathroom.

"Hello? Nick? I don't want to be late. This is a really important day for Grace, and I want to be there."

Nick paused in the doorway but didn't turn around to face Callie. "You can go on ahead. In case you forgot, I have my car here since I just drove almost five hours to come see you."

Callie didn't need to see Nick's face to know that he was speaking through gritted teeth. Before she could respond, he walked into the bathroom and closed the door behind him.

—ele—

"Hey, Callie! Where's Nick?" Tiny looked over Callie's shoulder disappointedly.

Not wanting to be late for the grand opening of Cupcakes by Grace, Callie had driven to the event by herself feeling simultaneously guilty and annoyed by Nick's comment. She hadn't asked him to drive up this weekend. Or any other weekend for that matter. In fact, as far as she could remember she had never actually *asked* him to do it. It was just an unspoken understanding that he would come visit every other weekend because it was something he wanted to do.

"He should be here any minute. He wanted to take a quick shower after the drive."

"Makes sense. I don't blame him. Making that drive every other weekend must be exhausting."

"Nick's a big boy, Tiny. He makes his own choices," Callie replied, sounding harsh.

Tiny's eyes grew wide, and he held up both hands. "Whoa, no need to bite my head off. Just saying that driving for ten hours every other weekend can't be all that fun."

Callie hadn't meant to snap at Tiny, but the truth of his words stung. Maybe she had been taking it too much for granted that Nick would drive to Seneca Springs so they could spend time together. Early on in their relationship, she had made it abundantly clear that she had no interest in revisiting the frenetic energy of the city. She had left it all behind for a reason, and she had no intentions of going back. And, after all, she had a business to run. She couldn't leave The Summer Breeze whenever she felt like it. She had guests and staff that she was responsible for.

Still, none of this was Tiny's fault, and Callie regretted her words. "Sorry, Tiny. Where's Grace? The bakery looks beautiful."

"It does, doesn't it?" Tiny, happy for the change of subject, asked with obvious pride. "Every hour I wasn't at the bed and breakfast, I was here with Grace, and we were working our tails off. Grace is a tough boss, but she had a clear vision on how she wanted the bakery to look. My parents upgraded the kitchen a few years ago, but the rest of the place needed a cosmetic refresh. We put in new floors, a new awning, new lighting, changed out all the displays. The works."

Callie looked around at the gleaming display cases filled with rows of beautifully decorated gourmet cupcakes. The modernity of the glass and metal cases was offset by the rustic, distressed dark hardwood floors and vintage seating. Everything worked together to create a cozy yet elegant bakery that was brought together by an exquisite, and unexpected, crystal chandelier.

Callie recalled the day she and Grace had rummaged through a storage room at the back of The Summer Breeze's basement in search of any vintage finds Grace could use for the bakery. The O'Connors had explicitly told Callie that everything they left behind when they sold her their home was hers for the taking. But she had always been so busy getting the bed and breakfast and the restaurant up and running, she had never spent the time to go through all the dusty boxes and shelves.

When Grace mentioned to her one afternoon that she was on the hunt for furnishings for the bakery, Callie had offered to go through the storage room with her. They had spent a surprisingly enjoyable afternoon discovering remnants of the O'Connor family's past. Fortunately for them, Papa O'Connor had kept the storage room as well organized as he had everything else in the home. Each box came clearly labeled with a list of its contents and the shelves were all arranged by room. There was an entire section for the kitchen and dining room that Callie and Grace had started with.

Grace had found several sets of dishware and serving utensils which she had claimed for the bakery, and Callie had found a handful of small crystal vases that would look lovely on the dining tables at The Terrace with fresh cut flowers from her garden. They were getting ready to call their scavenger hunt a success when Grace let out a loud squeal. Startled, Callie had screamed out reflexively in fear, thinking Grace had seen a spider or, worse, a mouse.

"What did you see? Where is it? Was it a mouse? Please say it wasn't a mouse!"

"Relax, Callie! It wasn't a mouse. Come look at this!"

Relieved, Callie had looked inside the very large box Grace was holding open. Inside was a beautiful, albeit very dusty, crystal chandelier in perfect condition. Together, they had carefully lifted the heavy fixture out of the box.

"Wow, not a single crystal is missing." Grace said breathlessly.

"It's beautiful, Grace. With some elbow grease and careful cleaning, it will be exquisite."

"I wonder if all the lights work."

"Let Tiny worry about that. He can fix anything."

Grace looked at Callie and then back down at the chandelier. "How much do you want for it," she asked, her voice sounding tentative.

"You're kidding me, right? I'm not going to charge you for it."

"You have no idea what it's worth. Maybe you should have it appraised first."

"I know exactly what it's worth. If it's sitting in a box, under a pile of other boxes, in a storage room that no one ever goes into, it's worth exactly zero."

It had taken some convincing, but Grace had finally agreed to take the chandelier on one condition. She had practically forced Callie to agree to free cupcakes for life. All in all, it had been a satisfying trade for both women, and now, the gleaming chandelier had taken its place as the pièce de résistance at Cupcakes by Grace.

——ele——

"I had no idea she was so talented."

"I'm in so much trouble."

Nick laughed and wrapped his arms tighter around Callie. "How many cupcakes did you have?"

"Mini. Mini cupcakes," Callie emphasized.

"Fine, how many 'mini'-cupcakes did you have?"

"At least half a dozen."

"And the deal is that you get a free cupcake any time you go to the bakery?"

"Correct."

"You are in trouble."

Callie playfully punched Nick in the stomach. "I'm pretty sure you kept up with me bite for bite, if not more!"

"Yeah, but I don't live here. I won't feel the need to pop into the bakery every time I'm in town."

"Don't remind me."

Nick kissed the top of Callie's head and then gently tilted her head up so that he could look into her eyes. "I'm sorry about earlier. I shouldn't have snapped at you. I was tired, but I had no right to take it out on you."

"I'm sorry, too. I never tell you how much it means to me that you drive up to see me. Maybe we can find a weekend where I can come down to the city."

"Really?" Nick asked, not wanting to get his hopes up too high.

"Yes, but of course, it will have to be after my summer busy season ends."

"Of course."

"And then there's the rush to see the fall foliage."

"There is that."

"And Thanksgiving will be with our families. How about some time after that?"

Chuckling, Nick replied, "Perfect, I'll pencil it in on my calendar."

Tabloid Fodder

"Hey Callie," Lynette said as she walked onto the back porch balancing her open laptop in her hands. "Come here for a second, I need to show you something."

Callie stood up and wiped her soiled hands on her jeans. Before joining Lynette on the porch, she took one last look around at her handiwork. Her first attempt at naturally deterring at least some of the critters that were feasting on her garden had been to plant herbs that let off a strong odor. So far, she had planted a mix of rosemary, thyme, sage, onion, and garlic around the perimeter of two of her raised vegetable beds. If they were effective, she would do the same for the remaining beds. It was hard work, but Callie relished the time outdoors.

"What's up?" Callie asked as she walked up the stairs towards Lynette who had taken a seat on the back porch swing.

"Did you manually do the bookings for next week?"

"Not that I recall, why?"

"When we did a quick check earlier this month, we saw that the whole house was booked, right?"

"Yup. Every suite, booked solid through the end of the month."

"Well, I was just doing some prep for next week when our new guests arrive, and every suite is reserved by someone who entered 'RP.'"

"Maybe it's a big group traveling together?"

"Yeah, but whenever we get those, someone usually puts at least some information in the comments section. These have nothing. Just 'RP.' And get this. Every appointment at the spa is booked by 'RP.' Every single appointment."

"Strange." There was only one person Callie knew who had the initials RP, and she had a pretty good hunch about what might be going on. "Has everything been paid for?"

Lynette clicked a few keys on her laptop and a report popped up showing that both the rooms and the spa appointments had been paid for in full, including a very generous gratuity.

"Scroll down to the payments section."

As soon as the credit card information popped up on the screen, Lynette and Callie drew in their breaths simultaneously.

"Rita Pearson?" Lynette said, sounding surprised. "Wow, she must be doing really well for herself to be able to drop that kind of money."

Callie looked at Lynette and rolled her eyes.

"What's that for?"

"Lynette, I don't think Rita booked The Summer Breeze for herself. I think the Westons might be coming."

Lynette's bottom jaw fell open. Despite the week they had spent with the surprisingly down-to-earth Westons the year before, Lynette was still star struck by the famous couple. "Really? Do you really think they're coming here again? I mean, they can go anywhere they like. Private beaches, Paris, the Amalfi Coast, anywhere! I don't get it. Why are they coming back here?"

"Lynette! What kind of question is that? You know how much they appreciated the time they got out of the limelight when they visited us the first time. Maybe they're looking for the same thing again."

"Maybe," Lynette acquiesced dubiously. "But why haven't we gotten any advanced prep list from Rita like we did last time."

"Maybe because they know we'll take good care of them without all that stuff, which they never ended up using anyway."

"But why wouldn't she just call us like she did last time? I completely understand their need for privacy, but why the secrecy from us? This just seems a little odd to me."

"I guess it does, doesn't it?" Callie asked rhetorically, wondering why the very demanding Rita Pearson hadn't just picked up the phone and barked orders at her like she had the first time the world-famous celebrity couple had come to stay at The Summer Breeze.

"Mmmmm, what is that smell?" Callie asked as she walked into the kitchen.

"Z'atar seasoning. We've been eating too many sweet things lately, time for a little savory. I made soft scrambled eggs with z'atar and chives. Cut yourself a slice of sourdough, pile on the eggs and add some sliced avocado."

"Sounds delicious," Callie said, doing as she was told.

"Hot sauce is in the fridge," Tiny added, anticipating her next question.

"Have you spoken to Lynette yet?"

"About what? When I came in this morning, she was hunched over her laptop acting very secretive."

Callie looked over her shoulder to make sure none of the other guests were around and then walked over to where Tiny was standing at the counter cutting a variety of fresh melons for the breakfast service. She came to a stop just inches behind him, and he sensed rather than saw her.

"Why are you standing so close to me?"

"I need to tell you something," Callie whispered.

"You can't tell me from a comfortable distance?"

"I'm serious, Tiny. This is important."

Tiny put down his knife, wiped his hands on his apron, took a giant step sideways that put about two feet of distance between him and his boss, and finally turned around to face her.

Callie looked over her shoulder again to confirm that no one had snuck into the kitchen unnoticed and whispered, "The Westons will be here next week."

"*The* Westons?" Tiny asked without bothering to whisper.

"Shhhhhh!"

"Who is going to hear me?"

"I heard you! Heck, anyone within a fifty-foot radius could have heard you!" Lynette exclaimed as she walked into the kitchen carrying her laptop. "You guys are not going to believe what I just found out."

Lynette sat down, opened her computer, and pointed at the screen. "Come look at this. It is not good."

Callie and Tiny hunched over Lynette to read the headline splashed across the front page of an online tabloid: "Sean Weston Spotted Near London with Nanny!" Below the headline was a photo of Sean Weston pushing a stroller. Next to him was a tall blonde-haired woman carrying a large diaper bag, and they were both flanked by the Weston's personal bodyguards.

"What on earth? Since when does walking next to a person garner a headline?"

"That's why I don't bother with that drivel," Tiny pointed out sanctimoniously before going back to cutting melons.

Callie was about to sit down to eat her breakfast when Lynette inclined her head towards the laptop and said, "I think you should keep reading."

Taking a large bite of the perfectly seasoned, creamy eggs, Callie scanned the subheading. What she saw there made her food catch in her throat and her stomach sink. She nudged Lynette with her elbow, "Move."

Lynette got up from the table and Callie sat down in her spot, her partially eaten breakfast abandoned. She read aloud in a disbelieving voice. "'Where is Rina Weston? The usually inseparable new parents haven't been seen together in over a month!'"

In the background, the sound from Tiny's knife against the cutting board stopped.

"Keep reading," Lynette prompted again.

Callie scrolled to the main body of the article. "'The last time the Westons were photographed together as a family was on the set of Sean Weston's new movie being filmed in England. The highly anticipated new sci-fi blockbuster has been plagued by budget overruns and scheduling delays. Delays, insiders tell us, caused by Mr. Weston's erratic behavior. A person with direct knowledge of the situation tells us that a verbal altercation between the Westons ended in a tense and embarrassing state of affairs when Mrs. Weston literally stormed off the set leaving Mr. Weston, the baby, and the nanny alone in his trailer. That was one month ago. And since then, work on the movie has come to an abrupt halt. And until yesterday, the Westons were nowhere to be found. Is this the end of the notoriously "perfect" couple? Has Sean Weston started a new family with his nanny?'" Callie's voice trailed off as she tried to process the information.

"I don't believe it," Tiny said, almost defensively. "Sean would never cheat on Rina. And Rina would never, never leave that baby. We saw them together with our own eyes. There was love there. Real love. And joy over the pregnancy."

Callie wanted desperately to believe Tiny, to believe in happy endings. But between the information in the article and the secrecy surrounding the room reservations by Rita Pearson, Callie felt the beginnings of doubt.

Lynette, mirroring Callie's concern, said, "I wonder if Rina is coming here to escape? That poor thing. What she must be going through."

"What if it's not her? What if it's him coming to stay?"

Lynette paused for just a moment to consider this possibility and replied heatedly, "I hope he's not planning on coming here with *that* woman. I will call in sick the entire week before I watch him playing family with a woman who is half his age! He has got some nerve bringing that baggage here!"

"If he thinks for a moment that I'm going to cook his favorite dishes for him, he is in for a rude awakening. I will quit before I cook for that philandering fool."

Callie stared at her uneaten breakfast dejectedly and wondered what would happen if she, too, left The Summer Breeze for the week.

In This Place

"I can't believe I let you convince me to be here."

"And you know how much I appreciate it, Lynette."

"I just want to be upfront about one thing. If I see any funny business going on in front of me, I am going to take him to task, do you understand me? And do not try to stop me."

Callie held up her hands in a sign of defeat. "You have made that abundantly clear." Adding under her breath, "At least a dozen times."

It had taken slow, constant pleading mixed with a healthy dollop of guilt to convince both Lynette and Tiny to come to work on the day "RP" was scheduled to arrive. In the end, they had acquiesced, just as Callie had expected they would.

"Any word on what time they'll get here? It feels weird being here without any other guests around."

The house had been empty since the previous guests had left the evening before. The rooms had all been cleaned, and Lynette had given Evie a few days off from her cleaning job. She and Callie had decided that given how aggressively Evie had behaved around the Smiths, she would be even worse around a famous celebrity, whether it be Rina or Sean Weston. And they had great doubt in her ability to keep any aspect of the visit confidential.

Lynette had been ready for Evie to push back since she always seemed to be in need of money, but Evie had jumped at the opportunity. She had even bought Lynette's obvious lie that there were no reservations for the entire week, going so far as to look pitifully at Lynette for having failed to secure bookings.

Callie looked at Lynette blankly and shrugged, "I don't know anything beyond what's in our reservations system. Which is basically nothing."

As it turned out, no one arrived that day. Or the next.

—ele—

Callie was sitting on the back porch swing working on a crossword puzzle when an unfamiliar, nondescript sedan with dark tinted windows pulled up the driveway and came to a stop. At that moment, Lynette came out of the back door and asked, "Whose car is that?"

Her question was left unanswered as the front door opened and a stranger stepped out. The middle-aged woman, dressed in matronly jeans and an oversized t-shirt that incongruously said, "Europe or Bust," shielded her eyes from the bright early afternoon sunlight and looked around the property. As if satisfied with what she saw, she walked towards the porch.

"Hi there, are you looking for directions?" Callie asked.

"You must be Callie." No sooner did Callie and Lynette hear her voice than they realized that standing in front of them, looking nothing like what they had imagined, was none other than Rita Pearson herself.

"Ms. Pearson?" Callie asked, trying to hide her surprise. She had been expecting at least one of the Westons. And she certainly hadn't been expecting someone who had rented the entire B&B to drive up in an old rental car.

"Is there anyone else here?" Rita barked in response.

Callie thought she noticed Lynette shiver almost imperceptibly, but she couldn't tell if it was out of fear or annoyance. If she had to guess, she'd guess the latter.

"Nope, it's just Lynette and me. Our chef Tiny has gone into town on an errand."

Without acknowledging Callie's response, Rita walked back towards the car, opened the driver's side back door and said something to someone waiting inside. Callie felt her heartbeat quicken. Maybe one of the Westons was going to be staying with them. She hoped it was Rina.

But the faint sound of a man's voice responded to Rita, and it was Sean Weston who slowly emerged from the car. He looked blankly up at the house and the two women standing on the porch as if he didn't recognize them.

Lynette sucked in her breath upon seeing his appearance. The once "Sexiest Man Alive" looked like a shadow of himself. His hair and his clothing were unkempt, and his normally clean shaven face now sported a dark five o'clock shadow that matched the dark bags under his eyes.

"I can't believe it's him. What happened to him? Has he been drinking? Is that what all this is about?" Lynette whispered quietly to Callie.

"Shhh, they'll hear you!"

Callie and Lynette watched in silence as Sean bent inside the open car and slowly reemerged cradling a squirming infant. Without saying a word, he gently placed the baby in Rita Pearson's waiting arms and gave the woman a quick kiss on the cheek. He then walked around the front of the car and opened the back passenger's side door and held out his hand.

"I swear if that's the nanny, I'm outta here."

"Shhh!"

Callie and Lynette were completely unprepared for what they saw next. Wearing a colorful scarf around her head, and also looking like a faded version of her former self, was Rina Weston. In what looked like an oft-practiced maneuver, Sean effortlessly scooped her up into his arms and slowly walked towards the house. As he climbed the stairs, tears started flowing from his eyes. Rina rested her head on his shoulder and reached up to wipe his tears. "It's okay, my love. Everything is going to be okay."

Sean smiled through his tears and finally acknowledged Callie and Lynette. "This was the only place she wanted to be. She kept asking me to bring her here and as soon as the doctors gave us the go ahead to travel, Rita made the booking."

"Callie...," Rina reached out her hand weakly, and Callie gently took it in hers. "Lynette. I'm so happy to see you both. Is Tiny here?"

"He should be back any minute. We're so happy to see all of you." Unsure of what else to say, Callie added, "Please, tell me what we can do to help you. Anything you need."

"I just need to be here. In this place. With all of you. I never forgot your kindness, and I've been wanting to come back here ever since this nightmare started."

Rita joined them on the porch carrying the baby who had managed to grab a handful of her hair and was cooing happily.

"Let's not talk about that right now, sweet girl. Sean needs to get you upstairs, and I need to change this little one's diaper. Don't I little love bug? Yes, I do."

When Rita wasn't barking orders, Callie thought to herself, she had an almost pleasant voice.

"By the way, I'm Rita and this little cutie is Rian," she said, just before turning her head towards the sound of a large pickup truck pulling in behind the rental car. Her voice went back to a bark. "Who is that? I thought you said no one else was here!" In response, Rian squealed happily and grabbed another handful of Rita's hair in his pudgy little fingers.

"It's just Tiny. Sean and Rina both know him."

"It's okay, Rita," Rina whispered weakly.

As Tiny stepped out of his car carrying a large pastry box, he took in the scene on the back porch. After a moment's pause and without saying a word of greeting, he ran up the stairs, put down the box, and gently took Rina out of Sean's tired arms. "Which room?"

———

It took a lot of work and cajoling, but in the end, Callie and Lynette knew it was the right thing to do. They each made several phone calls to all the guests who were scheduled to stay at The Summer Breeze the following week to let them know their reservations were being cancelled due to an unforeseen emergency. To make things easier for the Westons to extend their stay by a week, Rita had offered to add an incentive. Anyone who agreed to reschedule their stay would receive a five hundred dollar voucher, a deluxe wine country tour, and two spa treatments. Callie thought it was more generous than necessary, but it had certainly made the process a little easier for her and Lynette.

"That's the last of them. Do you want to let Rita know?"

"Let me know what?" Rita asked as she came down the stairs with Rian who seemed to be very attached to her.

"We managed to cancel all the reservations for next week! Come here you little cutie," Lynette said holding her arms out to Rian. Happy to go to everyone, the chubby baby grabbed a handful of Lynette's hair without missing a beat and continued babbling contentedly.

"How is Rina feeling today?"

"Stronger than yesterday and even stronger than the day before. Now I see why she wanted to come here. I know I can be difficult to deal with, and I'm not going to apologize for that, but I do want to tell you how grateful I am for what you're doing for these wonderful people. They're like family to me. When Rina was first diagnosed, their world fell apart. I knew what I had to do the moment I heard. I moved into their house to help with the baby while continuing to manage everything related to their careers. It wasn't easy trying to keep things secret, which is why we finally decided to move her to London to be closer to Sean and for treatment. But relocating involved finding the best doctor, the best hospital, a house, a private plane, security guards, a cook, a nanny, and so much more. It was a ton of work, but I'm proud of everything I accomplished, and I like to think that I helped Rina on the road to recovery."

Callie took a closer look at Rita and realized how tired she must be. In the days since the Westons had arrived, Rita, who was at least a couple of decades older than Callie, had been on the go from morning to night. When she wasn't caring for Rian, she was on the phone or her laptop managing an endless stream of media inquiries and working desperately to save the careers of two of Hollywood's biggest stars. She vacillated between being demanding and rude to being deferential depending on who she was talking to. But above all, she was loyal to the Westons and fiercely protective of their privacy.

Feeling overcome by emotion, Callie impulsively hugged Rita and gave her a kiss on the cheek.

Rita chuckled in response. "I'm not as bad as you thought, right?"

"You're wonderful. And it's obvious how hard you work. Listen, I know that you and the Westons don't know my spa manager personally, but I give you my word that Kirsten will respect your privacy as much as we do. She is an absolute miracle worker when it comes to massage and relaxation. Please, let me ask her to come in and schedule some appointments for you."

Instinctively trusting Callie, Rita nodded her head once.

A Surprise Visit

Tiny let out a wolf whistle as Sean Weston entered the kitchen. "Looking good, my friend. What's the occasion?"

Sean smiled and adjusted the apron he had borrowed from the kitchen the night before. "My wife is coming downstairs today to have breakfast, and I'm going to make it for her."

"Really? That's fantastic. What's on the menu?"

"I have absolutely no idea," Sean beamed and looked almost like his old self again.

"I think we can come up with a few options."

Sean rubbed his hands together in anticipation and said, "Put me in coach."

By the time Rina was ready to come down, Sean's white apron was stained with strawberry juice, flour, and a few egg splatters. But the table was set to perfection with a baked French toast casserole, a large plate of steaming hot home fries seasoned with smoked paprika, and a heaping bowl of beautiful berries.

"Everything looks great!"

"It does...everything except you. You look like Rian does after a bowl of that baby food Rita feeds him," Tiny quipped.

Sean looked down at his apron and laughed. "You know what? She won't care. And neither do I."

At the sound of Rian's cooing coming from the hallway, both men looked up and were surprised to see Rina walk in on her own strength. She looked noticeably healthier, and the color had started returning to her skin. Days spent out on the balcony off her room had done wonders for her. She had also made a conscious decision to remove her head scarf, and although her hair was still very short, it added to the air of confidence she seemed to be exuding.

And not only did she walk in on her own, she walked in carrying her baby. Something she hadn't had the strength to do in a long time. Sean was about to rush to her side but thought better of it. Rian, sensing rather than understanding his mother's fragility, did not fidget or try to pull her hair.

Instead, he babbled and placed his hands on Rina's cheeks. She bent towards him, and he looked innocently up at her so that she could place a kiss on his rosebud mouth.

Moved to tears, Sean walked over and embraced his family while Tiny tried not to burst out sobbing.

"Rina, you look beautiful. You folks enjoy your breakfast," Tiny managed as he removed his apron and headed for the door.

"Where do you think you're going? Sit down. I helped make this breakfast for all of us to eat together in the kitchen like we used to."

"What smells so goo...Rina, I wasn't expecting to see you downstairs! You look absolutely beautiful!" Callie wasn't exaggerating. Rina's cropped hair looked like a crown perched atop her stunning facial structure. And her green eyes were brought to life by a spectacular pair of emerald and diamond tear drop earrings. It was no wonder she was considered one of the most beautiful women in the world. She could still stand to gain several pounds, but there was no denying that Rina Weston was an absolute knockout.

"Thank you, Callie. And you were right, Kirsten is a miracle worker. I'm starting to feel like myself again. I don't know how she convinced me to lose the head scarf, but I'm glad she did."

"I'm starving. Let's eat," barked Rita Pearson as she strode into the kitchen, cutting through the celebratory atmosphere like a knife. "And someone get me a strong cup of coffee!"

She didn't have to ask twice.

—*ell*—

"Hey there."

"Hey, gorgeous."

"What are you up to?"

"Had that dinner meeting I was telling you about, and now getting ready for bed. Hoping you'll sneak into my dreams."

Callie smiled and pictured Nick lying in bed with one arm behind his head. "You can count on it."

"How was your day? Your mystery clients doing okay?"

"They are. Kirsten got her hands on them today, and that helped, too."

"You're really not going to tell me who they are?"

"You know I can't."

Nick sighed with a mixture of frustration and pride. He was desperate to know who all the fuss was about and couldn't understand why Callie didn't trust him enough to tell him. But on the other hand, he was proud of her for sticking to her guns and honoring her confidentiality agreement.

"Not even a hint?"

"Not even a hint." Changing the subject, Callie asked, "Are you working the rest of the weekend, or will you finally get some down time?"

"I have to meet some clients out on Long Island tomorrow morning, maybe see some friends for dinner, and then I'm pretty much free until the work week starts up again. You?"

"Mostly just working on the garden. Will try to get a couple of workouts or hikes in. I might pop into Cupcakes by Grace to try some new flavor combinations she's working on."

"Mmmmm...thinking about you licking the frosting off your fingers is just what I needed right now."

"Happy to oblige."

Callie had been prepared to have a difficult time finding a parking space, but the surprisingly quiet tree lined street had several spots open. After parallel parking with some difficulty, despite all the sensors in her rental car, she grabbed her overnight bag and stepped out onto the street. Although there wasn't a lot of vehicle traffic, there were plenty of pedestrians walking along the sidewalk, giving the street a friendly feel. And the distant sound of cars honking and the occasional yellow cab pulling up to pick up or drop off a passenger gave Callie an unexpected feeling of nostalgia. Maybe the city wasn't as bad as she remembered it, maybe her last couple of years living there had tainted her memory.

But none of that mattered right now. All Callie could think about was Nick's expression when he opened the door. She was fairly certain that he had absolutely no idea she was coming to visit him, despite her very pointed questions about his weekend plans when she had called him the night before. In fact, she hadn't even been sure she was going to make the five-hour drive until she mentioned it in passing to Lynette earlier that morning when they were on a walk.

"Do you think you and Tiny could hold down the fort until tomorrow evening? The Terrace is fully staffed, and the Westons barely require any work."

"Sure. You planning on a quick trip to see your family?"

"Nope. I'm thinking about driving down to New York City to surprise Nick." It had taken Callie a moment to realize that Lynette had stopped walking alongside her. "What?"

"Nothing. I think it's a great idea, and we can definitely take care of the b and b while you're gone. In fact, it'll be nice not to have you around for a change."

Once Callie had said it out loud, it made complete sense to her that she should visit Nick. In fact, she had realized it was something she should have done a long time ago.

Callie looked up at the beautiful brownstone that bore the number 167. The brick façade was a warm brown, as were the steps leading up to the front door. Holding on to the ornate wrought iron railing, Callie climbed the stairs, her heartbeat quickening with each step. The dark wooden double doors were inlaid with glass, and Callie could see a small light glowing towards the back of the house. Taking a deep breath, she rang the doorbell and waited.

After waiting for what felt like a very protracted minute, she rang the doorbell again. Maybe, she thought, he hadn't heard it the first time. Maybe he was watching TV. Or maybe he was in the shower. "Or maybe he's not even home," Callie mumbled aloud. She jabbed the doorbell several times in a row in frustration, dropped her overnight bag onto the front landing, and reached into her purse for her phone. How, she wondered, would she be able to convince Nick to come home without letting on that she was standing on his front porch like a fool. Dialing his number without any idea of what she would say, she waited for him to answer.

Faintly, from behind her, she heard Nick's ringtone chiming in time with the ringing in her ear. Turning around slowly, she saw him standing at the bottom of the steps staring up at her with his mouth wide open. He was dressed casually in khaki dress shorts and a black polo shirt and carrying what appeared to be Chinese takeout. It took a moment for him to gather his wits, but as soon as he did, a smile spread across his face, and he climbed the stairs two at a time.

Callie knew in that moment that she had made one of the best decisions of her life. She also knew that the Chinese food would get cold before they got around to eating it.

Pest Control

"Where'd you disappear to the past couple of days?" Sean asked as he and Rina joined Callie on the back porch.

"Sean, don't be nosey."

"I'm not being nosey. Just curious."

Rina noticed a slow blush spreading across Callie's cheeks and blurted out, "Callie! Did you go see a man?"

"Who's being nosey now?" Sean asked, and then added, "Answer the question, Callie. Did you go see a gentleman friend?"

Blushing fiercely and grinning like a fool, Callie nodded her head. "I did. I drove down to the city to see Nick."

"Spill. And don't hold back," Rina commanded, taking her favorite seat on the porch swing.

Half an hour later, after some of the most intense grilling Callie had faced in a long time, Sean and Rina had somehow managed to convince her to call Nick and ask him to come up for a quick visit so they could meet him. When he threatened not to come until she told him who her mystery guests were, they had told her to switch to a video call. It took one look at the easily recognizable couple to make up Nick's mind.

—ele—

"You know, I don't think I've ever told you what an amazing thing I think you're doing here."

"I don't know about that. The herbs around the raised beds are helping deter some critters, but there's still something eating away at my plants. I swear every time I see a vegetable starting to ripen, something else gets to it first. It's so infuriating! If I really want this to work, I may have to give in and build some sort of fencing." Callie bent forward to snip a few more sprigs of rosemary and added, "At least Tiny has plenty of fresh herbs and garlic to work with."

Nick chuckled and walked around the vegetable beds towards Callie. "I'm not talking about the garden. I'm talking about the bed and breakfast. There's something magical about this place. And I think it's you."

Callie squinted at him for a moment before bursting into laughter. Imitating his voice, she mocked, "'There's something magical about this place. And I think it's you.' Seriously, Nick?"

"Sounded cheesier than I intended, but I'm serious. Come here, you beautiful woman." He reached out and put his arms around her, pulling her close for a kiss. And then he crinkled his nose, "What is that smell?"

Callie laughed again. "That's my magic fairy dust! Also known as fertilizer. Also known as chicken manure."

Letting go of her, Nick took two large strides backwards. "I would think you could keep the critters away just by that stench."

"Doesn't quite work that way."

"Have you figured out what exactly is eating each of the veggies?"

"Nope. Everyone has an opinion on it, but I figure it's a combination of a few different things."

"And you refuse to use any pois—"

"Don't even finish that sentence," Callie interrupted angrily. "There has got to be another option."

Nick held up his hands in a gesture of agreement and said, "Maybe the first step is to figure out which animals are coming around here. Then you can find targeted, non-lethal, solutions."

"That's actually not a bad idea."

"You could install a couple of motion activated security cameras with night vision." Nick walked around the vegetable beds and pointed to two locations, "Mount one on that tree and one on that tree over there. Those vantage points would cover just about the entire yard."

"I just worry about how my guests would feel. What if they think I'm infringing on their privacy?"

"Unless your guests are out here digging around in the garden, I don't think the cameras will cover much else. The outdoor dining space is far enough away that you won't be able to overhear any conversation." Nick could see that Callie was almost convinced and added, "Why don't you ask the Westons? No one values their privacy more."

<center>~~~</center>

"There, see? The cameras are only picking up the area around the vegetable beds and a couple of the outdoor dining tables. I don't think you have anything to worry about."

Callie was pleasantly surprised by how quickly Nick's idea had come together. As soon as she had gotten the green light from the Westons, Nick had made the twenty-five minute drive down to a hardware store on the south end of the lake and come back with two small cameras that fit in the palm of his hand. It had taken him, Tiny, and Sean an hour of tinkering amid good-natured camaraderie to get the system set up.

They even installed an app on Callie's phone and laptop so that she could get notifications and view the videos whenever she wanted.

—ele—

"Callie, if I could stay here for another two weeks and keep eating Tiny's food, I would. That pappardelle was sublime."

Sean reached over and put his arm around his wife's shoulder. Rina was looking more radiant than ever. "I know, babe. But we have to go back for your check-up, and I have to get back on the set. There are a lot of jobs and a lot of money at stake."

Rina nodded and kissed his hand. "It's not that I don't want to go back to England. It's just that I'm not ready to face the paparazzi again with all their questions and prying and false assumptions."

Nick picked up his glass of wine and swirled the ruby red liquid around pensively. "Why not just give them what they want?"

Sean and Rina both looked at him. "What do you mean?" Sean asked.

"Look, from what I've seen and from what you've told me, Rita is an absolute master at managing media relations. So why not use her connections in the media? Issue a press release telling the press everything. Share some photos of Rina during her treatment. Give them facts. Take all the guesswork out of the situation. You control them, instead of them controlling you."

Silence descended on the table. Sean and Rina looked at each other and then at Rita. "It's not a bad idea. If we're not hiding anything, the press won't be running around trying to look for something. We're scheduled to leave tomorrow, and between the private plane and the private airport, we can stay under the radar for a few more days. That should give me enough time to write up the release and get it to all the big media outlets in one fell swoop."

"When did we tell the studio I'd be back?"

"A week from Monday."

"That'll give us plenty of time to get resettled."

"You know what else might be a great idea?" Rita asked, her media relations gears spinning, "A press conference the morning you return to the set. Fifteen minutes, no holds barred. Answer all their questions and put an end to their curiosity."

Callie poured herself a glass of water and leaned back against the kitchen sink. Apart from the hum of the refrigerator, The Summer Breeze was completely silent. The Westons and Rita had left earlier in the day, and not a single eye had been dry at their departure. Callie would miss them almost as much as she would miss Nick, who had stuck around for another hour before heading out for his long drive home.

The feeling of loneliness was one she hadn't felt in a very long time. Not since she had been living at her parents' house after leaving her life in New York City behind. But there was a subtle difference in the quality of the emotion this time. When she had once again been sleeping in her childhood bedroom and trying to put the pieces of her life together, trying to forge a path for herself, her loneliness had felt heavier. She was surrounded by people who loved her, and yet there was a melancholy mixed with the loneliness that left her feeling empty. Until she came up with her plan to open up The Summer Breeze. That idea had brought her back to life and given her purpose.

The loneliness Callie was feeling now seemed somehow lighter, she realized. Her life was everything she wanted it to be. Her family was close by, she was surrounded by friends who were like family, and her business was more successful than she had ever imagined it could be. This loneliness, she admitted, stemmed from missing the person she loved having with her all the time.

Pulling her phone out of her back pocket to call Nick, she saw an unfamiliar notification waiting for her on the screen. She clicked on it realizing it was from the security camera and eagerly logged into the app hoping to catch the culprit, or culprits, in the act.

"Gotcha!" Callie said aloud to her empty house.

The F Word

"Are your homemade repellants working?"

"Yes and no."

"I'm intrigued."

"They're keeping the pests away and the garden is thriving, but it smells horrible out there! I certainly wouldn't want to have a meal amidst the stench." Callie sighed in frustration. "Every day I waste trying to get this figured out is a day I waste in adding our outdoor dining area. I'm already a month behind on my soft launch date."

"There is one other option."

"Don't even say the F word."

Nick interrupted Callie before she could continue. "Callie, listen to me. You need to stop being so stubborn about this."

"Nick, if you think you're going to convince me to put in some hideous fenc—"

Speaking over her, Nick continued, "When I was driving back from my meeting on Long Island, I drove by some really nice homes, and a lot of them had fences. Like everything else, it got me thinking about you. Anyway, I got home and did some online research, and I can't believe I'm doing this, but I'm sending you some photos. Of fences. They're covered with vines and flowers, and I think they could be the perfect solution."

"I told you not to say the F word. I do not want to add a fence to the backyard! It would ruin the ambiance."

The only response Callie got was the ping of her incoming message notification. "I'm telling you, you're wasting my time. I am not going to install a...ooooh, these look so pretty! What kinds of plants are these?" Callie asked scrolling through the photos Nick had sent her.

Nick leaned back in his bed and smiled the kind of smile that made Callie's heart skip a beat. The kind of smile she would have loved to kiss.

———

"You would have saved yourself a lot of effort if you'd just listened to everyone in the first place."

"I know, I know."

"Not to mention the time and money you would have saved."

Lynette had a point, Callie thought to herself. It had cost her a small fortune to get everything done once she had decided that installing a fence was the right thing to do. Between purchasing the materials and mature plantings and then paying for the labor to get the work done quickly, it had been a lot more than she had bargained for. Thankfully, both the B&B and The Terrace were bringing in enough revenue to help cover the extra costs. Not to mention that her father and Jack had driven down over the weekend to help with everything.

"Point taken, Lynette. I did it in the end though, right?"

"I'm just saying. The garden would have been thriving, the outdoor restaurant would have been open, and you wouldn't have had to spend so much money to buy mature plants to put around the fence. Or beg your family for their help."

"You're not going to let this go, are you?"

"My current plan is to bug you about installing the fence for as long as you ignored my advice. I'd say you have another month or so to go."

Callie ran her hands lovingly over the beautiful white picket fence partially hidden by fragrant light pink roses and clematis and lavender-blue wisteria. The vegetable garden and outdoor seating area were nestled within the enclosed space and at both ends of the house, Jack had flexed his woodworking mastery skills by building two arched garden gates that were also covered with growing vines. The effect was just lovely.

Unbothered by Lynette's teasing, Callie laughed good naturedly. "You're a real pain, you know that?"

"Right back at you!"

"You know what else is a pain? Having to drive down to the hardware store every time I want something." Callie had had to make the fifty-minute round trip drive several times over the weekend to get everything needed to get the job done.

"You may have to drive even further if the store goes the way of the shopping mall."

"What are you talking about?"

"The mall is closing. You didn't see the signs?"

"Really? That's awful. A lot of jobs will be lost. Maybe it's a good thing they're re-opening that hotel down that way."

"Maybe."

"When were you down there?"

"Last night. We went for a drive and to check out that new Italian restaurant everyone's been raving about."

"How was it?"

"Eh, so-so. It's got nothing on Tiny's cooking. But I suppose if you live around there and you're looking for a nice restaurant, it works. Although I thought the prices were exorbitant."

"Exorbitant, huh?" Callie knew that Lynette's modest up-bringing hadn't caught up to her new lifestyle as the wife of a very wealthy man, and she guessed it never would.

Lynette nodded. "You know who I saw there? Evie. Dressed to the nines and having dinner with a man that looked like he was twice her age."

"Maybe it was her father."

"Trust me, with what she was wearing, it was definitely not her father. There was so much exposed skin, I was tempted to offer her my dinner napkin as cover."

Laughing, Callie asked, "Did you talk to her?"

"I was not planning on it, but I ran into her in the bathroom. Needless to say, it was awkward. She complimented me on my dress, so I complimented her on her earrings. And that was that. I avoid her as much as possible when she's here, and I have no desire to socialize with her outside of work."

"She's not that bad."

Lynette rolled her eyes.

"What?" Callie raised her hand and counted off three things with her fingers: "She's usually on time, gets her work done relatively well, and doesn't cause us any major problems."

Lynette reciprocated, counting off on her fingers: "She's always a little late, she can be sloppy sometimes, and she tried to cause a problem with the Smiths."

"I guess it's the difference between seeing the glass as half full versus half empty."

"You just don't want to bother with trying to find a replacement."

—ele—

Slipping into her hot bath, Callie reclined her head and thought about her day. The relief she felt over finally installing the fence and taking a major step towards opening the outdoor meal service was tempered by her conversation with Lynette.

As with so many things, Lynette was right about Callie not wanting to bother with trying to find a replacement for Evie. It was easier to leave things as they were so that she could focus on the things that needed to get done.

The new, outdoor tables and chairs she ordered had been delivered and were still sitting unopened, stacked up in her gym making the space completely unusable. She needed to order string lights, and outdoor candles, and tablecloths. If she couldn't find anything useful in the storage room she and Grace had already scavenged through, she'd also need to order more place settings and utensils. Not to mention that Tiny had been dropping hints that she should also order a large outdoor grill.

Sighing, Callie stood up and wrapped herself in her robe. For now, she would focus on getting the outdoor restaurant up and running. But she knew she'd have to turn her attention to Evie sooner or later.

And if Lynette knew that on more than one occasion, she had found Evie laying down on the guest room beds checking her phone when she should have been cleaning, Callie feared it would be sooner. Much sooner.

On Main Street

C allie wiped her mouth and sat back in her favorite bar stool at Paolina's. "That was one of the best meals I've had, Paolina. You've outdone yourself."

"Grazie," Paolina beamed. Callie was a woman after her own heart. A true foodie who relished a good meal and was effervescent and sincere in her praise. After a bumpy start as a standoffish food snob, the former newest resident of Seneca Springs was now a weekly regular during the lunch rush and well-versed in the local tradition of applauding when the food was served.

"Between the delicious zucchini blossoms and the corn, sweet onion, and avocado on the pizza, I feel like I've got the taste of summer in my mouth."

"You know, Callie, sometimes, when Marco and I drive down to the farmer's market, he'll pick out ingredients with you in mind." Imitating her husband's deep voice and strong Italian accent, Paolina added, "'What do you think Callie will like? How can we come up with something new for Callie?'" And then raising her voice, she threw in, "There was a time when that man cooked to please *my* palate. But now I've been replaced."

Overhearing his wife's comment through the open service window as he was meant to, Marco let out a big guffaw. He came out of the kitchen, grabbed his wife, tipped her back and planted a passionate kiss on her lips. The lunch crowd, who habitually clapped before the lunch service, erupted in applause for the second time during the meal.

—⁓ele⁓—

As Callie stepped out of Paolina's and turned right onto Main Street towards her parked car, she wondered if she should pop into Grace's shop to see if her friend needed any help. "Yeah, right," Callie mumbled to herself, laughing. "You know the real reason you're going there."

Apparently, Callie wasn't the only person who had decided to "pop into" Grace's shop because there was a small line of people forming out the door of the bakery, some chatting amiably with each other, others hunched over their phones.

Callie quickened her step wondering what was going on and then realized that most of the people in line were unfamiliar to her. As she took her place at the end, several more people queued up behind her, many looking like college students who had just rolled out of bed.

Turning towards the person standing right behind her, a young woman wearing a college sweatshirt and jeans with her hair in a messy bun, Callie asked, "Hey, do you know what's going on here?"

The girl looked at Callie with a strange expression, as if wondering why anyone would be waiting in a line if they didn't even know what it was for. "Yeah, the owner of this place had a booth set up at our school orientation fair over the weekend. She was giving away free samples and handing out flyers that anyone who came in today would get a dozen cupcakes for the price of six."

"Got it. They are delicious, aren't they?"

"Yup," the girl said as she pulled her phone out of her back pocket and started clicking away at it, putting a decided end to the conversation.

Callie considered making her way through the front door to see if Grace needed any help, and then decided to just go around to the back of the shop to avoid the appearance of cutting. As she stepped out of line, she noticed a couple of people look at her as if she was making a mistake. She was also pretty sure she noticed at least one young man check her out. It put a little spring in her step and a smile on her face.

The back door of the bakery was propped open by a large rock and the sound of voices could be heard drifting into the small alleyway behind the row of shops. Walking in without knocking, Callie was unsurprised to find two of her favorite people working in the kitchen.

"Hey, you two!"

Hank looked up and smiled at Callie. Even though she spent so much time with Tiny, Callie was always surprised that there could be another man almost as large as him. Tiny's father was a couple of inches shorter than Tiny but still taller than any other man Callie knew. And like his son, his size was completely incongruent with his demeanor. He was the epitome of a gentle giant.

"Callie! I hope you're here to work?" Bertha's question seemed more like a statement. A question she immediately answered herself without waiting for a response from Callie. "Grab an apron and go help Grace out front. It's been crazy ever since we opened this morning. We thought she might be busy which is why Hank and I came in to prep, but this is more than we bargained for."

Doing as she was told, Callie grabbed one of the bright pink aprons with the words Cupcakes by Grace embroidered in elaborate black lettering across the front. She slipped the apron over her head and tied the strings around her waist as she walked to the front of the bakery to see how she could help. Callie reminded herself to let Lynette know she'd be back late as soon as there was a lull in the traffic coming through the front door.

"Callie! Thank goodness you're here. Do you know how to assemble the boxes?" Seeing the blank expression on Callie's face, Grace inclined her head towards a bright pink stack sitting on the back counter and went back to helping the customer waiting at the display case.

"No, I'm sorry, we don't have any more of the white chocolate and raspberry cupcakes. We sold out of them first thing this morning. Apparently one of the sororities on campus is having an alumni event and their colors are pink and white."

"Another reason not to like those girls," the young lady, dressed in black from head to toe and sporting several tattoos on her bare arms, laughed nervously. "I was really looking forward to having one of those. What other flavors do you recommend?"

"If you like something fruity, we just added a strawberries and cream flavor that is delicious." Grace turned to the display and pointed. "These ones, with the candied strawberry on top."

The woman considered for a moment, but then shook her head. "Been there. Done that. What other fruity flavors do you have?"

Listening to the conversation, Callie thought that if Grace talked to each customer for as long as she was talking to this one, her line wouldn't be getting shorter any time soon.

"Do you like mango?"

The woman nodded her head vigorously.

"Then I recommend trying the mango cupcake with the passionfruit curd filling."

The woman's eyes lit up, and she clasped her hands together eagerly. "That sounds delicious. How much is it for one?"

"One cupcake is five dollars. You get half a dozen for twenty-eight, and today only, if you buy half a dozen, you get another half dozen for free."

"Oh, no thank you. Just one for me please."

Grace reached into the display case and pulled out a cupcake topped with a bright yellow-orange frosting. She turned towards Callie with her hand out expectantly and seeing that Callie had no idea what she was waiting for, Grace reached past her and grabbed one of the flattened boxes and quickly assembled it.

"I don't need a box. I'm just going to eat it at one of the tables."

"Great! Finally, someone who has time to slow down and eat a cupcake in the bakery. Callie, can you hand me one of the small plates?" Turning back to the woman, Grace asked, "Would you like a cup of coffee with that?"

The woman hesitated for a moment and then pulled a few crumpled dollar bills from her pocket and some loose change. "How much is it for the coffee?" she asked in a low voice and looked over her shoulder, seemingly embarrassed that someone would overhear her question.

"It's on the house," Grace replied, feeling suddenly sorry for her. "And so is the cupcake."

At this, the woman stood up ramrod straight and said, "No, thank you. Just the cupcake please." She counted out the money and laid it on the counter.

"I'm sorry," Grace said gently. "I hope I didn't offend you."

"It's fine. Just the cupcake please." She pushed the money towards Grace and took the plate from her. "Thank you."

Callie and Grace exchanged glances but didn't have the time or the privacy to talk about what had just happened. They did, however, watch as the woman sat down at a table near the front window. She looked down at her cupcake almost reverently before taking a small bite and closing her eyes in apparent bliss.

"You know that shiny piece of expensive technology you carry around in your purse?"

Callie walked past Lynette and into the living room without answering, knowing full well that she was in for a short lecture. She fell back on the sofa, exhausted. And in a feeble attempt to assuage the lecturer, said, "I know I should have called you, but Grace needed help, and I lost track of time."

Lynette looked closely at Callie and noticed that her boss looked more tired than she usually did after an afternoon spent puttering around in her garden. Softening her tone, she asked, "You okay?"

"Yeah, just really tired. I don't know how Grace is going to be able to sustain this much business."

"Is she expecting it to be that busy every day? I'm pretty sure that won't be very good for the collective waistlines of our neighbors."

Callie nodded in agreement. "It certainly isn't helping me out." She rolled her shoulders and stretched her neck from side to side. "I think today was just extra busy because Grace had a buy six get six free promotion she was running."

"Hold that thought for one second." Lynette pulled her phone out and quickly tapped in a few words.

"Did you just order cupcakes?"

"Of course. I'd be a fool not to. Besides, it's important to support locally owned businesses."

"Do not bring any cupcakes around here!"

"Don't worry, they're not all for us. I'll send half of them to my parents."

Callie sighed and closed her eyes. "You know, I saw something today. It's none of my business, and I know you're going to tell me the same thing, but I can't stop thinking about it."

Callie quickly filled Lynette in on the conversation she had overheard between Grace and the woman who had ordered just the one cupcake.

"Maybe she only had enough money with her for one," Lynette replied dismissively.

"I don't think so. When Grace offered her free coffee, the woman refused. As if her pride had been bruised. I mean, if she didn't have enough money on her, she could easily have said she'd come back later and pay Grace back."

"Maybe she doesn't live around here. Maybe she was just passing through."

"I thought about that, too, but there was just something about her. I couldn't put my finger on it." Shaking her head as if to clear the thought from her mind, Callie stood up. "Anyway, we'd better get ready for the dinner service."

"Just one more thing before you go."

"What's that?"

"Were you by any chance eating something with chocolate sprinkles on it?"

Lynette couldn't help but laugh as Callie rushed out of the room wiping her mouth with the back of her hand.

An Intruder

"There's a very, *very,* nice looking man sitting at one of our outdoor tables asking to see you, Callie."

"Really? Did he say why?"

Lynette shook her head. "Only that he met you a few years back and would," Lynette paused and made the universal gesture for air quotes with her fingers, "'Love to reconnect.' He's got some kind of accent that I can't quite put my finger on. I'm guessing European by the looks of his clothes."

"His clothes?"

"Well tailored shirt with the top three buttons open." Lynette wiggled her eyebrows, "And very tight, cropped pants. You know the kind where the guy's ankles show? Oh, and shoes with no socks."

"Hmmm...decidedly European. Did you get his name?"

"Nope, I was too busy drowning in his beautiful blue eyes."

Tiny tsked with mock disapproval, and Callie laughed knowing full well that Lynette was head over heels in love with her husband.

"That good looking, huh?"

"Gorgeous with a capital G."

"Point him out to me."

Callie followed Lynette out onto the back porch. "He's sitting over there," Lynette indicated, tilting her head towards a table at the far end of the outdoor seating area. "By himself with his back turned to us. The one in the white shirt."

From her vantage point, there was no way Callie could figure out who he was, and she realized she'd have to go over and be the polite hostess whether she wanted to or not. Taking a deep breath, she made her way over to his table and stood before him. "Hi, I'm Callie, owner of The Summer Breeze Bed and Breakfast and this restaurant. May I help you with something?"

The man rose from his seat in the effortless manner of someone who was in very good shape. He placed his hand on his chest. "Callie! How lovely to see you! And I'm heartbroken you don't remember me!"

Callie took a close look at him and willed her memory to recall who the stranger standing before her was. She was fairly certain that she wouldn't forget a face like his. With his light brown, thick curly hair, piercing blue eyes and chiseled jawline, he was exactly as Lynette had described him. Gorgeous. With a capital G.

"Please accept my apologies. If you could tell me your name, perhaps that would jog my memory?"

He waved his hand as if dismissing her concern. "Please, no need to apologize. Clearly, your beauty left an impression on me but mine had no effect on you whatsoever."

And with that very blatant, bordering on tacky, compliment about her looks *and* his own looks, he reached out, took her hand in his, and placed a whisper soft kiss on her knuckles. As he did, he looked up at her through slightly tousled hair and blinked ever so slowly, and a knowing smile spread across his lips.

Callie's stomach did a very unexpected summersault, and she quickly pulled her hand out from his with an uncomfortable laugh.

Knowing that he had gotten the exact reaction he had expected, the man stood to his full height and finally introduced himself. "My name is Jorgan Winther. We met several years ago when you attended my cousin's wedding in Norway. I believe you were traveling with a male companion. A politician if my memory serves me. Tell me, is the lucky man here?"

"You must mean David, my ex-fiancée."

"Well, I must say that I'm rather pleased to hear that he is no longer in the picture. Perhaps there's hope for me yet."

Not knowing what to say and still not recollecting who the handsome stranger was, Callie asked, "What brings you to Seneca Springs?"

"I'm here on some business for my family, and I'm also a guest lecturer at the university for the fall semester. Which means I can keep coming back here for the wonderful food and beautiful surroundings." Jorgan gestured out toward the waters of Cayuga Lake shimmering in the early evening light but kept his eyes on Callie. "Perhaps you'd be willing to join me for dinner one evening," he asked, sounding very much like a man who rarely received no for an answer.

Beginning to feel more uncomfortable by the direction of the conversation, Callie decided the best course of action would be to put a polite end to it.

"I really must get back to my other guests. It was a pleasure meeting you, Jorgan. Enjoy the rest of your meal."

———

Callie sat on the edge of her bed, hunched over her phone, scrolling through old photos until she finally got to the ones from the wedding she and David had attended in Norway back in the early days of their relationship. Zooming in on all the group photos from the reception, she finally found a few which included Jorgan. It was no wonder she hadn't recognized him right away. In the photos, his hair was cropped short, making it appear much darker than the light brown curls he had been sporting at dinner. But there was no mistaking his piercing blue eyes and roguish expression. In the photos, he had always been standing on the outer edges of the group, and Callie was now certain she had never had a conversation with him beyond a casual introduction.

Her curiosity partially sated, Callie crawled into bed and closed her eyes, waiting for sleep to come. But her mind kept wandering back to how Jorgan could have such a vivid recollection of their meeting and the details of her life at the time.

"Maybe he's just one of those people who never forgets a face," Callie muttered to herself. And at that, the image of Jorgan's face looking up at her through his thick curls as his lips lightly grazed the back of her hand popped unbidden into her mind. Her eyes flew open almost guiltily, and she took a deep breath to calm the sudden butterflies in her stomach. There was a time when Nick's face would fill her late-night musings, and this new face was an unexpected intruder.

"So, what's the story," Lynette had asked when Callie had returned to the kitchen earlier that evening. "You two seemed to have quite a lot to chat about."

Callie had shrugged her shoulders. "He claims we met at a wedding a few years ago in Norway."

"Why do you sound like you don't believe him? Did you go to a wedding in Norway or not?"

"I did. With David. But I have no recollection of Jorgan at all."

"Jorgan, huh? I kind of like the sound of that. Was I right about him or what?"

Callie nodded. "That's the thing. I mean, not to state the obvious, but he's not exactly the kind of man you'd forget."

"Not with those eyes. And that face."

Tiny cleared his throat, as if to remind Lynette that he was in the room.

Not one to back down, Lynette continued, "Not to mention that bod—"

"Don't go there, Lynette," Tiny admonished, chuckling to himself.

"Body," Callie, ignoring Tiny, finished Lynette's sentence for her.

"Do I need to remind you that this isn't a locker room, ladies?"

"Oh please, this isn't anything close to locker room talk." Turning towards Callie, Lynette asked, "Did he say what brought him to Seneca Springs?"

"Apparently he's a guest lecturer at the university."

"Can you just imagine?" Lynette burst out laughing, "Those co-eds are going to be lining up out the door during his office hours."

"I bet there will be plenty of *real* locker room talk then."

———

Callie closed her eyes, determined not to let the image of Jorgan's face intrude on her thoughts again. But as she thought about how the college girls would react to the blatant sex appeal that oozed from his pores, his blue eyes and sculpted jawline materialized once again. Squeezing her eyes shut, she willed herself to think about Nick.

Just then, her phone rang. It took her a moment to find it buried in her bed covers, and she answered it with a breathless and slightly guilty, "Hello?" knowing full well that there was only one person who would be calling her at this hour.

"If I didn't know any better, I'd wonder what you've been up to. Why do you sound so out of breath?"

"I couldn't find my phone."

"Hmmm...I thought maybe it was because you were dreaming about me."

Callie finished loading the few grocery items Tiny had asked her to pick up into her trunk and closed it. Looking down Main Street, she was surprised to see a line had started forming out the door at Cupcakes by Grace during the short time she had been in the grocery store. There was nothing in her purchases that needed to be refrigerated, and Callie decided she would pop into the bakery to see if Grace needed help with anything.

Excusing herself past the customers waiting in line, Callie stepped into the bakery and breathed in the now familiar fragrance of the freshly baked confections. The smell was reminiscent of her childhood days and immediately brought a smile to her face. Callie looked around and waved at a few familiar faces before making her way to the end of the display counter and walking towards the cash register where Grace was busy taking orders.

"Callie! You always seem to know when to show up!"

"And you always seem to have a line out the door!"

"I'm running another promo today." Grace counted out some change and handed it to a mom with twins in a stroller. "It'll take a few minutes to finish decorating. Would your little ones like a T-R-E-A-T on the house while you wait?" she spelled out discreetly.

Mouthing "thank you" in acknowledgement of Grace's courtesy, the woman said, "How about two of those mini ones? The C-H-O-C-O-L-A-T-E, please."

Grace laughed, picked out two of the mini cupcakes, and reached over the counter to hand the toddler boys a cupcake each. "Wait until your mommy says you can eat them, okay?" The boys squealed in delight and held the cupcakes like a treasure as their mom pushed the stroller out of the way.

Smiling, Callie asked her friend, "How can I help?"

Grace gestured over her shoulder where a stack of orders was printed out and waiting to be boxed up. "Those are all online orders. Just grab whatever you need from the display case, place them in the right sized box, seal it, and stick the order on each one so I know what's in what."

As Grace continued helping customers, Callie got to work prepping each order, pleasantly surprised by the sheer number of familiar and unfamiliar names in the stack. When she was finishing up the last order, Callie looked up and noticed the woman with the tattoos on her arms waiting patiently in line. She looked tired and, from her posture, Callie thought she also looked slightly defeated.

By the time it was the woman's turn to order, Callie had nothing left to do but was too curious about the stranger to leave. She decided to assemble extra boxes for Grace and stood within hearing distance of the counter.

"Hi! Welcome back! You're in luck today. I have the white chocolate with raspberry cupcakes."

"You remembered," the woman said, clearly touched by Grace's gesture.

"I make it a point to remember what all my customers like."

"That's the sign of a true chef," the woman replied almost deferentially.

The insightful statement caught Grace off guard. Spontaneously, she wiped her hands on her apron and extended one to the woman. "I'm Grace."

Looking at Grace's hand for a fraction of a second as if unsure of how to respond, the woman slowly raised her own hand and shook Grace's. "Alexis."

The two women locked eyes for a moment and smiled at one another. "Let me get you that cupcake."

"Could you box it up for me this time? I'd like to take it home for my son, Zayne."

Grace was about to ask if the woman wanted more than one and then thought better of it, not wanting to offend Alexis again. If she had wanted more than one, Grace reminded herself, she would have asked.

Callie, who had surreptitiously overheard the entire conversation, had a box ready. Grace carefully placed the cupcake inside and handed it to Alexis.

"Thanks, Grace. I'll see you next week." And with that, she walked out of the bakery with her head held higher than it had been when she had walked in.

Grace turned towards Callie and perfectly expressed what Callie had been feeling. "I don't know what it is about her, but I like her."

More Love

"My favorite kind of guests are staying with us for the next couple of weeks."

Callie looked up from her computer as Lynette walked into the kitchen carrying her own laptop. "Let me guess, older couples with no children who'll spend the majority of their days on wine tours and boating on the lake and then spend a lot of money eating at The Terrace."

Lynette sat down across from Callie and smiled like she had just won the lottery. "Yup. And they should be your favorite kind of guests, too. You know what else I love about them?"

"Enlighten me."

"They love to tell all their friends about the fantastic vacation they had at The Summer Breeze, and then those friends come to stay with us, too."

"Speaking of spending money at The Terrace, we've had a very good couple of weeks since we opened up the outdoor seating."

"You mean, since you finally listened to reason and put up the fence so that we could actually open it up? You could have been making money a lot sooner."

Callie glared at Lynette in response.

Lynette in turn checked her watch. "You've got at least another couple of weeks to go before I let up on the F word. Get used to it."

"I can't stand you sometimes, you know that?"

Lynette laughed, "I don't believe that for a minute."

—ɛɛɛ—

Mornings had always been Callie's favorite time of day, but lately, they felt even more special. She loved waking up before her guests awoke, while there was still dew on the lush green grass and the sun was just beginning to shine on her beloved vegetable garden beds. Everything she had planted was thriving and putting forth a variety of vegetables and herbs that Tiny was using with reckless abandon. Spotting several clusters of tomatoes that were ready to be picked, Callie used her clippers to harvest over a dozen of the plump red beauties and placed them in her wicker basket. Maybe, if she was lucky, she could find more of the ingredients Tiny needed to make gazpacho, her favorite summertime soup.

"You're up early."

Lost in her culinary daydreams, Callie hadn't heard Kirsten's car pull into the driveway. "Kirsten! You startled me."

"What'd you pick today?"

"Tomatoes. And I'm hoping to get a couple of small cucumbers, a bell pepper and a jalapeno."

"Gazpacho?"

Callie smiled and nodded. "Come up to the kitchen before the lunch crowd gets here. We can eat together. I feel like we haven't had a chance to catch up after everything that happened."

"I'd love to."

"What brings you here so early?"

"One of the guests wanted a morning massage. Plus, I need to spend some time doing inventory and re-ordering supplies. Again."

"Business is booming, huh?"

"It's been incredible. And it's not just the appointments. People are buying a ton of facial products. I feel like every time I give a facial, I sell at least a couple of creams and cleansers. And you know what else is flying off the shelves? The aromatherapy candles I've been making." Kirsten opened up her ever-present, very large bag and pulled out a brown box about the size of an apple. "Here. You'll love it."

Callie took the box and read aloud from the tastefully designed round label on top, "Aroma by Kirsten."

"That's the relaxation candle. Hold the box up to your nose and smell."

Callie did as she was told and was rewarded with a lovely fragrance. "Mmmm...I smell lavender and I think a hint of rose, but there's so much more. Complex and soothing all at once."

"It's got eucalyptus, ylang ylang, bergamot, chamomile, and a few other essential oils."

"I'm going to use it when I take my bath tonight."

"You won't be disappointed. I promise."

"See you at lunch?"

"Definitely."

As Kirsten headed towards the spa, Callie took another deep whiff of the candle and smiled. It had been just over a year since Kirsten had first brought up the idea of adding a spa to The Summer Breeze, and Callie was grateful she had. Not only had the spa been a boon for business, but Kirsten had become one of Callie's dearest friends.

Callie poured the highly anticipated, fresh from the garden gazpacho into two earthenware soup bowls and topped them off with garlic croutons she had made using half a loaf of day old, crusty French bread. She set the bowls down on the kitchen table next to one of the O'Connor's old vases filled with a colorful display of wildflowers and stepped back to admire her handiwork. Grabbing her phone out of her back pocket, Callie took some photos of the welcoming tablescape and sat down with the intention of waiting for Kirsten. A full minute passed before she was no longer able to resist her desire to have a quick taste. Callie looked around to make sure no one was watching, grabbed her spoon and took a sip of the chilled soup. The smooth tomato flavor was perfectly offset by the slight kick from the jalapenos and the coolness of cucumber. Looking over her shoulder again, Callie grabbed a crouton and popped it into her mouth.

"I can hear you crunching." Tiny chuckled without turning away from the stove and with his back towards Callie.

"Just making sure everything tastes good."

"I thought that's what you were doing when you were at the stove eating the croutons as you were making them."

Callie was about to retort with a comment about how it's the responsibility of the chef to taste, taste, and taste again when Kirsten walked into the kitchen.

Seeing Callie seated at the table, she asked, "You didn't start without me, did you?"

Tiny burst out laughing. "You didn't think she'd wait for you, did you?" Wiping his hands on his apron, he announced, "I'll leave you ladies to it. Most of the prep is done. I'll be back in a bit." And with that, he walked past the table, grabbed a handful of croutons, and walked out of the kitchen.

―――

The fragrance from the aromatherapy candle permeated Callie's bathroom, and she took another deep breath, feeling more relaxed than she had in a long time. All the guests staying with them this week were exactly as Lynette had predicted. Low maintenance and big spenders. The restaurant was doing very well, and as long as she and Lynette chipped in to help at almost every meal, things ran smoothly. They were still trying to hire a couple of more people, but Callie had learned that finding part time help was an exercise in patience. It would take time, but they'd get there.

Drying herself off, Callie thought back to her conversation with Kirsten who also seemed more relaxed than she had those first few weeks after discovering that Chad had a younger brother. Chad and JR were having video calls on a regular basis, and Kirsten could sense that their growing bond was helping each of them slowly let go of the pain from the past. And Jansen, knowing how important finding his brother was to JR, had also started calling Chad. All in all, the three men were handling things with compassion and respect for what each of them was going through.

"It'll take time, but they'll get there," Kirsten had said, adding thoughtfully, "It's like making a brand-new family, really. Or maybe more like adding new members to the family you already have. Either way, it's just more love coming our way, and that's never a bad thing."

—*ele*—

"I'm not sure I can handle Dr. Joshi and that Norwegian eye candy dining here at the same time."

"They're both here?" Callie asked Lynette.

"I'm not sure what you all see in him," Evie added unasked, as she placed some dishes near the sink. "He's losing his hair, and he's out of shape. Plus, he's kind of old."

Callie heard Lynette mumble under her breath, "I thought you liked older men," and shot her a warning glare not to start anything.

"The other guy, oof. I fully agree. Who is he anyway?" Evie continued talking, unaware of Lynette's comment.

Callie would have answered, but Lynette jumped in. "We're not sure. He's only been here one other time. Anyway, you'd better get back to work."

Evie shot Lynette a look that could turn a person to stone and walked out of the kitchen.

"You're going to have to make a choice pretty soon," Lynette said through gritted teeth.

"A choice?" Callie asked.

"Between keeping her," Lynette gestured at the door, "Or keeping me."

"Obviously, I'd keep you. But you know we need the help. Besides, she's not that bad."

"You keep telling yourself that, and I'm telling you that girl is going to cause problems."

"Look, if we find a replacement, I'll let her go. That's a promise. But until we do, we need to keep her around to get through our busy season."

Lynette sighed with resignation. "Fine. Fine. But I have a bad feeling about her."

No sooner were the words out of her mouth, than Evie came back into the kitchen smiling like the proverbial cat.

"His name is Jorgan Winther, and he's a visiting professor of investment strategy for the hospitality industry. He's here for the semester, living in a rental property near campus, and looking for new friends to show him around the area." And with that pronouncement, Evie grabbed two plates, smirked at Lynette and walked out of the kitchen, calling out, "I have to get back to work."

——ɛɛɛ——

In order to keep an eye on Evie, Lynette decided to circulate amongst the dinner guests to see how they were enjoying their meals. She even braved stopping by Dr. Joshi's table with a bottle of chili flakes before he requested them. Unfortunately, the few moments she spent talking to him only served to get her more flustered. The conversation had been completely innocent, but the way he poured every ounce of his attention on her made her feel like the only woman in the world. She could have stood there talking to him for hours, but she forced herself to come up with an excuse to keep mingling with the other guests.

After almost twenty minutes of watching Evie serve guests, Lynette begrudgingly agreed with what Callie had said. As far as servers went, Evie was not that bad. In fact, she was pretty good. She was polite, friendly, and worked at a decent pace. And since they needed the help, maybe Lynette was being too harsh on her. After all, Evie was a young, attractive woman. Of course she would be flirtatious and interested in meeting new men. Lynette remembered what she was like in her twenties, and while she may not have dressed quite as provocatively as Evie, she certainly enjoyed getting a man's attention.

Lynette was considering going back to the kitchen to tell Callie that she'd back off on Evie when Jorgan waved to get her attention. With butterflies fluttering madly in her stomach and a slow blush spreading across her face, Lynette walked towards his table. She wondered what her beloved husband would make of her behavior. Realizing that he'd probably have a good laugh with her and tell her how much he loved her, Lynette managed to pull herself together by the time she reached Jorgan.

"Good evening. May I help you with something?"

"Hello, yes." Jorgan ran his hands through his hair and looked up at Lynette with his spectacular blue eyes, setting the pesky butterflies aflutter again. "I'd like to meet the chef to personally extend my compliments to him for tonight's meal."

"Of course, I'll have him come out to your table. Have you ordered dessert yet?"

Jorgan shook his head, "No, I try to stay away from the sweet stuff. Watching my figure after all."

So am I, Lynette thought to herself. Aloud she said, "I recommend you make an exception this time around. It's peach season, and the chef has made a lovely peach cobbler. I'll have him bring some out for you."

Jorgan laughed, "In that case, I'm looking forward to it."

Lynette was about to leave when Jorgan continued the conversation. "Tell me, are you fully booked for the next couple of weeks?"

"Yes, actually, we're fully booked from now through the end of autumn."

"Really? That's impressive. I mean, Seneca Springs is relatively off the map. I wonder, how do people find out about this place? Do you do a lot of advertising?"

"Would you believe we stopped advertising a short time after we opened? Word of mouth, online reviews, and return customers have kept us fully booked ever since."

"That's quite an accomplishment."

Lynette smiled at the compliment with obvious pride. "Between the experience our guests have at the bed and breakfast and the food at The Terrace, we're probably one of the most successful establishments in this area."

"How's the competition?"

"There really isn't any. Of course, there are several bed and breakfasts, but they tend to be smaller and don't have a full-service restaurant and spa."

"You have a spa as well?"

Lynette nodded and pointed towards the spa building. "We have two treatment rooms housed in that building. If you're interested in a massage, you can schedule one online." Feeling slightly jealous that Kirsten would get to run her hands over Jorgan's bare skin, Lynette added, "Our massage therapist Kirsten is a miracle worker. We also have a small gym in that building which our guests can use."

Jorgan listened attentively to everything Lynette said and asked, "Have you ever thought of expanding?"

"Expanding?" Lynette almost laughed. "No. Definitely not. We have all the work we can handle right now and trying to find more help is our biggest challenge."

"I see. That's very good to know."

His last comment caught Lynette off guard, and it must have shown on her face because Jorgan quickly changed the subject.

"I'm really looking forward to that cobbler."

Butterflies

Lynette put down the phone and stared blankly at it for a moment before getting up from her desk and going to look for Callie. Not finding her at her usual spot at the kitchen table, she walked out to the garden and saw Callie sitting hunched over one of the dining tables. As she got closer, Lynette saw a spool of copper wire, some tubing, several hand-held tools, and two empty wine bottles.

"I'm not sure I want to know, but I feel compelled to ask what you're up to."

Without looking up, Callie continued using a pair of pliers to loop a length of the copper wire around an empty wine bottle. "I'm making a hummingbird feeder. We need to attract more pollinators."

"You know, you can buy a hummingbird feeder at the store. All you have to do is hang it off a branch. Done."

"I knew you were going to say that."

"And still you decided to take the harder, more time-consuming route."

Callie nodded. "I like making things with my hands."

Lynette watched Callie at work for a few moments, and decided that if she couldn't beat her, she may as well join her. "Hand me a bottle."

Callie looked up at Lynette with a big grin. "I knew you wouldn't be able to resist." She handed Lynette the supplies she'd need and explained the steps. The two women sat in companionable silence as each worked on her hummingbird feeder, until Lynette suddenly remembered the reason she'd come looking for Callie in the first place.

"I almost forgot to tell you. We had a cancellation for next week."

Callie stopped what she was doing and stared blankly at Lynette for a moment. "A cancellation?" she asked, as if unsure of what the word even meant.

"That's the same reaction I had. I can't remember the last time we had one."

"Did they say why?"

"Something about a first grandchild arriving earlier than expected."

"Well, at least it's for a happy reason."

"I guess."

"It'll give us some more downtime."

"Callie, I'm out here making wine bottle hummingbird feeders with you. How much more downtime do we need?"

Callie laughed. "Consider this an investment in our future."

―――

Lynette hung up the phone and was staring at it blankly once again when Callie walked in the front door.

"What now?"

"You're not going to believe this. Did the van leave?"

"Yes. I'm not going to believe what?"

"Who I just got off the phone with. Did all three couples get on the van?"

"Yes. Who did you just get off the phone with?"

"The Norwegian eye candy."

"Jorgan?"

"Is there another piece of Norwegian eye candy walking around Seneca Springs that I should know about?"

Callie rolled her eyes. "What'd he want?"

"A place to stay."

"I thought he had a place to stay."

"Apparently, he had a water leak, and now he needs a place to stay for a few days while they clean everything up."

"Wow, he's lucky we have a room available."

"That's one way to put it."

"What do you mean?"

"Think about it for a minute. When he was here last week, I specifically remember telling him we were fully booked through the end of autumn. Then we have the first cancellation we've had in who knows how long. And now, suddenly, on the first day we have a vacant room, he needs a place to stay and just happened to call us?"

"I think you're making a big deal out of nothing. He needed somewhere to stay, and we're probably the only place he knows around here."

"Maybe."

"Plus, he's been here to eat a few times, and he seems to really enjoy the food. I've seen Tiny stop by his table to talk to him. Maybe they've become friends?"

"He's not the only one."

"You mean Evie?"

Lynette nodded.

"I've seen her talking to him a few times as well. Even when he's not sitting at one of her tables. Maybe they've struck up a friendship, too," Callie added.

"Hmmm...and maybe you haven't been finding excuses to go downtown just to 'pop into Grace's bakery' for a free cupcake."

"That is not true! I have important errands to run," Callie said in defense.

Lynette laughed. Teasing her boss was one of the best parts of her job. "Of course you do. Anyway, Jorgan will be here in about an hour. Gird your loins."

⁓ꞏℓℓꞏ⁓

Callie sat back on her garden swing and looked out at the still waters of Cayuga Lake. The night sky was clear, and bright stars could be seen twinkling in the darkness. Most of the lights at The Summer Breeze were out, and she felt that now familiar feeling of contentment at where life had brought her. Or, she thought to herself, at where she had brought her life. Raising a wine glass to her lips, Callie took a sip of the cold, crisp Pinot Gris from Lakeside Vineyard, just a few miles away. The bottle had been an unexpected gift from Jorgan on the day of his arrival. Savoring the full-bodied wine with its equal parts sweet and spicy flavor, she thought about her unexpected, budding friendship with Lynette's so called Norwegian eye candy. Several times in the past few days, Callie had managed to convince herself that she had finally become immune to his good looks. But then he'd walk into the room and look at her with his beautiful blue eyes and run his fingers through his hair, and her stomach would start filling with butterflies again.

In an effort to assuage the little prick of guilt she couldn't deny feeling, Callie reminded herself constantly that these were not the same butterflies she felt when she was with Nick. Those never seemed to go away, often intensifying the more time she spent with him. And her relationship with Jorgan was completely innocent. They were always surrounded by people, and he seemed to be making friends with everyone at The Summer Breeze. When he wasn't in his suite working or sleeping, he found ways to spend his free time with Callie, Tiny, and much to her content, Lynette. He took a genuine interest in the workings of the B&B and was an excellent listener. Callie was looking forward to their hike tomorrow. It was the first time they were spending time alone together, but she hadn't been able to refuse his repeated requests to show her the picturesque gorges and waterfalls that these parts of the Finger Lakes were known for.

"I'm surprised you agreed to go hiking with him tomorrow," Lynette had said nonchalantly when she and Callie were alone.

"Why?"

"Don't be naïve."

"Don't be old school. You know full well that men and women can be friends."

Lynette stared at Callie for a moment before deciding to throw down the gauntlet. "Really? Name one single, straight man that you're friends with."

Callie thought for several seconds, and then begrudgingly admitted that she couldn't name even one. "Just because I don't have a single, straight male friend at this exact moment doesn't mean I can't have one. Besides, you know how I feel about Nick."

"Great, so I assume you've told him all about Jorgan? And that you're going to be spending several hours hiking out in the woods alone with him tomorrow?"

The little prick of guilt poked at Callie before she said, "Not yet. But I will."

"Good luck with that," Lynette had said, thankfully putting an end to their conversation.

Callie took another sip of her wine and picked up the phone to call Nick. She reminded herself again that there was nothing untoward happening, and there was absolutely no reason for her to feel guilty. She'd tell Nick about her plans with Jorgan, and that would be the end of that. As she waited for him to answer the phone, her stomach filled with butterflies again. But this time, she couldn't be sure if they were because she was excited to hear his voice, or maybe because she was just a little nervous over what she was about to tell him.

Gorgeous Gorges

"You're going hiking with the Norwegian? Just the two of you?" Nick had asked incredulously when she had told him about her plans.

"It's not a problem, is it?" Callie had bristled almost immediately. Her plan had been to tell him calmly, almost nonchalantly, and then provide him with reassurance if he needed it. Instead, she had thrown her plans at him like a challenge, just waiting for him to say something. "You trust me, right?"

"Of course I trust you. But do you trust him?"

"I wouldn't be going if I didn't."

"Callie, how well do you even know him?"

"Well enough."

"Okay, let me rephrase the question."

"Am I being interrogated?"

Ignoring her question, Nick asked, "How *long* have you known him?"

"He's been coming into the restaurant pretty regularly for a few weeks now. Plus, he's been staying in one of our suites for the past few days. If you don't trust my judgement, ask Tiny or Lynette. They've been spending a lot of time with Jorgan as well." Callie could feel herself getting more annoyed by the minute.

"I don't want to ask them. I'm asking you."

"Fine. We're going to a public park, and you know it's peak tourist season so there will be a lot of people on the trails. Look, I'm not sure I like having to defend myself. I'm a grown woman, I want to go on a hike with a new friend."

Nick sighed. "You're right."

Caught off guard, Callie asked, "I am?"

"Yes. I trust you. And if you trust him, then I trust him."

Callie listened closely to his response and gauged his words carefully. It was hard to be absolutely certain over the phone, but from what she could tell, Nick was being honest with her about his feelings. She felt the stress leave her shoulders, and she took another sip of her wine. "Good. And besides, why would I want to be with anyone else, when I have you?"

Nick sighed again, and Callie thought she heard him mutter, "Why indeed?"

Lynette was sitting on the back porch enjoying her second cup of coffee of the day and enjoying the relative peace before guests started arriving for lunch when Callie's car pulled into the driveway. Slamming the door shut harder than was necessary, Callie mumbled something under her breath before realizing that Lynette was watching her.

"Aarghhh."

"Hello to you, too. What happened? I thought you wouldn't be back for a few hours."

"What happened? I'll tell you what happened." Callie sat down on the back porch step and drew in a deep breath to calm herself down. "Evie happened."

On hearing her least favorite person's name, Lynette rolled her eyes. "Now what?"

"We somehow managed to find a parking spot, and when we got to the trailhead, would you believe Evie was there? Dressed like a sexy hiker and doing stretches."

"'A sexy hiker?'"

Callie nodded. "You know, like those Halloween costumes they have. Sexy nurse, sexy doctor, sexy witch. Evie was dressed as a sexy hiker."

"Do I detect a hint of jealousy?" Lynette teased, giving Callie, who was dressed in old jeans and a plain white t-shirt, a once over.

"Not a chance."

"What was she wearing?"

———

Callie and Jorgan had been chatting away amiably when they pulled into the parking lot by Callie's favorite hiking spot in the area. She hadn't been on a hike in far too long, and she was looking forward to the challenging trail and beautiful views. This particular trail wound its way through hilly woodlands along a deep gorge and ended at a spectacular waterfall. The distant sound of water could be heard, and Callie felt like a little kid excited about going on a big adventure.

Callie had grabbed her small backpack filled with a couple of water bottles, some light snacks, and a first aid kit out of the car and was putting her arms through the straps when she noticed Jorgan waving at someone. Considering that the man barely knew anyone in the area, she turned in surprise, wondering if maybe he had seen someone from the university. The site that met her eyes had been the farthest thing from her mind, and Callie's jaw dropped open.

Standing at the trailhead, waving at them, and beaming from ear to ear was Evie wearing a low cut, very form fitting white tank top which was perfectly tucked into a pair of very short shorts. A pair of hiking boots in pristine condition finished the outfit. The effect was comical and looked to Callie like a perfect "sexy hiker" Halloween costume.

"Hi! Jorgan, what a nice surprise! Callie, I didn't know that you knew about this place! I didn't think you ever left the bed and breakfast!"

Biting her lip and reminding herself to be civil, Callie forced a smile on her face. "This is one of my favorite trails. Jorgan wanted to explore the area, so I suggested we come here."

"Just the two of you? How nice." Evie's friendly tone of voice said one thing, but Callie caught the slight glint in her eyes which conveyed something else altogether.

"What are you doing here? I didn't know you liked to hike." Unable to control herself, Callie gave Evie's bare legs a pointed stare and added, "I hope you're wearing mosquito repellent. I wouldn't want you to leave here covered in mosquito bites or worse, poison ivy."

Ignoring the jab, Evie smiled at Jorgan and batted her perfectly mascaraed eyelashes. "Oh, I love the outdoors. I try to explore every chance I get." She bent down to tie her shoes in what looked like a well-practiced maneuver. Callie watched as Jorgan had exactly the reaction Evie had been hoping for and wondered if he even noticed that Evie's hiking boots looked brand spanking new.

And then Jorgan said the words Callie had been dreading. "Are you hiking by yourself? Why don't you join us?"

Evie stood up and looked at him in surprise. "I wouldn't want to be a third wheel."

Knowing full well that the comment was meant for her, Callie had felt she had no choice but to respond, "Not at all. You're welcomed to join us if you like."

—⁓—

"You mean to tell me that you actually invited her along?"

"What choice did I have?"

Lynette chuckled. "You gotta give it to her. She goes after what she wants."

"What do you mean?"

"You don't think it's awfully coincidental that she happened to be at that particular trailhead at that particular time?"

"You haven't even heard the half of it."

Lynette took a sip of her now tepid coffee and looked at Callie with anticipation, eager to hear what happened next.

"We hiked for about half an hour. And you know what that trail is like. The first half mile is steep and only wide enough for two people to walk side by side. For the first few minutes, Jorgan and I were walking next to each other, but it quickly became obvious that Evie needed help. She was stumbling and kept falling behind. At one point, Jorgan had to hold her hand to help her along, and she somehow managed to push me out of the way so that the two of them were walking next to each other and I was bringing up the rear."

Lynette giggled, "Sounds like something out of high school."

"And then, out of nowhere, Evie suddenly stumbled and fell onto her hands and knees."

"What did she trip over?"

"Nothing! I'm telling you, the path was steep but well-maintained and smooth. No rocks, no roots sticking up. But of course, Jorgan didn't notice that."

"Of course not."

"He put his arms around her to help her stand, and I had to help clean up her knees which were scuffed up from the fall. And then when she tried to walk, she made this strange little whimpering sound and said her ankle hurt."

"From tripping over nothing?"

Callie nodded, "Exactly. Anyway, to make a long story short, she said we should keep going and she'd get herself home somehow. Jorgan obviously immediately objected to that and offered to drive her home in her car. And that, my friend, was that."

"Like a well-choreographed dance."

"I guess I should look at the bright side."

"Oh? What's that?"

"I have the rest of my afternoon free. And let's just suffice it to say that Nick will not be disappointed at how things turned out."

———eee———

Callie tilted her head back and drank the last few drops of orange juice in her cup. Fresh squeezed just the way she liked it, courtesy of Tiny. Making sure no one was watching, Callie stuck her finger in the cup and scooped up some of the pulp remaining around the edges.

"That looks refreshing. Is there any more left?"

Callie was startled as Jorgan joined her in the kitchen and hoped she didn't have any pulp stuck between her teeth.

"Of course. Let me pour you a glass."

"Is there anything to eat?" Jorgan asked, sounding considerably less friendly than he usually did.

Callie handed him a glass of orange juice and took a closer look at his face. In a word, he looked exhausted. There were bags under his eyes and his skin had an unhealthy pallor. Jorgan's sexy hair was always a little disheveled by design, but today, it looked limp and a little oily.

"Are you feeling okay? You don't look so good."

"That obvious, huh? Remind me never to go out with that girl again."

"What girl?" Callie asked, confused at first and then suddenly realizing that he might mean Evie.

"Evie."

"You went out with her? I thought her ankle was hurt and that's why she didn't come in for her shift last night." Callie hoped her voice sounded normal and not tinged with the mixture of annoyance and, she'd be lying to herself if she didn't admit, a mild case of jealousy.

"We never actually left her apartment. Honestly, I'm not even sure how she managed it, but before I knew it, she had convinced me to stick around for dinner as her way of saying 'thank you' for coming to her rescue. That turned into a bottle of wine, which turned into another bottle, and well, you know how that goes. And then it wasn't safe for me to drive, so I had to stay over. She just now dropped me off."

Callie's eyes grew wide as Jorgan finished telling his story. She had always suspected that Evie got around, but she had never heard it told from a firsthand point of view.

"You know what? On second thought, I think I'll skip the orange juice, and just go lay down for a bit." Jorgan pushed his untouched glass away and walked out of the kitchen, leaving Callie standing there alone.

Not wanting to waste a perfectly good glass of orange juice, Callie felt she had no choice but to drain this one, too.

Callie and Lynette were going over their weekly accounting reports at the kitchen table, a chore most people would have found tedious. But for Callie, it was a special time, almost like a weekly affirmation that the drastic changes she had made in her life over the past year and a half were worth it. Not just for her, but for everyone connected with the bed and breakfast. Each week that she saw the income her business was generating was proof that she had done the right thing for herself in charting her own course. She was particularly proud of her ability to create well-paying jobs for her employees while also supporting local vendors and suppliers. Rarely did the revenue she generated in Seneca Springs get spent outside of Seneca Springs. In her own small way, she was helping to revive the economy of this quaint, lakeside town that had become her home.

Lynette, who thrived on organization, looked forward to these meetings almost as much as Callie did. She was proud of knowing every detail of how the bed and breakfast was running. She could recount inventory levels, reservation statistics, and expenses down to the penny. Without her, Callie knew she wouldn't have been able to accomplish half as much as she had.

"You were right about our guests last week. Just look at these numbers. They spent a lot of money."

Lynette nodded, "And we have another batch coming on Sunday."

"Which reminds me, Jorgan will have to check out."

Sighing, Lynette added, "I'll be sad to see him go."

"You know he spent the night at—" Before Callie could finish her sentence, Grace walked into the kitchen carrying a large tray covered with a cloche which could only mean one thing.

"Got a few minutes to taste some new recipes I'm trying out?"

Callie groaned, knowing she wouldn't be able to say no. "Why couldn't you have opened up an all you can eat salad bar?"

"Speak for yourself. I'm happy to taste everything you make, Grace. That's what good friends are for."

Grace laughed, placed the tray on the kitchen table and removed the cloche with a flourish, revealing three different varieties of cannoli. "Ta-da!"

"These aren't cupcakes," Callie stated the obvious. "You're not making cupcakes anymore?"

"I'm expanding my repertoire. People can't just eat cupcakes all the time. So, I thought I'd try something new. A revolving menu of different specialties every week. Or every month. I haven't decided yet." Pointing at the delectable mini-cannoli, Grace added, "We have the traditional with candied orange peel and ricotta dipped in pistachios. My favorite, filled with candied lemon ricotta with a candied lemon peel wedge. And what I think will be Callie's favorite, dipped in chocolate and filled with hazelnut crème."

Callie and Lynette exchanged eager glances before reaching out and selecting the one they wanted, Lynette opting for the traditional and Callie choosing the hazelnut, leaving the lemon for Grace.

"This calls for a cup of coffee."

While Callie was making a fresh pot, Grace leaned forward and whispered conspiratorially to Lynette, "Is the eye candy still here? You know, he came into the bakery yesterday. Picked up a couple of cupcakes and had them packed to go."

"I haven't seen him yet today. I wonder who the cupcakes were for."

Callie, who had overheard the conversation, served the coffee, and sat down. "I know who they were for. And the reason you haven't seen him yet today, Lynette, is because he spent last night at Evie's. Came back a little while ago, hungover and exhausted and went straight up to his room."

Lynette's jaw dropped open, and she sat staring at Callie. "Do you mean to tell me that we've been sitting here going over the ledger, and this whole time you've known that bit of gossip and have kept it from me?"

"I was about to tell you, but we got distracted by these absolutely scrumptious cannoli." Callie took another bite and added, "Crispy on the outside, smooth on the inside and not too sweet."

"Cannolis," Lynette corrected.

"What?"

"You said cannoli when you should have said cannolis. With an 's' at the end. Plural." Lynette picked up her cannoli and smiled smugly. "You're not the only one who can correct a person's grammar, you know," she said, using the cannoli to emphasize each word before taking a bite.

"Actually, Callie is right. Cannoli is the plural version of the word. The singular is cannolo."

Callie tried to hide her laughter behind her raised coffee cup.

"I hate you both."

"It's a common mistake," Grace said trying to make Lynette feel better.

"Kind of like doppledanger and doppelgänger," Callie chimed in unhelpfully.

Seeing Lynette's reaction and anticipating her unladylike response, Grace changed the subject. "So, tell me about the Norwegian. He really spent the night at Evie's?"

Callie filled Grace in on Evie's hiking "injury," and Jorgan's behavior and appearance when she had seen him earlier in the day.

"People are a mystery to me. He seemed like a decent guy. Flirtatious, yes, but how could he not be looking the way he does? When he came into the bakery, he asked to sample some of the flavors, and before I knew it, I was feeding him a mini cupcake. Thank goodness Dominick wasn't around to see that."

"Did he do that thing with his eyes? Where he looks at you through his hair and blinks slowly?"

Grace nodded, and the three friends sighed almost simultaneously.

"I'll be sad to see him go," Lynette repeated.

"You know, I saw him talking to Alexis briefly as well. She was in the bakery picking up her weekly cupcake, and he managed to strike up a conversation with her in the ten minutes he was there."

"Have you learned anything else about her?"

"Who's Alexis?" Lynette asked.

"The woman from the bakery I told you about a while ago. The one who didn't seem to have enough money to pay for her cupcake."

"The one who's business you were trying to snoop into?"

Callie nodded and motioned for Grace to continue.

"I know she works at the university, cleaning fraternity and sorority houses. A job she hates. And I know she has a son whom she adores. But that's about it." Grace paused, seemingly unsure of whether to continue. "Well, there is one other thing."

Callie leaned forward in anticipation. "What?"

"Her knowledge of flavors is off the charts."

Callie sat back disappointed. "Oh. I was hoping for something juicier than that."

Undeterred, Grace continued, "If I make even the slightest variation to a recipe, she picks up on it. Like the other day, I made a chai flavored cupcake and asked her to taste a sample. As soon as she bit into it, she closed her eyes and listed off every spice I put in. Ginger, cloves, cardamom, black pepper, cinnamon, nutmeg."

"Chai spice is ubiquitous. Every coffee shop serves some version of it."

"But most casual drinkers have no idea what comprises it."

"That's true." Lynette chimed in. "I have no idea what's in it."

"You're like Nick. He'll eat anything without ever questioning the ingredients."

"Speaking of Nick, when is he coming to visit?"

"Tomorrow."

"You mean he'll be here at the same time as the Norwegian eye candy?"

Callie nodded. "He has a name, you know. It's Jorgan."

Ignoring her, Lynette added, "If Dr. Joshi comes in for dinner, and Nick is here, and the Norwegian eye candy recovers enough to join us for a meal, it'll be a veritable feast for my eyes. I wonder if we could seat all three of them at the same table."

Floodgates

N ick poured two glasses of wine and joined Callie on the back porch swing. The heat of the day had dissipated and a slight breeze off the lake made the night weather perfect for spending time outdoors.

Callie took the glass Nick held out to her and smiled up at him, "Thank you." Tilting the glass up to her nose, she inhaled deeply and luxuriated in the aroma before taking a sip.

Nick sat down and placed his arm gently around Callie's shoulders. "I'm glad I came down this weekend."

"Me, too."

"Glad I got a chance to meet Jorgan. Lynette's right on point with what she calls him. He really is eye candy."

Callie laughed, "I'm glad you agree."

"I'll admit I was a bit jealous when I heard about him on the phone. But now that I've met him, he seems all right. Maybe a little too friendly, but he's that way with everyone, men and women alike. And very curious about the restaurant and the b and b. I've never heard someone ask so many questions."

"He's some sort of professor in the hospitality industry."

"Yeah, he mentioned that. Still, I found his curiosity about The Summer Breeze a little much."

"To each his own," Callie said, dismissing Nick's concern and attributing his little criticisms to lingering jealousy.

"I feel like the restaurant is getting busier every time I visit," Nick observed, changing the subject.

"It's doing incredibly well. Sometimes, I feel like the bed and breakfast is becoming the side business."

"Does that bother you?"

Callie thought for a moment and then shook her head. "I'm happy with everything I've created here. The success of each is dependent on the success of the other. As more visitors from out of town come to visit the bed and breakfast, the restaurant and Tiny both garner more fans. They spread the word, and we get more guests from far and wide. And as more people come to eat at the restaurant, the more they tell their friends and families about the b and b. It's all interconnected. Today's a big day, you know."

"Oh? How so?"

"I have officially broken even on my initial investment in The Summer Breeze." Seemingly as an afterthought, Callie added, "Almost one year ahead of schedule."

Nick let out a long whistle and raised his glass, ever amazed by the woman he was fortunate enough to be with. "Congratulations! That's an incredible achievement."

Callie smiled with immense pride in her accomplishment. When the idea of opening her own bed and breakfast had first started taking shape, she had known she would be taking a financial risk. But as she had researched the idea, and then found the perfect location and slowly hired employees who had become like family to her, she had felt certain the risk would be rewarded. And today, it had been. In less than two years, she had turned her dream into reality. A reality that benefited her, her employees, and her new community of Seneca Springs.

"I owe it all to a lot of people. Including you." Draining the last of her wine, Callie stood up and held her hand out to Nick. "It's starting to feel a little chilly. Why don't we go inside?"

She didn't have to ask him twice.

"With Nick and Jorgan gone, and Dr. Joshi on vacation for the next few weeks, how will we entertain ourselves?"

"I'll work, and you'll go to the city for a few days with Mr. W," Callie responded, not taking the bait.

"You're no fun. Are you sure you'll be all right? We're fully booked all week. And reservations for The Terrace are out the door."

"Yes, you deserve some time away from here. Besides, I hear your husband has already bought tickets for a couple of Broadway shows."

Lynette rubbed her hands together eagerly. "I know! I can't wait. Can you believe I've become a theater junkie? I never understood what people used to love about the theater, but now it's one of my favorite things to do when we go to New York."

"I can count the number of shows I went to see on one hand. I never took enough advantage of everything the city had to offer. I'm glad you're doing it."

"By the way, you never told me about your surprise trip to see Nick. Did you two lovebirds take in any shows? Have any good restaurant recommendations for me?"

Callie blushed thinking about the two days she had spent with Nick in New York. Two days during which they never once left his apartment. "Not unless you want to eat take-out for every meal."

Lynette threw her head back and laughed. "That good, huh?"

"Better."

—ell—

Callie had just drifted off to sleep when her phone rang. Assuming it was Nick calling her again to say good night one more time, she answered groggily, "Hello? Do you miss me already?"

A voice she hadn't been expecting answered back, sounding rather frantic. "Callie? It's me, Sean. Sean Weston."

Suddenly wide awake, Callie sat up in bed and wondered at the probability of one of the biggest movie stars in the world calling her on a Sunday night.

"Is everything okay? Is Rina okay?" Callie could hear Sean's anxious tone mirrored in her own voice.

"Yes, yes, she's fine. I mean, health wise, she's okay. I'm sorry, I didn't realize what time it was on the East Coast. I didn't mean to wake you. Go back to sleep. We'll call you in the morning."

Callie could hear Rina saying something in the background that sounded a lot like, "She's already awake now. Just ask her about—" She couldn't hear the rest of the sentence or anything at all for that matter because Sean put the phone on mute.

After several seconds of waiting, which only served to rouse Callie's curiosity further, he came back on the phone. "Sorry about that Callie. You must think we're crazy. Thanks for not hanging up on us."

"Not at all. Is everything all right?"

"Listen, you go on back to sleep, and we'll call you in the morning."

"I'm already awake. Please, tell me why you called." Callie replied as patiently as she could, agreeing with Rina's logic. She was already wide awake and anxious to know what was going on. The thought that the Westons were going to come back to visit fleetingly crossed her mind, but she doubted they'd call at this hour to make reservations.

"Do you remember the earrings Rina was wearing when we were at the B&B last time?"

Callie rubbed her eyes. This conversation was getting stranger by the minute. Before she could respond, she heard some muffled conversation on the other end of the line. This time, Sean hadn't hit the mute button. It seemed like he had just put his hand over the phone.

"Callie, it's Rina. Sorry to wake you. On one of our last days at The Summer Breeze, the day Sean had made breakfast with Tiny, I was wearing a pair of rather large earrings. Do you remember which ones I'm talking about?"

Callie was glad Rina had wrestled the phone from Sean and finally gotten to the point of their call. Closing her eyes, she recalled the exact moment she had seen Rina that morning, standing in the kitchen and looking absolutely radiant. The earrings had been hard to miss. If Callie had had to guess, she would have figured the emeralds alone were more than two carats each. Throw in the diamonds, and she was certain those earrings cost more than most people made in a year.

"The emerald and diamond tear drops?" Callie nodded as she spoke, even though Rina couldn't see her. "I remember them. They were beautiful."

"Yes, those are the ones. A little showy for breakfast at home, I know," Rina said almost apologetically. But her casual reference to breakfast at "home" was not lost on Callie. "Sean gave them to me when Rian was born. I've never worn them before, you know? Earrings like that are only for special events. Red carpets, awards shows, that kind of thing. Anyway, we have the opening of Sean's new movie coming up, and I was meeting with my stylists to plan out what I would wear. I'd been saving the earrings for just this occasion, but when I went to show them to my team, I couldn't find them. We've searched every corner of the house. Every square inch. And they're just not here."

Callie could hear the panic rising in Rina's voice as she spoke and could only imagine how she would feel if she lost something as special as those earrings.

"Have you worn them again after you left here?"

"No."

"Have you retraced your steps after you left? You flew straight to London to finish filming if I recall."

"Yes, that's right. I've gone over everything a million times." As if to prove her point, Rina continued. "After our breakfast that day, I put the earrings back in my jewelry pouch. I specifically remember doing it because Rian kept trying to grab them off my ears. When we went back to our room, I handed the baby to Sean, went into the bathroom, and took the earrings off. I placed them inside the box they came in and placed the box inside my jewelry pouch. And when it was time for us to leave, Sean and Rita packed up everything. Sean always keeps my jewelry in his carryon for safe keeping, and I remember he made a comment about it."

In the background, Callie heard Sean say, "I said 'Your jewels are in the inside pocket of my bag, my Queen.' I said those exact words as I was putting them in the bag."

"Those were his exact words. Sean always makes a point of doing a walkthrough of any place we're staying to make sure we don't leave anything behind."

Callie picked up the thread of Rina's recollection. "I remember that Lynette and I did a quick check of all the rooms as well, and we didn't find anything either." Without meaning to sound it, Callie thought she detected a hint of defensiveness in her tone.

Rina didn't seem to notice and continued, "Right. After that, we loaded up the rental car and went straight to the airport. We were on a chartered flight with no other passengers. The crew took our bags out of the car and loaded them into the cargo section of the plane."

"Everything except my carryon and Rian's diaper bag."

"I was just about to say that. Quit interrupting me. Anyway, where was I, Callie? Oh right, we landed at a small airport outside of London and then Sean drove our car, which was waiting there for us, straight to our home. Sean put the jewelry pouch in our safe, and I never took any jewelry out of it for the rest of our stay in England. Not once. And when it was time for us to return to the States, I remember Sean took the pouch out of the safe and put it right back into the inside pocket of his carryon. He never even opened it to check that everything was there because we had no reason to believe anything would be missing."

"I should have checked."

Callie could almost picture Sean shaking his head in frustration.

"It's not your fault, sweetheart," Rina comforted. "When we landed in California, it was the same thing all over again. That carryon bag never left Sean's sight. No one ever carried it but him, and when we got home, he placed the pouch in our safe at home."

"So, the last time you had the earrings was when you were here at The Summer Breeze," Callie said contemplatively.

"Yes. I'm certain of it. And when I went to show them to my stylist, I opened the safe, took out the pouch, opened the box and the earrings weren't there. It was just an empty box."

Callie took a deep, shaky breath, unsure of what to say.

Thankfully, Rina kept talking. "I hate to trouble you, Callie, but would you mind looking around the rooms we stayed in to see if we may have missed something?"

Feeling slightly relieved by Rina's request, Callie replied, "Yes, that's not a problem at all. I can definitely search the entire property. But...," Callie hesitated for a moment before continuing, "I have to tell you that we've had several sets of guests stay at the bed and breakfast after you left. The rooms have been cleaned and turned over each time. If the earrings were here, I'm certain they would have turned up by now."

Rina sighed shakily as if she was holding back tears. "I was afraid you were going to say that. In that case, we would need to know the names of all your employees and the guests who've stayed there."

Her statement hit Callie like a slap across the face, especially coming from a woman who valued her privacy above much else. Before she could even formulate a response, Sean came on the phone.

"Sorry about that, Callie. Rina's really upset, but I don't think we're quite there yet. I don't want to ask you to violate your guests' privacy or anything like that. If you can just please do a search, maybe check under the beds or behind furniture? I think that would be a good starting point."

Callie let out the breath she didn't realize she had been holding. "I can definitely do that."

"Okay, let's start there. Are there guests right now in the room Rina and I slept in?"

"Yes."

"Okay," Sean repeated as if trying to comfort Callie and himself, "It's late. Why don't you go to bed and maybe you can take a look around when the room is being cleaned tomorrow."

"Okay."

"Give us a call and let us know how it goes."

"I will."

"Thanks, Callie. And I'm sorry about all this."

Sean disconnected the line.

"So am I," Callie whispered to no one.

———ele———

Callie woke up the next morning feeling unrested and unwell. Her conversation with the Westons had left her deeply troubled and unable to sleep. While they hadn't come right out and accused someone associated with The Summer Breeze of having anything to do with the missing earrings, there was no doubt in Callie's mind that that's what they were thinking.

She had tossed and turned for much of the night, wondering how Sean and Rina could be so certain they hadn't misplaced the earrings. Callie replayed the conversation over and over in her mind. But if everything they said was true, that after Rina had worn the earrings the one time at the B&B and then had placed them in the box and never worn them again, then there really was very little doubt that the earrings had most likely gone missing at The Summer Breeze. The only thing Callie could think of was that Rina, distracted by her baby, might not have actually placed them in the box. Maybe she had put them on the bathroom vanity for a moment and planned to place them in the box, but then never got around to it. That would be the only explanation for the empty box traveling around the world with them.

But if that was the case, then why hadn't the earrings turned up already? Why hadn't one of her employees or guests come running down the stairs and announced, "I just found a pair of earrings!"? Callie was fairly certain that if anyone had seen those particular earrings, they would have known almost instinctively that they were valuable. She knew that earrings with gemstones as large as those would feel heavy in the palm of anyone's hands.

Callie fought the urge to check which guests had stayed in the room the Westons had slept in when they were at the B&B, but after what felt like an eternity of tossing and turning, she threw the covers off in frustration and pulled her laptop onto her bed. Quickly logging into her reservations software, she pulled up the historical report of guests and scanned through the list of names. Three couples had stayed in that room after the Westons' departure.

There was the newlywed couple who had found each other late in life and were enjoying a very low-key road trip honeymoon. They had been pleasant and courteous, but clearly very much in love and not interested in spending time with anyone but each other. When they did leave their room, they usually were out on the lake or visiting the local vineyards. Callie recalled that they dressed well and drove a very nice car. Other than that, they seemed like two regular people enjoying time together.

It was the same for the two sets of retired couples who stayed in the room after them. They seemed well to do and were simply enjoying their sunset years at their own pace. They had eaten at the restaurant several times, ordered expensive wines, and showed off photos of their grandchildren to anyone who asked.

Callie couldn't, and didn't want to, imagine any of them stealing Rina's earrings. But her mind started playing tricks on her, and before she could stop, she found herself picturing each of them finding the earrings and hiding them inside their luggage.

"No. Stop it. Stop it right now," Callie said aloud, slamming her laptop shut. If she was going to start doubting her guests and accusing them of thievery, she may as well close down The Summer Breeze that very minute. Opening up her home to strangers, so many of whom had become friends, had been the whole point of owning a bed and breakfast. Meeting new people and giving them a unique experience that left them feeling pampered gave her immense pride, and now, here she was wondering if they were hiding stolen goods in their suitcases.

Callie gave her pillow a fierce fluffing and laid back down. She pulled her sheets over her head hoping to hide from her own thoughts.

"Breathe," she reminded herself. "Slow down."

After several moments of deep, intentional inhalations and exhalations, Callie could feel herself calming down and thinking more clearly. And then, unbidden, another, even worse thought suddenly popped into her head. What if it wasn't a guest who stole the earrings? What if it was one of her employees? A person she had hired and trusted.

The sour taste of bile rose in Callie's stomach, and she found herself feeling unexpectedly nauseous. At that point, the floodgates of negative thoughts had opened up, and try as she might, Callie had been unable to stop them.

Clue

"Good morning, Callie." Tiny walked into the kitchen and put two large shopping bags he had been carrying onto the kitchen island. "I stopped by the store on my way in, picked up a bunch of staples we needed. Salt, sugar, some spices. I need to get started on those muffins. Are you going to help me?" When he didn't get a response from Callie who had been sitting quietly at the kitchen table lost in her own thoughts, he prompted, "Hello? Earth to Callie?"

Still not getting a response from his usually chirpy boss, Tiny walked over to the table and sat down across from her. Callie watched his reaction as he got a closer look at her face and knew there was no hiding how she felt. Her drawn expression and the bags under her eyes belied her emotions, equal parts sad and frustrated.

"Everything okay? Anything I can do to help?" Tiny asked gently, concern for his friend coming through.

Callie looked up at him and quickly turned away. She couldn't bear to look at this man who had become such a close friend without feeling horribly guilty at the thought she had had just hours ago - wondering whether Tiny had gone up to the Weston's room to help bring down their luggage, and whether he had seen the earrings and quietly put them into the pocket of his apron.

Nodding her head, Callie managed to say, "I'm okay. I...I don't think I can help you with the muffins today. I'm so sorry."

Callie hastily walked out of the kitchen, knowing her apology was for so much more than not being able to help with making breakfast.

———

With Lynette still in New York City, Callie had to manage the front desk on her own, whether she was feeling up to it or not. And by the time she got through all the suddenly grueling small talk and fake smiles necessary to get her guests out the door on their excursions, she felt like she was ready to burst into tears.

Taking a deep breath, Callie checked her watch and wondered when Evie would arrive. Her plan was to inspect each room while her guests were out, and she wanted one other person with her at all times. As she was straightening up the desk, the phone rang, and Callie jumped to answer it, hoping it was Lynette. She wanted desperately to talk with one of the most grounded, logical, reasonable people she knew. And although the thought had briefly crossed her mind the night before that Lynette had opportunity to take the earrings, she had been able to rule her out almost immediately. The earrings were incredibly valuable, but Callie also happened to know that the ring on Lynette's finger was equally valuable. And she had a pretty good idea of what Lynette's husband was worth. Lynette may have had opportunity, but Callie was absolutely certain that she didn't have any motive to take the earrings.

"Hello?"

"Callie? Oh, good. I'm glad you answered and not Lynette."

Disappointed, Callie recognized Evie's voice on the other end of the line.

"Listen, can I come in an hour later today? I have some things I need to take care of."

"Not today, Evie. I need you to come in now. We have a lot of rooms to turnover before our guests return."

"I can get them done quickly. It's just an hour, what's the big deal?"

Callie, already frustrated, snapped, "It's always 'just an hour.' I give you plenty of advance notice of your schedule, and I expect you to be here on time."

"Okay, okay, take it easy," Evie soothed.

Callie could sense from Evie's tone that she was caught off guard by her usually agreeable boss and likely annoyed that she wasn't getting her way. But Callie couldn't be bothered by any of that. Instead, she doubled down. "I'll expect you here in 10 minutes. In addition to cleaning the rooms, I need you to help me do a thorough search of all the rooms."

"Oh? What are you looking for?"

"Something one of our VIPs left behind," Callie said vaguely.

"Let's start in the bathroom. That's where they were last seen."

"Where what was last seen? It would be helpful if you tell me what I'm looking for," Evie said with ill-concealed displeasure.

"A pair of earrings. Trust me, you'll know them if you see them." Callie began her search by methodically opening each drawer in the vanity one at a time and running her hand along the inside.

Evie watched Callie for several seconds before saying, "I've cleaned this room a bunch of times in the past few weeks. If you tell me when the earrings were lost, I may be able to think back to that cleaning."

"It's been a few weeks. Look, let's just get this over with. Okay? Why don't you start looking around the baseboards and under the vanity, in case they got stuck on the floor somewhere."

Surprisingly, Evie didn't protest. She got down on all fours and started running her hands along the baseboards and under the vanity. Then she sat up and pulled the small bathroom trash can towards herself. She removed the plastic bag, placed her hand inside the can, and slowly pulled it out again.

"Are these the earrings you're looking for?" Evie held out her open palm to reveal Rina Weston's beautiful, shimmering, diamond and emerald tear drop earrings.

Callie's heart leapt with a combination of joy and relief as she took the earrings from Evie. "Yes! I can't believe we found them so fast! Where were they?"

Evie stood up and brushed dirt that wasn't there off her pants. "They were in the garbage can. Under the bag. Hidden in the folds of the extra bags I always leave at the bottom of the cans."

"Amazing! I can't thank you enough, Evie! You know what, once you're done cleaning the rooms, you can skip your shift at The Terrace tonight. I'll cover for you. You've earned the evening off."

"With pay?" Evie asked, sounding inexplicably disappointed.

"May I speak to Rina, please?" Callie asked the unfamiliar voice who had answered the phone number Sean had told her to call.

"May I ask who's calling?"

"This is Callie. The Westons are expecting my—" Before Callie could finish her sentence, Rina's voice came on the line.

"Callie! It's Rina. The phone was on speaker and as soon as I heard your voice, I ran over and grabbed it from Rian's new nanny. Please, please tell me you have some good news."

"We found them. We found your earrings."

Rina let out a sound that seemed part sob and part laughter, and Callie knew exactly how she must be feeling because it was exactly the same way she had felt when Evie had held out her hand with the earrings nestled safely on her palm.

"Sean, she found the earrings!" Rina yelled before saying, "I don't know how to thank you, Callie! How did you find them? Where were they?"

Callie could hear Sean whooping in the background and smiled. "You won't believe it. They were at the bottom of the garbage can in the bathroom of the room you and Sean slept in. From what I can tell, our cleaning crew usually keeps extra empty bags at the bottom of each can. And when it's time to empty the garbage can, they just pull out a new bag from inside. I'm guessing the earrings somehow fell inside and got covered by the extra bags at the bottom."

"So that would mean I never put them inside the box." Although it sounded more like a question than a statement, Callie assumed it was a rhetorical one and didn't answer. "I must be losing my mind, because I swear I remember putting them in the box."

"Babe, I told you, you're not losing your mind. Anyway, it's not a big deal. What's important is that Callie found the earrings!"

"You're right. You're absolutely right. Thank you, Callie. Thank you so much."

"There is one small problem though."

"Oh?"

"How am I supposed to get them to you?"

Rina laughed with renewed relief. "I'll let Rita sort that part out."

Callie walked into the kitchen rubbing her hands together in eager anticipation. "Are there any muffins leftover from breakfast? I'm starving."

Tiny stopped chopping the pile of carrots on his cutting board and stared at Callie who looked like a completely different person than she had a few short hours earlier. "Feeling better, I see?"

"Much."

"Want to talk about it?"

"Nope. Maybe later."

"Zucchini."

"What?"

"Zucchini muffins. I saved a couple for you."

Callie smiled from ear to ear, walked over to Tiny, and gave him a hug. "Thank you."

Taken aback, Tiny laughed. "They're just muffins."

"It's more than that. You're a great friend, you know that?" A better friend than I've been, Callie thought to herself. Shaking off the guilt she felt, she promised herself she'd do better to be the kind of friend Tiny deserved.

Tiny squinted his eyes at Callie as if wondering at the mysteries of womanhood, and, deciding he'd never be able to understand it. Instead, he simply shrugged his shoulders and seemed happy that she was herself again. "Go on. Get your muffins, and I'll make you a cup of coffee."

"Lynette! You're back!" Callie walked around to the back of the desk and gave a startled Lynette a hug.

"What's gotten into you? Of course I'm back. I said I'd be back today."

"I'm just so happy to see you."

"Have you lost your mind?"

"What? No. Can't a girl be happy to see her friend?"

"If you don't cut it out, I'm going to walk out that front door and not come back."

Callie laughed, knowing full well that Lynette was teasing her. And knowing full well that her relief at finding the earrings was making her giddy.

"There's been a lot going on the past couple of days, and I'm just happy to see you."

Lynette squinted her eyes at Callie much as Tiny had done the day before. "Spill."

"Maybe later," Callie replied.

Not as easily dismissed as Tiny, Lynette pushed. "In the living room. Now."

Without waiting for an answer, Lynette walked into the living room and sat down on one of the sofas. "Sit," she commanded and pointed at the chair next to her.

Callie did as she was told, knowing that resistance was pointless. Lynette would get the story out of her one way or another.

"It's really not that big a deal."

Lynette crossed her arms and stared at Callie.

"I'm not even sure what to tell you."

Lynette sat back and got comfortable.

"The Westons called me on Sunday night. Late." Callie could tell from Lynette's expression that she had her full attention. With a rush of words, she told Lynette all the details of the phone call and all the thoughts that had raced through her mind after she had hung up.

"It was just awful, Lynette. I literally couldn't stop myself from trying to figure out who could have taken those earrings."

"Of course you couldn't. I think it was a perfectly natural reaction to a very stressful situation."

"You do?"

"Yes. I'm curious, did you think it was me?"

Callie wasn't sure what to say. She didn't want to lie to Lynette, but the thought of telling one of her closest friends that she had momentarily suspected her of theft was mortifying.

"You did!" Lynette quickly deduced from Callie's silence. She burst out laughing and asked, "What made you rule me out as a suspect?"

Without meaning to, Callie's eyes drifted towards the enormous diamond on Lynette's finger, which only made Lynette laugh harder.

"You are something, you know that?"

"I'm sorry, I really am. But I promise it was just a fleeting thought."

"What about Tiny? Did you suspect him?"

Callie nodded guiltily.

"Did you tell him?"

Callie shook her head.

"It's like that board game. What's it called? The one where you accuse someone of something? It was the cook in the kitchen with his spatula!" This thought made Lynette laugh even harder. "I'm just sorry I missed out on all the fun! What was the big deal about these earrings anyway? What'd they look like?"

"Spectacular diamond and emerald teardrops."

No sooner had the words left Callie's mouth than the laughter immediately died from Lynette's.

"Like diamond studs with an enormous emerald dangling from each?" Lynette whispered.

"Yes. Why?"

"I've seen them before. But not on Rina."

—ele—

"Thanks for coming in on your day off," Callie said flatly.

"I hope you'll remember this when it comes time to give me a raise."

Callie stared at the woman in front of her with barely disguised disgust. "Lynette and I wanted to talk to you for a minute. She's waiting in the living room."

"About what?"

Without answering, Callie led Evie into the living room where Lynette was standing and waiting.

"What's going on?"

"Callie tells me that you found a pair of earrings belonging to one of our guests."

"Yeah, in the garbage can. She was standing right there when I found them," Evie replied defensively.

"Do you remember when we ran into each other in the bathroom at that new Italian restaurant down by the lake?"

Evie seemed to slowly freeze before their eyes. Her face became almost entirely expressionless.

"Because I do," Lynette continued. "I remember you paid me a false compliment about my dress, and I paid you a real compliment about your beautiful earrings. And when you walked away, I remember thinking to myself that your costume jewelry looked good enough to be the real deal. And now, I realize, that that was because they *were* the real deal."

Evie listened quietly as Lynette spoke, her eyes utterly emotionless and her countenance unchanging. When Lynette finished, it was Evie's voice that belied her true feelings. "You can't prove anything," she seethed defiantly.

At that moment, Callie and Lynette knew for certain that they had a thief in their midst. Evie's turn of phrase was, without a doubt, an admission of her guilt. An admission that she had gone through a guest's private belongings, stolen valuable jewelry, and then brazenly worn it in plain sight. Callie shuddered to wonder what else she had stolen from previous guests. She was shocked that no one had called her to complain about missing items, and simultaneously dreading the day that someone would.

Lynette, who had been right about Evie all along, was about to speak when Callie put a restraining hand on her shoulder.

"I got this Lynette." Callie turned to look Evie right in the eye and spoke in a strong, confident tone. "From the moment I first met you, little red flags started going off in my mind. When you wouldn't let me talk to your previous employers, I wondered about you. But I gave you a chance. When I found you sleeping on the job, I overlooked it and gave you a chance. When I found you flirting inappropriately with our guests, I justified your actions and gave you a chance. But you never deserved those chances. I may not have listened to my instincts then, but I'd be a fool to ignore the truth in front of me now. You are rotten to the core, Evie. And you. Are. Fired." Callie punctuated each of her final words with a jab of her index finger towards Evie's face.

Evie turned red, and she looked from Lynette to Callie as if trying to find a way out. As if trying to find a way to convince them to let her keep her job. But she knew she had crossed the line.

"I should never have brought those earrings back. You fools would never have been the wiser."

"Not true." Now it was Lynette's turn to speak. "Because your type of rot eventually starts to stink. And people can smell it from a mile away." Lynette paused and pointed her finger at the door for effect. "Out. Now. Do not ever set foot in this house again."

"You owe me money! I worked over the weekend!"

Appalled by the gall of her demand, Lynette took one menacing step towards Evie before the girl tucked tail and ran out of the living room.

—⁂—

"What a day," Tiny said as he removed his apron. "Despite the drama from earlier and being short staffed, that was one of the best dinner services we've ever had. You really stepped up your game today, Callie. Being a server is no easy task."

Callie nodded her agreement. "We have got to find some more help."

"Correction," Lynette added. "We have got to find some more *good* help. And if our little red flags go up with anyone, this time we heed them."

"Agreed."

Lynette pointed her finger at Callie. "I'm going to hold you to that."

"No doubt," Callie muttered under her breath.

"You know what's really been bothering me all day?"

"I'm too tired to guess."

"I can't figure out *when* Evie took those earrings in the first place. She wasn't even supposed to be working on the days the Westons were here!" Lynette said ruefully, shaking her head.

"I don't think we'll ever know the answer to that question."

"I still can't believe she stole those earrings and then had the nerve to wear them around town." Tiny shook his head and grabbed his car keys out of the drawer.

"And then had the nerve to bring them back to the house and pretend to 'find' them," Callie chimed in.

"Well, believe it. Anyway, I'm sick of talking about Evie." Lynette spat Evie's name out as if it had left a bad taste in her mouth. "And I'm exhausted. I'll see you tomorrow."

"Good night. Oh, and Lynette, one more thing."

"Yes?" Lynette asked turning towards Callie.

"Thank you."

Lynette smiled and gave her friend's hand a quick squeeze. "You're welcome. We're a team, right?"

"You two might be a team. I'm just the 'cook in the kitchen with his spatula.'" Tiny laughed as he walked out of the kitchen.

Insatiable

Tiny rubbed the back of his neck as he drove home after the long day. He still couldn't get over everything that had taken place. He had grown up in Seneca Springs, and as far as he could remember, nothing like this had ever happened. But, then again, he reminded himself, no one as famous as the Westons had ever stayed in Seneca Springs.

His sleepy small town had been gradually changing and growing ever since Callie had opened The Summer Breeze. And Tiny was smart enough to know that as a town got bigger and wealthier, it often attracted an unsavory element. The hardest part for him to get his head around was that Evie had essentially gotten away with stealing. When Lynette and Callie had first told him about what had happened, he had been shocked and demanded that they call the police to have Evie arrested. It was only after their patient reasoning that he realized there really was no proof that Evie had stolen the earrings. Even if Lynette testified that she had seen Evie wearing them, Evie could always say that she had bought fake, look-alikes.

As he turned onto Main Street, Tiny was lost in his thoughts and driving along the familiar street on autopilot until he saw a faint light shining through Grace's shop window.

"What are you doing here at this hour?" he wondered aloud. Not seeing Grace's car parked on the street, he decided to drive around to the alley behind the bakery. As he turned the corner, he was surprised when his headlights didn't illuminate her car parked there either. But a thin sliver of light was shining through the door, which appeared to be propped open by a rock.

Tiny pulled up and parked next to the open door and got out of his car. He was even more surprised when he heard the faint sound of someone singing from inside. As he approached the door and looked inside, he could see a small but beautifully decorated cake on the counter and a set of hands holding a pastry bag. Not wanting to startle Grace, Tiny cleared his throat loudly before opening the door while saying, "What are you doing here so late, sweetheart?"

And then he screamed.

The woman screamed in turn, dropping the pastry bag she had been holding and brandishing an electric hand mixer instead. "Stay away from me! I know how to hurt you with this thing, and don't think I won't!"

Tiny stared at the woman who stared back at him. Almost simultaneously, they both recognized each other.

"I know who you are!" Tiny exclaimed. "You're the woman with the tattoos and the great palette. Gracie's told me all about you! What are you doing here? Where's Grace?" Tiny asked, looking around as if Grace might be hiding somewhere.

Recognizing the giant as Grace's fiancé, Alexis slowly lowered the electric hand mixer and placed it on the counter. She smiled sheepishly as she tried to buy herself some time to come up with a reasonable explanation for why she was in the kitchen of a bakery, which she didn't own or work at, this late at night.

Alexis decided that honesty would be her best policy. She clasped her palms together and beseeched, "Look, please don't call the cops. I can explain."

Tiny wondered again at what kind of element was making its way into Seneca Springs. But he doubted anyone else would be alarmed by a woman baking a cake. He had no intention of calling the police, but he certainly wanted an explanation. "I'm listening."

"Tomorrow is my son Zayne's birthday. He's turning five. And every year since he was born, I've baked a cake for him. But this year, I...I couldn't afford the ingredients for it." Alexis looked around the kitchen as if realizing for the first time what she was doing.

"I'm so sorry. I don't know what I was thinking. I'm so ashamed." And then Alexis burst into tears. Sitting down on the floor and covering her eyes with her hands, she quietly wept until she heard the beep of Tiny's phone as he made a call.

She looked up at him and wiped the tears from her eyes, readying herself for the consequences of her actions. "I don't blame you for calling the cops. If I found some crazy woman in my kitchen, I'd do the same thing. Oh man...how am I going to explain this to my family?"

Tiny had kept a steady eye on Alexis and listened to what she said as he waited for the phone to be answered.

"Gracie? It's me. Can you come down to the bakery?" Tiny paused as Grace responded and then added, "It's important, sweetheart. I'll explain when you get here." He hung up the phone and stepped into the kitchen. Grabbing a glass from one of the cabinets, he filled it with water, sat down on the floor next to Alexis and handed it to her without saying a word.

She whispered gratefully, "Thank you."

By the time Grace arrived, Alexis had calmed down considerably. Tiny had given his assurance that neither he nor Grace were going to call the police. They were still sitting on the floor when Grace, wearing pajamas with colorful little cup-cake designs, walked through the back door looking noticeably frazzled.

"Dominick! What on earth is going...Alexis?"

Alexis looked up at Grace and waved her hand once. "Hi Grace. I'm sorry to have made you get out of bed so late at night. I know bakers have to be up early."

Grace looked quickly from Alexis to Dominick who was sporting a ridiculous grin on his face. And then she noticed the cake sitting on the counter. It was beautifully decorated with bright colors and exquisite fondant work.

"Who made that cake?"

Again, Alexis raised her hand and waved it once. "Guilty."

Grace looked at Alexis, back at the cake, and then back at Alexis, at first unbelievingly. And then, slowly, realization dawned that she wasn't all that surprised. There had always been something about Alexis that drew Grace to her and now, at last, she knew what *it* was. Sitting down on the floor across from Alexis and Dominick, Grace crossed her legs. "Tell me everything."

"First, I want you to know that I'll pay you back for every-thing I used today. I will work for free for you, doing whatever you need, until I've paid you back or I'll find a way to work more hours at my other jobs."

"Let's not worry about that right now," Grace replied gently, not wanting to start off on the wrong foot by hurting Alexis' pride. "Where did you learn to bake like that?"

"Two years at culinary school. Summer jobs doing scut work at some amazing restaurants and then finally making my way up the ladder at one. Hours spent pouring over cookbooks I'd check out from the library. And tasting, tasting, tasting."

"You do have an amazing palette."

Alexis nodded with pride. "That was something my instructors and co-workers always complimented me on. I was going places, you know? And my parents, who had worked so hard to give me every chance to succeed, were so proud of me." At the mention of her parents, Alexis' voice shook, and she looked like she might cry again.

Grace and Dominick waited patiently as Alexis rubbed her eyes and took another sip of water to calm herself.

"They went without so many things and had saved up enough money to help me pay for school. And then I went and blew it all. On what? A guy." Alexis shook her head in frustration and looked from Dominick to Grace. She laughed ruefully.

"Can you believe that? I had my whole future ahead of me, a promising future! And I threw it all away on a man."

"It wouldn't be the first time, Alexis. Let me guess, he was one of the chefs you worked for?"

Alexis nodded her head. "You know the type. Almost a decade older than me, at the top of his game. And so conceited. He was after me from the moment I started working at his restaurant. I resisted him for almost two months, but he was a charmer. And very persistent. I wanted so badly to impress him, to make him happy. I thought I was falling in love with him, even though he was such a terror in the kitchen. Always screaming and cursing and throwing food at people. But he was a master of flavor and demanded perfection. Especially when it came to the five French mother sauces."

Dominick noticed the quizzical expression on Grace's face and placed a hand on Alexis' shoulder, signaling for her to pause, so that he could clarify. "The five French mother sauces are Béchamel, Velouté, Espagnole, Hollandaise, and Tomate."

"That's right," Alexis nodded. "He expected every chef in his kitchen to be able to make each sauce to perfection. One night, desperate to perfect my technique, I stayed in the kitchen to practice after almost everyone had gone home. And of course, he found me there. I sometimes wonder whether I stayed to become a better chef or because I wanted him to find me." Alexis sighed heavily. "One one-night stand was all it took for him to lose interest in me. The next day, it seemed everything I did was 'trash' or 'inedible.' By the end of the week, the restaurant manager 'suggested' that it was time for me to move on. I went home to lick my wounds and get ready for my final year at culinary school. But by that time, I realized I was pregnant. I just couldn't face everyone's disapproval, so I never went back."

"So, he doesn't know?"

Alexis shook her head. "I read somewhere that he had become chef de cuisine at some Michelin starred restaurant in Paris."

"I can think of a few words to describe a man like that," Dominick said to try to ease the tension.

"Oh, trust me, I've said just about all of them."

"You moved back in with your parents and had Zayne," Grace prompted.

"I did. And he's the best thing that's ever happened to me. For the first few years after Zayne was born, my parents kept working to make ends meet so that I could stay home with my baby. But they were getting older, and it was getting so much harder for them. And then they'd get home and there would still be housework that needed to get done. I'd try to do whatever I could to help, but Zayne was a handful and constantly needed my attention. By the time he was ready for preschool, we had decided that I would go back to work so that my parents could finally retire. Money was incredibly tight, and it seemed like Zayne always needed things. New clothes, new shoes, new toys to satisfy his insatiable curiosity."

Alexis took another sip of water and continued. "We always knew he was a smart little guy, but then the school called to tell us that he was off the charts on some assessments they had conducted. Top one percentile or something like that. They highly recommended that we enroll him in a private school for gifted students. And, well..."

"Private schools cost money," Grace finished Alexis' sentence for her.

"A lot of money. But this was my baby's chance to finally get the intellectual stimulation that he always seemed to crave, and I was going to do whatever it took."

"Let me guess, you're working multiple jobs."

Alexis nodded and held up two fingers. "Restaurant jobs don't pay much when you're not a culinary school graduate. And I couldn't bear to work in some dump. So, I started bartending at events and cleaning houses during the day. Right now, I have a steady gig cleaning some of the sorority houses on campus and I try to pick up as many events as I can."

"Which means you don't have much time to spend with your son."

"Or time to cook," Dominick added.

"It's just all such a mess. Look at me. Sitting on the floor of a kitchen that I broke into so that I could steal ingredients to make a cake. To see if I still *knew how* to bake a cake."

"Speaking of which, how did you get in here?" Grace looked around the room as if searching for a broken window or some other evidence of breaking and entering.

"I hid in the bathroom until you went home for the night."

"Clever," Grace said amused by the thought of someone hiding in a bathroom so that they could bake a cake.

"I thought so."

"Well, I don't know about you ladies, but I've had a long day filled with crime drama." Tiny stood up and held his hands out to help both Grace and Alexis up.

"What now?" Alexis asked.

"We can figure that out later. For now, let's all just go home and get a good night's sleep."

Alexis nodded in appreciation.

"Let's get this cake boxed up first," Grace added with a smile. "I think I have some ribbon around here, too."

Sous Chef

There was rarely a time when the aroma of something delicious wasn't wafting out of the kitchen at The Summer Breeze. But as Callie walked up the back stairs after having spent the morning running long overdue errands, she thought the aromas smelled especially enticing.

Dropping her purse and keys off in her room, she quickly made her way to the kitchen eagerly anticipating whatever Tiny had been cooking up. As she made her way down the hall, she thought she heard two voices. Hoping Grace had stopped by with some new cupcake or cannoli flavors to taste, Callie quickened her step. She turned into the sunny room and stopped dead in her tracks.

A woman she had never expected to see in her kitchen was moving confidently about as if she had done it a hundred times. As if she belonged there.

"Alexis?"

Alexis stopped what she was doing and stared at Callie. "You know my name?"

"Grace has told me a lot about you. What are you doing here?"

"We'll get to that later. Sit," Tiny said. "It's time for lunch."

Confused but curious, Callie did as she was told.

"I'm trying out some new recipes for The Terrace. We have here a mushroom wellington with portobello, shiitake, and oyster mushrooms sauteed with shallots, garlic, thyme and then baked inside a handmade puff pastry."

Callie listened to Tiny describe the first dish he placed in front of her with barely concealed amusement, wondering why he was speaking as if he was the host of a televised cooking show. She also thought she noticed a slight British accent.

"Here we have for you a delicate butternut squash ravioli in a white wine cream sauce, topped with parmesan."

"It looks and smells delicious!"

"Shhh, I'm not done yet. And here," Tiny pointed to a bright blue dutch oven that was sitting on the table, "We have for you a garden-to-table summer ratatouille." He lifted the lid with a flourish and seemed to be awaiting applause.

Callie indulged him if only to hurry him along so that she could eat. Her stomach was growling mightily, and her mouth was watering.

Satisfied with her reaction, Tiny rewarded her by finally serving the food into three plates. He and Alexis took their seats at the table and all three of the self-professed gluttons dove in and savored the food in silence for several minutes.

Callie helped herself to more ratatouille, and managed to ask between mouthfuls, "Are these ingredients from our garden?"

Tiny wiped his mouth before confirming. "As many as we could get. That's why it tastes so good."

"It's delicious. It's all delicious. We've never added three new menu items at once. Your fans are going to go wild."

The meal she had just eaten had been truly exceptional. The pastry crust on the wellington had been flaky and crisp while the mushroom filling was oozing with umami and earthiness. The ravioli was light and fluffy, and the sauce was absolutely divine. Smooth and silky and flavorful. The balanced notes of the ratatouille - sweet, peppery, and tangy - was superb. Callie hoped there would be enough leftovers for her to sop up with a nice crusty piece of bread.

"They may not be my fans."

"Huh?" Callie asked, confused.

"I didn't make these dishes."

"You didn't?"

Tiny shook his head as a grin spread slowly across his face. "She did." He paused and gestured towards Alexis. "Callie, Meet my new sous chef."

Callie shifted her gaze between Alexis and Tiny trying to absorb what she had just been told, wondering how Alexis could have made these spectacular dishes. And then, suddenly, it all made sense. Alexis' affinity for flavors, her palette, and the connection Grace felt with her. Alexis was a chef. There was no doubt about it.

Mistaking Callie's silence for hesitation, Tiny added, "I made the hiring decision on your behalf. And if you don't agree with me, I quit." He threw his napkin on the table to emphasize his point.

Callie rolled her eyes at his theatrics. "Pass me another wellington. And of course, I agree with you."

Alexis' eyes grew wide, "You do?"

"Welcome to The Summer Breeze."

⌇

From the moment Alexis started working at the B&B, it was as if she had always been a part of The Summer Breeze family. Her intense focus while she was cooking was offset by her surprisingly playful behavior when she wasn't. Between her myriad tattoos, jet black hair, and perennially all black clothes, her appearance gave off the impression of a tough, hardened, and unapproachable woman. But she proved to be easygoing and quick to laughter. A proud mom who was always ready to share a photo of Zayne or boast about his many accomplishments to whomever was willing to listen.

"I can't believe we're finally going to meet the little man himself. I'm so glad Alexis is bringing him and her parents in for lunch today."

"I'll be honest with you, Callie. I'm a little nervous. From what I can gather, that kid is smart as a whip. What if he asks me something that I can't answer?"

"Tiny, he's five. I wouldn't worry too much."

"I guess," Tiny replied, unconvinced.

"I was going to tell her that lunch would be on the house, but I didn't want to offend her."

"It's probably better that way. She's very proud of her independence, and I think we should continue to encourage it and support her."

Impressed by his insight, Callie said, "Good point. See? You are very smart."

"I guess," Tiny repeated. "Did Grace tell you that Alexis started working at the bakery a few hours a week? And the first thing she did with her first paycheck from you was to pay Grace back for all the supplies she had used to make Zayne's cake the night we found her in the bakery."

Callie nodded, "She's a class act."

"And an amazing chef. With her classical culinary training and a couple of years of experience, she's going to be a lot better than me. Word will start getting around, and she's going to be in high demand. I wonder where she'll end up."

"Let's cross that bridge when we get to it. For now, I'm just happy eating whatever she's cooking."

"I heard she made eclairs yesterday. With a blackberry pastry cream filling. Grace said they were amazing."

"What? How come no one ever told me?"

"Relax, boss. I brought some for you." Alexis walked into the kitchen carrying a small signature pink box from Grace's bakery and set it on the table. "Three blackberry eclairs. All for you. I would have brought more, but Grace said you'd just eat them all and then be mad at me for giving you so many."

Callie laughed and peeked inside the box. Three eclairs, identical in width, length, and color, and decorated with an understated fondant and topped with fresh blackberries. The fruity scent of the berries escaped from the box and made its way up to Callie's nose. Callie shut the box and made a mental note to thank Grace for only allowing Alexis to bring three.

"Thanks, Alexis! I can't wait to try these."

"Mommy?" A little dark-haired boy called out as he came into the kitchen, shyly at first, and then beaming as soon as he saw the person he was looking for. "Mommy!"

"Hey, Zayney!" Alexis lifted the boy easily into her arms and gave him a big kiss on the cheek.

"Is this where you cook?"

"It is! And these are the people I've been telling you about. Tiny and Callie."

"Put me down Mommy," Zayne said, squirming. As soon as Alexis set him down, he walked over to Callie and held out his hand. "Hi Callie. You made my mommy happy."

"Hi Zayne. Trust me, the feeling is mutual." She shook his tiny little hand and then, remembering that the child was only five, Callie went on to clarify. "That means—"

"Oh, I know what it means." Turning towards Tiny, Zayne tilted his head back to look him in the eyes. "You must be Tiny. Which is a very incongruous name for a man as big as you. I'd like to thank you for not calling the cops on my mommy. Can I give you a hug?"

Tiny nodded, feeling self-conscious and unsure of himself.

"Well, you'll have to bend down."

Tiny got down on one knee, and Zayne threw his arms around the man who must have seemed like a giant to him. Callie took one look at Tiny's face and knew that Zayne had instantly made a friend for life.

"When do I get to see you? It's been more than two weeks."

"I know. I'll try to make it up this weekend."

"If I didn't know any better, I'd think you were trying to avoid me."

"In that case, it's a good thing that you *do* know better."

"Maybe I should start dropping Jorgan's name again. Would that help."

"Not in the least," Nick chuckled at Callie's attempt to bait him. "I haven't heard much about him lately. What's he been up to?"

"He came into the restaurant the other day, asked about Evie. I wasn't sure what to tell him, so I just said that she doesn't work here anymore." Callie thought back to her conversation with Jorgan and added, "He almost seemed happy to hear it."

"Maybe he didn't like her either."

"I don't think it was that. Actually, I don't mean 'happy' as in he was happy that he wouldn't have to see her. More like 'happy' that she was no longer employed. I don't know how to explain it."

"I still can't get over how you and Lynette confronted her."

"It's been high drama in Seneca Springs these past two weeks."

"Theft. Breaking and entering. High drama indeed."

"And you missed out on all of it."

"The only thing I miss is you."

"Does that line really ever work in real life?"

"You tell me."

"Say it again."

"The only thing I miss is you." Nick's voice sounded husky and full of emotion.

Callie's heart skipped a beat. "Yup. It works."

Norwegian Eye Candy

"The Norwegian eye candy is back," Lynette announced as she walked into the kitchen.

"That's like the third time he's been here this week."

Lynette shrugged her shoulders. "Who can blame him? His other option is to sit at home eating ramen or going to one of the faculty dining halls on campus."

"I hear the food there is pretty good, and there are other restaurants in town you know. Maybe we should recommend Paolina's."

"I have. He goes there for lunch almost as often as he comes here for dinner."

"Must be nice," Alexis chimed in. "Who is this guy anyway?"

"An exceedingly handsome Norwegian man."

Alexis laughed, "I gathered as much. Is he as good looking as Callie's Nick?" Alexis looked at Callie and wiggled her eyebrows up and down. "Because he is a legitimate hottie as far as I'm concerned."

Callie laughed in response. From the moment Nick had arrived, as promised, for the weekend, he and Alexis had hit it off. Their first meeting had been during the Saturday lunch service. Nick and Callie had walked into the kitchen holding hands, and Alexis had just stared at him with her mouth open for an awkward moment before Tiny had given her arm a gentle shove.

"You're staring."

"Sorry."

"Alexis, I want you to meet Nick. Nick, this is our new sous chef."

Nick extended his hand and said, "I've heard a lot about you."

Alexis shook his hand and shamelessly mouthed the word 'wow' at Callie.

Nick had let out a laugh and from that moment on, the two of them had gotten on as thick as thieves. Alexis because Nick had loved her cooking, and Nick because Alexis had loved his looks.

"Why is the 'Norwegian eye candy' in Seneca Springs?" Alexis asked, bringing Callie back to the moment.

"He's a visiting professor at the university. But from what I can gather, he comes from money," Lynette chimed in.

"Why do you think that?" Callie asked.

"Besides the fact that he spends a small fortune at The Terrace every week?" Lynette retorted, stating the obvious.

"I don't think that tells us anything. Professors make good money. Besides, Jorgan's housing is paid for. Plus, he's single with hardly any living expenses. Eating at The Terrace frequently isn't a reason to think he comes from money."

"That's true, but there's just something about the way he dresses and carries himself. The way he talks about traveling and attending events."

Callie wasn't convinced by Lynette's reasons. She just found Jorgan to be a typically well-cultured, well-traveled European. But since she'd been batting a zero lately as far as being a judge of people, she didn't want to get into another situation with Lynette which would give her friend one more opportunity to say, 'I told you so.'

"Three times in one week is a lot, even for Jorgan," she added lamely, trying to change the subject.

Thankfully, Lynette took the bait. "He says he loves all the new dishes we've been adding to the menu. Asked to talk to Tiny again about his 'creative process'."

Tiny wiped his hands on his apron and turned toward Alexis who appeared to be engrossed in stirring something in a pot.

"Nice try, Alexis, but I know that pot is empty."

Alexis stopped stirring but continued looking into the empty pan.

Callie and Lynette exchanged quizzical expressions and wondered what was going on.

"It's time," Tiny said gently.

Alexis shook her head. "I can't. I'm not ready. I just got back into the kitchen, and I don't want to mess things up again."

"You're not going to mess things up. You need to go out there and take credit for your dishes. People need to know who you are." And then Tiny added the one sentence he knew would help convince Alexis. "A true chef understands that people deserve the chance to meet the person who made their food."

"Low blow."

"I tell it like it is."

Alexis sighed and finally looked up at Tiny. She nodded her head once and took off her apron. Turning towards Callie, she asked, "Do I have any food on my face?"

"No. You look great."

Alexis straightened her shoulders and lifted her chin in determination. "Lead the way, Lynette."

Callie, feeling sweaty after a long early morning hike with Lynette and Grace, stepped into her shower and let the cool water refresh her. It had been too long since she'd exercised, and she recommitted herself to getting at least a couple of workouts in each week.

If someone as busy as Nick could make exercising a priority, then so could she. The thought of Nick working out unavoidably led to the thought of his body, and Callie blushed, thankful she was in a cold shower. She imagined him going to the gym and, while she was confident in his feelings for her, she was certain that plenty of women checked him out. She wondered how many boldly approached him in an effort to start a conversation that could lead to something more. Feeling the pinch of jealousy despite her confidence, Callie put her head under the shower and let the cool water distract her.

She pumped shampoo into her hand and worked it into a nice lather in her hair. While Alexis had been downright transparent in her appreciation of Nick's physique, she had made it a point to be abundantly clear that she was not interested in starting anything with anyone of the opposite sex. Most especially not her new boss' boyfriend. But Alexis' reaction to Jorgan, and, for that matter, Jorgan's reaction to Alexis, had been something altogether puzzling to Callie.

Callie had accompanied Lynette and Alexis to Jorgan's table the night before to hear his reaction to finding out that Tiny was not the only cook in The Summer Breeze kitchen. She had expected Jorgan to be effuse in his praise, and Alexis to be reserved in her acceptance. But Callie couldn't have been more mistaken.

Lynette had stopped at Jorgan's table and announced that she had a surprise for him. Jorgan had stood up as was his habit when a woman came to his table, and Lynette had stepped aside to reveal Alexis, who had been standing behind her.

"Jorgan, please meet Alexis, Tiny's new sous chef who has made several of the new dishes we've been serving at The Terrace."

The heavy lidded, flirtatious expression that Jorgan usually sported when speaking to just about anyone seemed to falter as soon as he saw Alexis. She stood before him, unsure of herself, and dressed in her quintessential all-black skintight jeans and black tank top. Her clothing accentuated her lean, lithe body and tattoos accentuated her well-toned arms. Alexis had tied her jet-black hair into a high ponytail, revealing the shaved portion underneath and had lined her eyes with black eyeliner. She looked every bit the polar opposite of Jorgan, with his light-colored clothes, curly light brown hair and blue eyes.

He stared at her awkwardly for a few moments before blurting out, "Hello Jorgan, I'm Alexis. Pleasure to meet you."

Alexis, who had been nervous at first, had taken one look at Jorgan in his cropped and extremely fitted pants, no socks, and tight white t-shirt, and decided that, despite the fact that he most definitely qualified as eye candy, he was not worth her time. Her nervous expression had fallen away and been replaced by a disdainful one. She looked him up and down once with ill-concealed distaste.

"Hello. *I'm* Alexis."

"Yes, yes, of course you are. Forgive me. It's just that your cooking is absolutely divine." And then, as if trying to regain his footing, he ran his fingers through his hair and added, "And so are you."

The compliment fell flat. Alexis, looking like she had just eaten something that had gone bad, turned on her heels and started walking back to the kitchen, and mumbled an unceremonious "Thanks."

Callie wondered what had gotten into both of them. Why had Jorgan, usually so well composed, stumbled and made such an embarrassment of himself? And why had Alexis been so dismissive of him? The whole interaction between them had been awkward and fraught with tension.

In a way, it reminded Callie of how she had acted when she had first met Nick. He had tried to flirt with her as he did with most other women, and she had shunned him every chance she had.

And then a strange thought crossed her mind. Maybe Jorgan, who flirted shamelessly with everyone without attaching any meaning to it, was actually smitten by Alexis.

—ele—

Callie lifted the spoon to her mouth in anticipation of the explosion of flavor which her sense of smell told her to expect. The aroma from the large bowl of late summer tomato risotto made with fresh herbs, white wine and parmesan was indescribable. She opened her mouth, closed her eyes, and took her first taste.

"Mmmmm..." Callie opened her eyes slowly and took another spoonful without saying a word. "Mmmmm...mmmm mm. Oh, Alexis, this is...I don't even know what this is. Why have I never had tomato risotto before?"

"Do you like it?"

"Do I like it? Do you have to ask?" Callie took another spoonful and smiled at Alexis. "It is absolutely delicious. Can we add it to the menu for tonight?"

Alexis nodded with obvious pride, and Tiny, who had been quietly watching the tasting, clapped his hands together once. "Consider it done. If Jorgan comes in tonight, he is going to be blown away. Don't be surprised if he asks to compliment you in-person. Again."

Alexis rolled her eyes. It had been two days in a row since the first time she had met Jorgan. He had come in to eat on both days and asked to pay his compliments to the chef. Each time, he had been more awkward than the time before, and each time, Alexis had come away feeling annoyed.

"Jorgan's not a bad guy, Alexis. I don't get why you don't like him. He's obviously got a thing for you."

"Thanks, but no thanks. I wouldn't go near him with a ten-foot pole."

"Oh, I would. I'd go near him with a much, much shorter pole." Lynette opined unasked.

Alexis laughed. "I'd stop you. Trust me, I know the type. Zayne's father was the type. Gorgeous, sexy, confident, well off. The kind of guy that knows he can walk all over anyone. And does."

"You think Jorgan is 'confident' around you? That man cannot form a simple sentence the moment he sees you. He's always stumbling and bumbling. He looks more like a man who would *fall* over rather than *walk* over you."

"Whatever. If he asks to see me, just let me know. It's kind of amusing to hear him 'stumble and bumble'."

Tiny shook his head and mumbled, "That poor, poor fool."

"Mommy, can we stop by Grace's?" Zayne looked up at his mother with his big brown eyes, and Alexis knew her answer would be yes, even though she still had errands to run. It still gave her such a thrill to be able to walk around downtown Seneca Springs with her boy and know that she could say 'yes' to him on the rare occasion that he asked her for something.

"If you promise me you'll only eat one cupcake."

"Not a mini?"

"Not a mini. You can have a regular sized cupcake."

"Deal." Zayne slipped his small hand into his mother's waiting hand, and Alexis' heart filled with love.

She recalled the first time she had stood in line at Grace's, desperate to step inside a real bakery to experience all the exquisite sights, sounds, and smells. Things she hadn't even realized she missed so very much. The anticipation of what flavor combinations the bakery had concocted was soured by the guilt she felt for wanting to spend some of her hard-earned money on something so extravagant as a treat for herself. Money she should have set aside for Zayne.

In the end, though, it had all been worth it. Going into the bakery that day had reset the course of her life in ways she could never have imagined. She now had two steady jobs that paid well, and she was doing what she loved most. And as if that wasn't enough, all her schooling and experience had come flooding back to her, and thanks to her palette, she had been able to step back into the kitchen almost as if she had never left it.

Alexis smiled as she opened the door to Grace's bakery and walked in with Zayne. Thankfully, it was one of the rare occasions when there wasn't a line at the bakery, and they were enthusiastically greeted by Grace.

"Hey, you two! Just the people I was hoping to see!"

"Really?" Zayne asked, his eyes growing wide.

"Really! I have something extra special just for you!"

"Does it have chocolate in it?"

"You'd better believe it does!"

Zayne clapped his hands with excitement.

"But this isn't just a regular chocolate cupcake."

"It's not?"

"It's a Boston cream pie cupcake!"

"Grace, you didn't!"

"I sure did. When you told me that Zayne loved Boston cream pie donuts, I knew I had to make a cupcake for him with those same flavors. Go on and sit down. I'll bring them out to you. Coffee?"

"Yes, please."

Alexis and Zayne sat at two of the empty seats facing the large window overlooking Main Street, both eagerly awaiting their first bite of the cupcakes.

"Do you want a glass of milk with—" before Alexis could finish her sentence, Zayne waved at someone on the street.

"Mommy, I think that man knows you. He was waving at you, but you didn't see him, so I reciprocated for you."

Alexis was about to comment on Zayne's use of the word "reciprocated" when it registered with her that the person waving at her son was none other than Lynette's Norwegian eye candy. As soon as Jorgan recognized Alexis, he raised his hand in a tentative wave, and looked back at the little boy sitting next to her with a surprised expression, wondering who he was.

Alexis raised her hand in a rather cold response, hoping that it would be enough of a signal to Jorgan to keep on walking. But unfortunately, she had no such luck.

Jorgan, who had been drawn to Alexis from the moment they had met, found his legs walking him towards the front door of the bakery.

Realizing that she wouldn't be able to get rid of him quite so easily, Alexis tried to disguise her mild irritation. "Fudge," she said indelicately.

"A glass of milk with fudge?" Zayne asked, confused as he scanned the display. "I don't see any fudge."

"Alexis! Hi. So good to see you. Who's this?"

Most men who were interested in Alexis either ran in the other direction when they saw her with the boy or ignored the child completely. Jorgan's direct question threw her off balance.

"This is Zayne, my son." She watched Jorgan's face closely to gauge his reaction to the news and was surprised by his genuine warm smile.

"Great to meet you Zayne! Let me guess, you're what? Six? Seven?"

"I'm five, but I'm above average height for my age, ninety eighth percentile actually. Which is probably why you thought I was older."

"I have a nephew who is five! But he doesn't know what a percentile is! Do you?"

"Yes, it's when you're at the top end of a range of numbers. On average, two percent of boys my age are taller than me, but the rest are shorter. Right, mom?"

Alexis nodded, beaming with pride and wondering how Jorgan would react to Zayne's obvious intelligence. Many people often started talking to him in a sing-song-y baby voice in a futile effort to make him act his age. To her surprise, Jorgan did not.

"You know, I think you have something in common with your mom because I think she's in the ninety eighth percentile when it comes to cooking."

Now it was Zayne's turn to beam with pride. "She's the best cook I know." Switching to a conspiratorial whisper, he added, "I think she's better than Mr. Dom and Grace. But don't tell them I said that."

"I think you might be right."

"What's your name? And what's that accent I hear? Scandinavian?"

"Norwegian, actually. I'm Jorgan."

"Nice to meet you, Jorgan. Would you like to join us for a cupcake? Please mom? Can he?"

For the second time that day, Alexis knew she wouldn't be able to say no to Zayne.

Kvæfjordkake

C allie walked into the kitchen blushing and feeling flustered. Dr. Joshi was back from vacation, and she had made the mistake of volunteering to take him his Calabrian red chili flakes. Then she had made the even bigger mistake of asking him about his vacation. For the next twenty minutes, he had regaled her with stories of going on safari in Tanzania and the spectacular sunsets over the Serengeti. Callie had stood in rapt attention as his words whisked her away to another place and made her feel as though she was riding in the open-air Jeep right beside him.

"You do realize you stood there talking to Dr. Joshi for almost half an hour, don't you?"

"I was powerless."

"That almost ties the amount of time Alexis has spent talking to Jorgan every time he comes in. Which I swear is every day."

Alexis, who was standing at the stove, looked over her shoulder at Lynette. "Not true." It was hard to tell if the rose in her cheeks was caused by the heat from cooking or the heat of embarrassment.

"Oh, please. When you took that dessert out to him yesterday, you didn't come back in until the last customer had left."

"He was asking me about Zayne," Alexis said in defense.

"If you say so."

"Has he asked you out yet?" Callie ventured.

"No! And I already told you, I know the type, and I'm not interested."

"Makes sense. Of course you're not interested in a man who is obviously crazy about you *and* your son."

"What doesn't make sense," Alexis said as she glared at Lynette, "is *why* he's crazy about me. Do I look like an easy target for a one-night stand? Is there a bullseye on my forehead?" Alexis suddenly choked back a sob as she put her worst insecurity into words.

"No!" Lynette, suddenly feeling protective of Alexis, exclaimed. "He is crazy about you because he loves your cooking! Because he thinks you are a wonderful mother to Zayne. Because your son is a whip smart little boy who makes interesting conversation." Lynette paused for effect and then said the statement that had been buzzing around in her mind for the past couple of days. "Because, I believe you are the yin to his yang."

Callie took a sideways glance at Tiny and mouthed, "Yin to his yang?" Tiny shrugged his shoulders and went back to listening to Lynette's acclamation.

"Besides, that is not you talking! That is Zayne's father talking. Are you going to let him control your life all these years later? Are you going to give him that power over you?"

Alexis let out a faltering breath, wanting more than anything to buy into Lynette's reasoning, and slowly, almost imperceptibly, shook her head.

But it was enough for Lynette. "Good! Now go out there and take his panna cotta with you!"

As Alexis did as she was told, Lynette turned towards Callie and raised a finger in warning. "Not one word about yin and yang, you got me?"

"I wouldn't dream of it."

The noise from the customers in the bakery was only partially blocked by the closed door to the kitchen. But it didn't bother Alexis, who was laser focused on the contents of the stand mixer in front of her. The egg whites and the sugar she was whisking had finally formed into the glossy, stiff peaks she was aiming for. Gently, she poured the meringue over the batter she had made earlier, being sure to form little peaks throughout for an appealing design. She sprinkled thinly sliced almonds across the meringue and placed the pan to bake in the pre-heated oven.

She may not be able to pronounce the name of the cake she was making, which included a lot of K's and vowels, but she was certainly going to do her utmost to make it as perfect as she could. Turning her attention to the vanilla custard filling, Alexis whisked sugar and egg yolks in a bowl and slowly added cornstarch until the mixture turned a pale yellow color. To this, she slowly whisked in hot milk seasoned with vanilla beans and heated the mixture until it thickened.

When the timer dinged to signal that the cake was done, she took it out of the oven and set it on the counter to cool along with the custard. Then she went into the bakery to make sure that all of the customers had gone so that she could start getting everything else ready.

"Did it turn out?" Grace asked as she saw Alexis.

"Time will tell. It needs to cool before I can do the final assembly."

"Don't worry, you still have plenty of time. No one will be here for a while."

"I know. It's just that I want it to be perfect, you know? I feel so bad for him. I can't imagine being so far away from family on your birthday."

Grace smiled knowingly but refrained from commenting.

"Anyway, it's not like I'm throwing him a party or anything."

At that comment from Alexis, Grace's self-control faltered. "No, it's definitely not like you're throwing him a party. After all, the only things you've done are invited a few people, baked a cake, and bought some balloons and decorations. That's not like a party at all."

Alexis stopped spreading colorful "happy birthday" confetti on one of the tables and looked up at Grace with a mildly shocked expression on her face. "I am throwing him a party, aren't I?"

"Most definitely."

In a feeble attempt to offer up an explanation, Alexis added, "He's always so patient with Zayne. Always making time to answer his questions and being genuinely interested in everything he has to say."

"Not to mention how he is with you."

"I...but...I don't know." Alexis faltered and could think of nothing more to say.

"My advice?" Grace asked gently. "Accept what's happening and lean into it. You might be surprised."

"Your mom made my birthday very special, you know that Zayne? Kvæfjordkake is my absolute favorite and it's not easy to make."

"It's not easy to pronounce, either," Alexis joked.

"She does the same thing for me every year. And for my nana and pop-pop. She bakes us our favorite cake. That's how she shows us her love."

Alexis looked down at Zayne and laughed uncomfortably. "Kids say the darndest things."

"Do they?" Jorgan asked, his voice suddenly hoarse with emotion.

Alexis was almost afraid to look back at him. But knowing that deep down she couldn't and didn't want to avoid it, she slowly turned to face him.

Without a word, he tucked a piece of stray hair behind her ear and gave her a gentle kiss on her lips, lingering almost to the point of no return.

Seeing the closed-eyed, almost blissful expression on his mom's face, Zayne wrapped one arm around her legs and the other around Jorgan's and held them close in a tight embrace.

—ℓℓ—

Callie kicked the bed covers off her feet and stared at the ceiling trying to calm her racing mind. It had been an eventful and busy week, and she wanted nothing more than to clear her head and get a good night's sleep. Between the constant stream of guests at the bed and breakfast and the diners at The Terrace, she was meeting more new people than she could keep straight. Earlier that day, she had mistaken the itineraries of two sets of guests and sent the wine loving pair on a nature tour and the nature lovers on a wine tour. Thankfully, they had all come back four hours later none the worse for wear and chuckling good naturedly at the mix up. The fact that Lynette had pulled some strings to get them upgrades for the correct tours for the following day also helped. As did the afternoon scones which Alexis made just for them.

Callie thanked her lucky stars for the millionth time at her good fortune. Not only because she had opened The Summer Breeze, but also because she knew for certain that the credit for the continued success and growth of her business lay almost entirely at the feet of her employees. As a team they were hard-working and dedicated to serving her clients. As individuals, they were caring people who were loyal to Callie and a whole lot of fun to be around.

Especially her dream team. Without Lynette, Tiny, and now, Alexis, Callie knew the B&B and the restaurant would be nowhere near as successful as they were. These days, it seemed that everyone was working at the top of their game. Alexis' budding relationship with Jorgan seemed to have added fuel to her culinary creativity, and she had started taking more risks with her dishes and plating. Her energy had, in turn, lit a fire under Tiny who proved over and over at every meal service why his reputation as an amazing chef was spreading far and wide.

And then there was Lynette. Lynette, who loved to tease Callie mercilessly but without whom, Callie knew she would be lost.

Callie made it a point to thank her employees as often as she could. She wanted each of them to know how much she appreciated them. She also made sure to pay them well. Most of the profits of the B&B and the restaurant were used to pay salaries. But somehow, these days, that didn't seem like enough. Callie wanted to express her gratitude in a meaningful way, and apart from paying out a monetary bonus, she couldn't think of anything else.

Frustrated, she got out of bed and went to the kitchen to get a glass of water. As she stood at the sink and looked out over the backyard and the waters of Cayuga Lake shimmering under the moonlight, an idea suddenly popped into her mind.

"Yes! It's time for another Evening under the Stars!"

Party of Six

C allie hung up her phone and typed a few more things into her laptop.

"That looks like a to-do list. And that usually means you're up to something."

Jumping, Callie slammed her laptop shut. She hadn't heard Lynette walk into the kitchen, and the last thing she wanted was to ruin the surprise she was planning.

"Yup, definitely up to something."

"Just trying to stay organized."

"Mm-hmmm." Lynette rolled her eyes in disbelief and hoped Callie didn't have any more expansion plans in mind. While the staffing problem seemed to have improved lately with the addition of Alexis and some part-time servers, Lynette knew the two of them couldn't handle much more work.

"What are you looking for?" Callie asked, hoping to change the subject.

"A cup of coffee. Maybe something sweet to go with it. Or maybe salty. I can't decide. Do we have any more of those pickles Tiny made the other day? Those are the perfect balance of everything I'm in the mood for."

"Sounds like that time of the month."

"It does, doesn't it? Which reminds me, I think it should be here next week. Or maybe it was last week. Ugh, I can't seem to remember anything these days."

Callie squinted her eyes and looked closely at Lynette.

And as she heard the words coming out of her own mouth, Lynette looked at Callie. "Impossible," she said. "Do you have any idea how old I am?"

Callie shrugged her shoulders noncommittally, and Lynette laughed nervously. She pulled her phone out of her pocket, opened the calendar, and gasped aloud.

"Holy sh—."

"Lynette!" Callie interrupted, not wanting any of her guests to overhear that kind of language coming from the kitchen.

"I'm three weeks late, Cal! What on earth! How could this happen?"

"Have you been careful?"

Lynette shook her head slowly, "Not always. But I thought we were too old for the runners to reach the finish line!"

Callie tried to suppress her laughter. The most organized woman she knew, who was a master at planning and logistics, had just had the rug pulled out from under her.

"Are you laughing at me?"

Callie shook her head and bit her tongue.

"What should I do?"

"Go home and take a pregnancy test. Then make a doctor's appointment because it's going to be positive."

"What am I going to tell Randy?"

"Who's Randy?"

Lynette looked at Callie as if she had just discovered that there really was such a thing as a stupid question. "My husband! Randolph, Mr. W., Randy!"

"I thought his name was James!"

"It is! James Randolph Whitmore!"

"I didn't know you called him Randy, but I suppose it's apropos in the current situation." Callie burst out laughing at her own cleverness, but immediately got herself under control when she saw the part-furious, part-nauseated expression on Lynette's face. Clearing her throat, she added, "My recommendation would be to tell him that he's going to be a father."

⁓

Callie had known she couldn't afford to leave the B&B for more than one night, but with Nick being so busy with his big project, she knew that a quick trip to New York was the only way for them to have any time together. As she parked her car in one of the few open parking spaces on his street, her heartbeat quickened in anticipation of seeing him again. It had been more than three weeks since his last visit to Seneca Springs, and while they spoke often on the phone, it didn't compare to talking to him face to face. And, Callie would be lying to herself if she didn't admit that absolutely nothing compared to waking up next to him.

Before she even reached the top step of the staircase leading up to his beautiful brownstone, the door flew open, and Nick ran out to greet her. He lifted her off her feet and planted a quick kiss on her lips.

"I am so happy to see you! It's been too long, and I'm so sorry I haven't been able to come up to visit. But guess what? I have some great news!"

Callie smiled at the reception he had given her and followed him up the stairs. "Don't keep me in suspense! What's the news?"

"We're finally back on schedule. Which means that this project will be wrapped up in a couple weeks, and then I'll finally have some time for myself." Nick paused and gazed steadily and deeply into Callie's eyes. *"For us."*

Callie's breath caught in her throat, and she wasn't sure quite how to respond. Fortunately for her, Nick asked her a question which put her back on solid ground.

"Are you hungry?"

"Famished."

"Go out? Or stay in?"

"Definitely stay in."

Nick smiled and planted another kiss on Callie's lips. This time, though, it wasn't quick. It was slow and sensual and everything that Callie had been craving.

———

Callie settled in for the long car drive back to Seneca Springs after what felt like the perfect weekend with Nick. Between talking almost nonstop about work and family and friends, they had packed in as much eating and together time as they could. They had even managed to go out for a quick walk to grab some of the bagels New York was so famous for.

In less than three short weeks, Nick would finally be able to come up and spend an entire week with her. Despite her old insecurities, which still managed to rear their heads every so often when Callie thought about being in a long-term relationship, she was looking forward to having Nick around more than she was ready to admit. He, however, did not hold back in his enthusiasm.

It would be the perfect time for Callie to throw her Evening Under the Stars party to show her appreciation for the role so many people played in her success. She had been busily making lists for many days and had even managed to convince Nick to let her bring her laptop into bed so that she could run some of her ideas by him. It was going to be a no holds barred gala event. Callie had invited a local college band to play and, after a great deal of internal debate, had finally taken her parents' advice to have the event fully catered so that Tiny and Alexis could take a very well-deserved break.

What made the timing even more perfect was that she had picked the week that the entire O'Connor clan would be staying at The Summer Breeze. After they had sold her their family home, she had renovated it into the B&B and they had been her very first guests. The entire family, including Nana and Papa, their children and all their grandchildren had come out for a vacation the year before and had unanimously decided that it was the perfect location to start a tradition of annual family reunions in the house where they had so many fond memories.

Arrangements for the food, music, and beverages were all progressing nicely, and the only thing left for her to do was to finalize the guest list. Her family would, obviously, attend and would arrive the day before the event to help out with whatever was needed. All of her employees and their families would be invited, as would the local business owners and tradespeople who had provided goods and services to her along the way. People like Mr. Blake, the contractor who had worked on the renovation, Alicia, her former employee, and so many more. She'd also remember to invite Mr. Blackhawk who had played such an important role during the early months of The Summer Breeze renovation, both as a supplier of fresh produce and a purveyor of many jokes, both good and bad, which had provided oft-needed comic relief on many mornings.

Callie, not wanting to forget anyone, decided to pull over at one of the ubiquitous fast food rest areas along the highway so that she could add the names of everyone she wanted to invite to her spreadsheet. She found an empty picnic table, opened up her laptop and started typing. By the time she was done, her list had well over one hundred invitees on it. A smile spread across Callie's face. It was heartening to see how many people had helped her along on her journey. She closed her laptop and breathed in the fresh air, feeling well loved and grateful for everything she had. Wanting to savor the moment, she lingered at the picnic table a little longer watching the cars and people coming and going. Life was good, she thought to herself, life was good indeed.

Callie ran her finger down the reservations list for dinner service at The Terrace, scanning the names, some familiar and some new. When she got to one name, she paused and looked up at Lynette.

"Kirsten is coming in for dinner tonight? Party of six?"

Lynette shrugged her shoulders and took a bite of her banana chocolate chip muffin. "If that's what it says," she said with her mouth full. "I didn't take that reservation."

"How are you feeling, by the way?"

"Great. But I'm going to be enormous if everyone keeps plying me with snacks."

"And Mr. W?"

"He's still as giddy as he was the day I told him. He thinks he's some kind of macho man, impregnating his wife at his age."

Callie chuckled. "When are you going to tell everyone else?"

"At the end of my first trimester. Another few weeks."

"Do you think 'Randy' will be able to contain himself until then?"

"Technically, he's already proven that he can't contain himself." Lynette raised her eyebrows up and down shamelessly.

Callie rolled her eyes in response and changed the subject. "I wonder who Kirsten's having dinner with. Are her college friends in town?"

"Quit guessing. Just go ask her. And bring me another muffin and a glass of milk before you go." Seeing the expression on Callie's face, Lynette smiled angelically, patted her stomach, and added, "Please."

Callie sat in the soothing waiting room at the spa waiting for Kirsten. Assuming her friend was in the middle of an appointment and not wanting to disturb her, Callie quietly picked up a book of nature photography and began flipping through the pages. Between the silence and the heady fragrance from the scented candles and products Kirsten used, Callie could feel herself relaxing. Her eyelids began to feel heavy, and she slowly gave in to the urge to close her eyes for just a few minutes.

The sound of a car door closing nearby jolted her awake. Callie wiped what felt like drool off the side of her mouth and looked at her phone. She couldn't believe the time. The few minutes she had meant to close her eyes had turned into a forty-five minute siesta. She wondered, feeling embarrassed, if Kirsten and her client had already come out of the treatment room and snuck past her, not wanting to disturb her peaceful slumber.

Callie stood and listened for any sound of movement, evidence that there were other people inside the spa. Hearing none, she suddenly realized that even the peaceful sounds of the music Kirsten usually played and the tranquil sounds of the tabletop water fountain were absent. And then it dawned on her that she hadn't seen Kirsten's car parked in the driveway when she had walked over to the spa.

"Hello? Anyone here?" Callie's whispered questions sounded like a scream in the otherwise quiet building. Hearing no response, she hurried back to The Summer Breeze kitchen to see what needed to be done to get ready for the dinner rush.

"What'd Kirsten say?" Lynette asked. She was standing at the kitchen table, about to pour herself another glass of milk, when she stopped mid-action.

"Say about what? She wasn't even there." Callie said, feeling suddenly self-conscious.

Lynette squinted her eyes at Callie. "Where have you been for the past hour?"

"In my office. Working."

"Is that right?"

Callie nodded her head.

"So you didn't go over to Kirsten's?"

"I did, but she wasn't there. So I did some work instead."

Lynette laughed disbelievingly. "Sure. By the way, you may want to...ummm...touch up your appearance before people start coming in for dinner."

Without a word, Callie turned and rushed to her bathroom. One look in the mirror and there could be no question why Lynette had laughed at her. Some of the hair on one side of her head was plastered against her cheek while the rest was puffed up and frizzy. And a thin grey line of dried drool was visible from the side of her mouth down to her chin.

Callie sighed and knew she had just given Lynette enough material with which to tease her for the foreseeable future.

―――

Callie walked between the outdoor tables at The Terrace chatting with some of the regulars and welcoming any new guests she saw. She was making her way towards Jorgan's table when she heard a familiar voice behind her.

"Hi Callie."

Callie turned with a smile already on her face, excited to see Kirsten making time for a nice night out at The Terrace. But when she saw the rest of her friend's party, the smile fell from her face, and she glanced quickly at Kirsten for any cues on how to react. What she saw put the happiness back on her face. Kirsten looked as carefree as ever. Wearing one of her signature flowy, floral, ankle length dresses and a variety of beaded jewelry that all seem to come together harmoniously, she radiated peace and joy.

"I brought my family in for dinner."

Callie gave Kirsten a hug and turned her attention to the rest of the group. "Chad, it's been too long since we've seen you!"

"Hospital is keeping me busier than ever. And whenever I'm not working," he added, laughing, "I'm at home packaging up Kirsten's candles to ship out all over the country." Chad turned towards the couple standing behind him, "You remember my parents."

"Of course! It's such a pleasure to see you again! Welcome back to The Summer Breeze."

"Thank you, dear. This place holds so many wonderful memories for us. It really was a lovely wedding."

"And you know Jansen, and my brother JR."

Callie nodded and grinned, feeling particularly pleased to see this group of wonderful people all together. "It's such a pleasure to see you again! I'm only sad you're not staying with us!"

Jansen chuckled and responded, "We suggested it, but Kirsten wouldn't let us. She insisted on all of us staying at their place."

Callie's eyes grew wide. She had been to Kirsten and Chad's house on several occasions, and while it was brimming with charm and character and perfect for a young couple, it certainly wasn't large enough to house six people comfortably. "How's that working out?"

"It's perfect. We're constantly bumping into each other and making a mess of the place, but I wouldn't want it any other way." JR's voice was full of emotion as he reached over and put an arm around his big brother's shoulder.

Chad smiled, the pure joy of finding a brother he didn't know he had clearly reflected in his eyes, and teased in pure big brother fashion, "Dude, don't start crying again...."

JR laughed and turned to Callie, "I'm starving. What's on the menu for tonight?"

"Come on, let me get you seated, and you can take a look at our menu." Callie led the group to a large table set for six that was right next to Jorgan. "I'm not sure if you've heard but we hired a new sous chef. Alexis has added some spectacular new dishes to our repertoire."

At hearing Alexis' name, Jorgan perked up. "I like to think of it as elevated comfort food, very similar to Tiny's cooking, but Alexis puts her own twist on things." Jorgan stood up, "Apologies for intruding on your conversation. But if you haven't eaten here lately, I recommend the tomato and white bean tart and the eggplant rollatini. The house marinara is sublime."

"Sold!" Jansen said good-naturedly, and added, "Jansen Smith. Pleasure to meet you."

Jorgan shook the hand Jansen extended to him. "Jorgan Winther."

Ever the hostess, Callie made introductions all around. After some brief pleasantries, JR reminded everyone that he was starving. Jorgan returned to his seat, and Callie got Kirsten's party settled and took their rather large order. Jansen was treating, and between JR and Chad, they had somehow managed to order almost everything on the menu.

___ele___

"Who's still out there? I don't think I can make another dish tonight." Alexis rubbed the back of her neck and did a few shoulder rolls to release the tension.

"Just a few groups lingering over their coffee and desserts. Why don't you head out for the night? We'll finish up here."

"Are you sure?"

Tiny nodded. He could only imagine how tired Alexis must be. She had spent several hours at the bakery helping Grace before running home to pick up Zayne from school. After spending the afternoon with him, she had rushed back to Seneca Springs for the dinner service.

"Thanks, Tiny. I owe you." Alexis took off her apron and, trying to keep her voice casual, asked, "Is Jorgan still out there?"

Tiny nodded and smiled knowingly.

"I'll just say good night to him before I head out. He insists on walking me to my car."

"As it should be. Good night, Alexis. Great job tonight."

Alexis waved and made her way to Jorgan's table, surprised to see that Kirsten and her family were still there as well. A man she didn't recognize along with Kirsten's husband seemed to be in conversation with Jorgan, and Alexis wondered what they could possibly have to talk about. She managed to pick up the tail end of their conversation before Jorgan noticed her walking towards them.

"...expanding the research and treatment center. We're also looking to purchase or build a place for the families to stay."

"You're doing incredible work," Jorgan said to the man Alexis had never seen before. And then, as usual, he stood up as soon as she approached his table. Clapping his hands together and grinning like a fool, he said, "The maestro herself! Allow me to introduce Alexis, your sous chef extraordinaire."

Alexis blushed and accepted the enthusiastic compliments they heaped on her with humility and grace. "Thank you. I'm so glad you enjoyed your meal."

"It was a pleasure meeting you." And with that, Jorgan took Alexis' hand gently in his and walked her to her car. It was a few minutes before she actually got in and started driving, but she felt a type of contentment she hadn't felt in a long time.

(Another) Evening Under the Stars

The evening weather was starting to get a bit cooler, and Callie worried the event she had been planning for weeks might not be as perfect as she wanted it to be. She wondered for the tenth time whether she should have an enclosed canopy tent set up, but then dismissed the idea again. With a large white tent overhead, the party wouldn't exactly be "under the stars." Reminding herself that she couldn't worry about everything, she finished getting dressed. She gave Nick, who was still fast asleep, a quick peck on the cheek and made her way to the kitchen to help Tiny get breakfast ready for the rambunctious O'Connor family.

Thankfully, the only people who were already awake were Nana, Papa, and their two eldest daughters. Callie was thrilled to find them busily helping Tiny.

"Good morning!"

"It's a fine day," Papa agreed.

"Callie, you're on eggs."

"Two dozen?"

"Yup. Half sunny side up, half scrambled."

"Heard, chef. I'll start the scramble now and the sunny sides to order."

Callie saw Tiny smile as he turned his attention back to assembling a large breakfast galette. The dough had turned out perfectly, and all he had left to do before popping it in the oven was to finish assembling the thinly sliced layers of potato and summer squash, caramelized onions and cheese.

With everyone working together in companionable silence, breakfast was almost ready by the time several sets of footsteps were heard coming down the stairs.

"Here we go! Callie, start the eggs. I'll start making the pancakes. Nana, can you take the galette out of the oven? Just pile everything up on the island and everyone can take what they want."

The silence which had been so companionable just a few moments earlier was slowly shattered by the sound of children laughing, parents admonishing them to eat some fruit with their pancakes, and the clinking of dishware. Callie looked around at the suddenly full kitchen and smiled. This, she thought, is what life must have been like when the O'Connors lived in The Summer Breeze.

Nick, who had woken up soon after Callie left, entered the kitchen and caught the contented expression on Callie's face. This, he thought, was exactly the kind of life he wanted to create with her.

—ele—

Callie reached into her closet and pulled out the dress she had ordered just for her Evening Under the Stars. It was a tad over the top and something she would never have worn back in her New York hobnobbing days. But today, she didn't care because it was absolutely perfect for her party. She had kept it hidden in a garment bag at the back of her closet lest Nick get curious and start snooping around for it. Callie unzipped the bag and pulled out the champagne colored, low cut, above-the-knee dress that was positively dripping with sequins. She walked to her full-length mirror and held her dress in front of her. Even the slightest movement caused the sequins to shimmer and shine in myriad ways. It took her breath away, and she was certain it would do the same to Nick.

"That poor, poor man." Callie said aloud, grinning mischievously. "He won't even know what hit him."

As she slipped out of her clothes and into the dress, she went over her final checklist one last time. Thankfully, Lynette had had the foresight to plan a half-day, family friendly excursion for the O'Connors. Those several relatively quiet hours had given Callie just enough time to help get the caterers situated in the kitchen and the band set up in the backyard. She could hear the faint hum of their final sound check wafting in from her windows. While she had initially resisted the suggestion to outsource so much of the party, in retrospect, she was very glad she did. Tiny had gone home soon after breakfast was over, and Callie had given Alexis a much needed day off to spend with Zayne.

Callie managed to zip up the back of her dress with some amount of difficulty, wiggling and bending her arms at strange angles to reach the tiny little pull tab. Satisfied that she had zipped it all the way up, she turned to look at her reflection in the mirror.

A smile spread slowly across her face. "That poor, poor man," she repeated to herself.

She was about to touch up her make-up when there was a gentle knock on the door.

"Who is it?"

"It's me."

"I told you I'd meet you outside! I know what you're here for, but there's no time! Now go away!"

Callie could hear Nick chuckling faintly and could imagine him shaking his head.

"I'm not here for that. I promise. I forgot my watch."

"Oh," Callie mumbled, feeling a little bit disappointed. "Hold on, I'll get it for you."

As she walked towards her dresser to get Nick's watch, she heard him open the door and gasp.

"Nick! I told you to wait outside!"

"I thought you said come get it!" He started walking towards her, and his intentions were written all over his face.

"I said I'll get it! Do not come any closer."

"You look amazing," he said taking another couple of steps towards her.

"We're going to be late. Stop right where you are."

"I don't know what time it is. I don't have my watch," Nick said innocently and held out his unadorned left wrist as proof.

Callie took another step back and bumped up against her dresser. Her heart was pounding in her chest and a familiar warmth was spreading through her body.

Nick closed the distance between them and came to a stop just inches from her. "That dress is...." Without finishing his sentence, he let his gaze slowly travel down the length of her body. When his eyes finally met hers again, she could see his desire clearly reflected in them. "You look spectacular." As he said the words, he allowed his lips to brush against hers, and Callie leaned in for the kiss she knew he was going to give her.

But instead, Nick cleared his throat loudly and reached around her. "Here it is," he said picking up his watch and looking at it. "Would you look at the time? We'd better get going or we'll be late."

Nick turned and winked at her as he walked out of the room.

Callie stood open mouthed, watching his retreating back and knowing she had just been played. Well, she thought to herself, two can play this game. She went into her closet to pull out her secret weapon. A pair of sparkling high heeled strappy sandals that would drive Nick wild and make him forget about time altogether.

~ele~

"Speech, speech, speech!" The chanting grew louder as the well-fed and increasingly noisy crowd cheered Callie on. The lead singer of the band stepped aside with a flourish as if yielding the stage to a celebrity.

Callie smiled at him and stepped up to the microphone. "How about the music, huh? And the food?" The crowd erupted in applause on cue. Callie looked out at all of the smiling faces with immense happiness. Her party had gone exactly as she had planned. The caterers had outdone themselves with fan favorites and exceptional service. The bartenders had admirably kept up with the steady demand, and the band had chosen the perfect dinner music. Until that point, the party had felt like a lovely social affair, but Callie knew that as soon as she stepped away from the microphone, a full-on celebration would break out.

This was her moment to say all the things she wanted to say to the family and friends she had gathered around her. She cleared her throat and unfolded the piece of paper she had been holding in her hand.

"Thank you all so much for coming tonight. Many of you have traveled this journey with me from the very beginning." Callie looked around at all the familiar faces and paused when her eyes met Lynette's and Tiny's. Feeling the emotions starting to build up, Callie cleared her throat, determined to get through her speech before the tears started.

"So, this might sound familiar to you." She glanced down at the paper and realized she knew all the words by heart. Because she had written them from her heart.

"To you who have journeyed with me, to my family and friends,

To you who've learned my to-do lists never seem to end.

For your love and support, I thank you all,

For without you in my life, I was sure to fall.

The B&B is a roaring success, it was no small feat,

With joy and gratitude, my heart and soul are replete."

A hush had fallen over the crowd as Callie spoke. She looked around and saw that everyone was listening to her with rapt attention, and Tiny was wiping his eyes. A tear slowly trickled down her own cheek as she finished her speech.

"So, on this evening under the stars, this moment I'll seize,

To thank you all for my beautiful – *our* beautiful – Summer Breeze."

"Great party, Callie. Thank you so much for inviting me up for it. It was the perfect excuse to get away from my grandkids for a while."

Callie laughed in response to Mr. Blackhawk's obvious humor.

"Those kids never stop talking. And you know what? They don't laugh at my jokes! They say my jokes are worse than their dad's jokes. And that is no joke!"

Callie gave Mr. Blackhawk a hug. "I'm so happy you were able to make the trip up. It means so much to me to have you here. I would have been lost without your help those first few months."

"You won't hear me arguing with that. I remember the day you told us you were posting 'help wanted' posters on the old community bulletin board outside of Grace's grocery store.

You were clueless." Mr. Blackhawk chuckled at his own comment and then seemed to grow serious. He looked at The Summer Breeze and the still crowded tables scattered around the backyard and then back at Callie.

"But no one would say you're clueless now, Callie. You've done an amazing job. I'm proud of you."

Callie swallowed back the tears she'd been fighting all night. She gave Mr. Blackhawk another hug and whispered, "Thank you. You're welcomed here forever."

Mr. Blackhawk nodded his head with emotion, both of them knowing that he wouldn't be coming back. "That ought to give me enough time to come up with some more jokes. I'll be seeing you." He waved as he walked off towards his car.

Callie swallowed again, grateful that at least she wouldn't have to say goodbye to anyone else that night. The O'Connors would be at The Summer Breeze for another couple of days. She was dreading the moment when they left, but at least she knew for certain they'd be back the following year.

The whole evening had been an emotional walk down memory lane for Callie. Seeing everyone from the contractors who had first worked on the renovations, including Mr. Blake, to employees who had worked at The Summer Breeze when it had first opened, including Alicia who looked like she could have her baby at any moment.

Callie knew it was important to look towards the future, but this evening, she was grateful for having celebrated the past.

—ele—

Nick helped Callie with the zipper on the back of her dress and then walked to her dresser. He opened one of the drawers and pulled out what he knew were one of her favorite pair of pajamas, shapeless grey pants and a ratty old college t-shirt. He knew they gave her comfort, and he knew that's what she needed more than anything else after the emotional evening she'd had. He held them out to her, and she took them gratefully. He waited until she put them on, took her gently in his arms, and let her have her cry.

Secrets Revealed

Callie wandered into the kitchen a little later than she normally did. She had been expecting to find everyone busy at work on breakfast and was surprised to see only Alexis and Tiny sitting at the dining table. Tiny was rubbing the back of his neck, while Alexis was rubbing the bottom of her feet. Both of them looked as exhausted as Callie felt.

"Never again," Alexis looked up at Callie accusingly. "No more parties. No more bands. No more dancing in heels. I can barely walk."

Callie laughed and dragged herself towards the coffee maker. "What's your excuse, Tiny?"

"My 'excuse' is that the love of my life is a foot shorter than me and never wants to leave the dance floor! My shoulders are killing me."

"Fair enough. Have you had your coffee yet?"

Tiny and Alexis both nodded and then mumbled something that sounded like they wouldn't mind another cup. Callie got to work making coffee for everyone and trying to figure out what to serve her guests for breakfast when she spied two large boxes on the counter. They weren't the familiar pink boxes from Grace's bakery, and Callie wondered what was in them. Too tired to walk over and investigate, she asked Tiny.

"What's in the boxes?"

"The caterers left them. Apparently, your dad added an assortment of breakfast pastries, muffins, and bagels to our catering order thinking that we might be too tired to cook."

"He thought right," Callie said and smiled. She'd be sure to call him later in the day to thank him for his thoughtfulness. "The O'Connors haven't come down yet?"

"Who are you kidding? Nana and Papa were in here when I arrived. Sitting next to each other at the table and having tea. They just went for a little walk. Holding hands."

"Gotta love 'em."

Tiny nodded. "Speaking of love, you and Jorgan were inseparable last night. Especially certain parts of you when you were on the dance floor."

Alexis blushed and tried to deflect Tiny's comment. "We both enjoy dancing."

"Is that what we're calling it now?"

Alexis' blush deepened. "Was it that obvious?"

"It's been that obvious for weeks," Callie chimed in.

"I don't know what I'm thinking. It's just that Zayne is crazy about him, and Jorgan is so good with Zayne."

"Don't do that," Tiny admonished gently. "Zayne wasn't even there last night."

Alexis sighed. "It's just that I'm not sure if I'm ready for this. I haven't felt this way about a man in a long time. And the last time ended so very badly."

"But that time, you were younger and more impulsive. You ignored the behavior you had seen with your own eyes. You ignored your instincts. What do your instincts tell you about Jorgan?"

"That he's an open book, but also that he's almost too good to be true."

—ele—

Alexis pulled into one of the open spots on Main Street. She considered herself lucky to have found enough room to parallel park almost directly in front of Paolina's. Although Zayne was a huge fan of her cooking, on rare occasions he asked for food made by someone else, and today she had promised to pick up his favorite pizza from Paolina's.

She walked into the restaurant and deeply inhaled the aroma of freshly made pizza sauce and dough cooking in the wood fired oven. The sounds of people talking and laughing put a smile on her face, and she looked forward to going home to her own family. These days, there was plenty of talking and laughing around her dinner table, too. Her parents were incredibly proud of everything she had accomplished in such a short time. Alexis knew that without their support, all the hours they worked so hard and all the times they cared for Zayne, she would never have been able to cobble her life back together.

"Hey Alexis! The Zayne special, right?"

"Yup. Extra cheese, extra pineapple, and easy jalapenos. I don't know where he gets that flavor combination from."

"Don't knock it. We added it as a special the other day just to see how it would sell."

"And?" Alexis asked, laughing at hearing this news and knowing how excited Zayne would be when she told him that Paolina had served his favorite pizza as the daily special.

"Sold out."

"Are you kidding me?"

"Nope, something about the combination of salty, sweet, and spicy."

"What're you calling it?"

"Zayne's Special. Not very creative, but..." Paolina shrugged her shoulders.

"It's perfect."

"I figured you'd think so. Tell Zayne we said hello. And this pizza is on the house."

"Oh, no, I insist."

"I don't care whether you insist or not." Paolina handed the large pizza box across the counter to Alexis, who was about to retort when she saw the determined look on Paolina's face.

"Thank you."

Paolina winked at her and turned her attention to the next customer in line.

As Alexis walked to her car, she thought again about how much her life had changed since the first time she stepped foot inside Grace's bakery. The people of Seneca Springs had enveloped her and Zayne in a warm embrace. They had given her a leg to stand on, and a reason to hold her head up high. In the short time that she had been working for Callie and Grace, she had met many of the locals and she beamed with pride whenever they recognized her when she was out and about with Zayne. One look at his smile, and she knew that he felt that same pride.

Alexis placed the pizza box carefully on the roof of her car and unlocked her door. She threw her purse onto the floor and was about to place the pizza box on the passenger side seat when she heard an unfamiliar voice behind her.

"Alexis?"

Alexis turned around and smiled, "Yes?"

"I'm Evie, nice to meet you."

The name sounded vaguely familiar to Alexis, but she was fairly certain she had never seen this woman before.

"I'm sorry, do I know you?"

"No, but we have a lot of things in common."

"Oh?" Alexis balanced the warm pizza box and waited for Evie to explain.

"I used to work at The Summer Breeze. And, well," here, Evie paused and leaned conspiratorially towards Alexis. "We both have Jorgan in common," she whispered.

"Jorgan?" The word caught in Alexis' throat, and she felt a hollow pit forming in her stomach.

Evie raised her eyebrows in a way that left no room for doubt as to what she meant.

Alexis felt as if the breath had been knocked out of her, and she stood staring dumbly at the stranger standing before her. And then she remembered where she had heard the name before. Callie and Lynette had told her all about Evie.

"You know, I'm not sure if I'm supposed to tell you this or not, but I think we women need to stick together." Without waiting for a response, Evie continued. "I followed him one day. You know, after we...well, *after*. And when I saw where he went, I decided to do some digging around about him. See what I could find out. As it turns out, stupid Lynette's 'Norwegian eye candy' isn't just a visiting professor. He's also here on family business. His family's *hotel* business. His company is the one renovating that boutique hotel on the south end of the lake. I could be wrong, but I have a feeling he's been snooping around The Summer Breeze trying to find the best people to work at his hotel. I wouldn't be surprised if he tries to get you and that giant to go work for him. Maybe that's why he's been spending so much time with you. Trying to butter you up."

Alexis swallowed the self-doubt that was fighting to pour out of her eyes as tears. She did not want to cry in front of this woman who she held in such low regard. "You'll have to excuse me. The pizza is getting cold."

And with that, Alexis awkwardly got into her car and shut the door. But not before she saw the smug, satisfied look on Evie's face as she strutted away. Alexis' hands were shaking as she turned the key in the ignition. She put the car in reverse and looked in the rearview mirror to check for traffic. But as soon as she saw her reflection, the tears that had been threatening just moments earlier burst to the surface and ran down her face.

All she could think about was how she was going to tell Zayne that the man they had both been falling in love with was no longer going to be a part of their lives.

Tears streamed down Alexis' face as she pulled off Main Street and onto the highway. She felt a roller coaster of emotions surging through her and needed more than anything to vent her rage. Rage at Jorgan for his betrayal, and ultimately, rage at herself for having been such a fool. Again. Turning the volume way up on her radio, Alexis gave herself permission to scream at the top of her lungs. It was only when her throat started to burn that she stopped and wiped the tears from her eyes.

"Think, Alexis. Think!" She admonished herself and took a deep, quivering breath to try to calm herself down.

Alexis replayed her entire conversation with Evie over and over in her mind. And by the time she pulled into her driveway, she was convinced that what Evie had told her was the truth. There was no reason Alexis could think of for someone, even someone as awful as Evie seemed to be, to lie about something that could so easily be verified.

It was the repercussions of that truth that would be hardest to deal with, and she was not ready to deal with them yet. She wanted more than anything to protect Zayne for one more night. And so, before she got out of the car, she touched up her makeup in an attempt to hide the puffiness around her eyes. And before she walked through the door carrying the pizza box that would make her sweet boy so happy, she plastered a smile across her face.

As she sat across from Zayne at the dining table, Alexis listened to his stories with rapt attention, and let him eat as many pizza slices as he wanted. She evaded the concerned looks from her parents who seemed to know that something wasn't right. By the time she put Zayne to bed, Alexis was exhausted and desperately in need of some alone time.

Alexis went to her room and quietly closed the door. She sat down on her bed, buried her face in a pillow and gave in to the deluge of emotions she had been suppressing all evening. They cycled between anger at Jorgan for lying to her and were then immediately overshadowed by her disgust with herself. As a mother, she knew it was her responsibility to protect Zayne, and instead of cautiously and slowly letting Jorgan into her own life, she had opened the door wide, and let him into Zayne's, too.

After her conversation with Evie, Alexis had wanted more than anything to drive straight to Jorgan's house to face him in person, but she knew her family was waiting for her. Now that she was finally alone, she wondered if she should give in to the urge to confront him. But what would she say? What if he tried to deny it? What if he tried to convince her it was for the best? Would she believe him? Or worse, what if he dismissed her? Shut the proverbial door in her face? Could she take that kind of rejection again?

Alexis' phone buzzed, and she didn't have to look at the screen to know that it was Jorgan calling to say goodnight. After a moment of hesitation, Alexis answered. It was better to get it over and done with.

"How many slices did Zayne manage to eat?" Jorgan asked without greeting.

"Is it true?" Alexis asked.

"Huh? Your voice sounds funny. Are you okay?"

"Is it true that you're in the hotel business? That you bought a hotel to compete against Callie? And that you thought you could lure me away to come work for you?" Alexis asked, unsure of the answer she wanted to hear. If he admitted it, his betrayal would be confirmed. If he lied about it, she knew that she could never trust him again. As she spoke, Alexis could hear her voice rising, fuming.

And with a loud sob, she added "And is it true about you and Evie?"

And when there was no response on the other end, she knew she had her answer.

"Goodbye, Jorgan."

"Alexis, wait! It's not what you think! Let me explain!"

But in his initial silence, Alexis had heard all that she needed to know.

Nick sat on the sofa in Callie's private suite and waited patiently for her to do her nightly walkthrough before getting ready for bed. He had learned the hard way that it wasn't something she was willing to rush or take lightly. She was very particular about the health and safety of her guests and had a specific routine she followed every night. Out of curiosity, he had done the walkthrough with her several times and was impressed by how seriously she took her responsibility. But by the third night, when he dared to venture some suggestions to speed things up, he was relegated to waiting in her bedroom.

Nick checked his watch and tapped his foot. Then he stood up, walked around the room a couple of times, and sat back down. He was feeling abuzz with energy. He had worried he might feel nervous about the conversation he was about to have with Callie, but he felt surprisingly confident. The past week at The Summer Breeze had been exactly as the name of the B&B implied – as joyful and rejuvenating as a summer breeze. He realized, in retrospect, what a perfect name Callie had chosen.

While Nick waited for her, Callie took her time and checked all the kitchen appliances once and the gas stove, which she had an irrational fear that someone would leave on by mistake, twice for good measure. Then she checked all the first-floor doors and windows. Satisfied that everything was as it should be, she walked back to her bedroom looking forward to curling up with Nick and a good book by a new author Lynette had recommended to her.

She walked through the door of her suite and smiled at Nick. "Hey there. Sorry, that took longer than I expected. The lock on those French doors leading out to the front porch always gives me a hard time."

"You know, there are companies that specialize in adding these tiny little devices to all your doors and windows. And you can check to see if everything is closed from the comfort of your own bed."

"Ha. Ha. I told you I'm not installing a security system."

"I just think it would make life a little easier for you."

"And I think it would detract from the mood we're trying to create here."

"Fair enough." Nick yielded the point knowing that Callie was right. While it might make her nightly routine a little faster, it would be jarring if an alarm beeped every time someone opened a window. "Come sit down for a minute, I want to talk to you about something."

"Sounds serious," Callie said as she sat down on the sofa and turned to face him.

"It is. I got a call last week from your friend Jansen."

"Jansen Smith?"

Nick nodded and refrained from asking how many other Jansens Callie knew.

"I didn't know you two knew each other."

"We've never met," Nick confirmed. "Everything I know about him comes from what I see in the news and from what you've told me. So, I was surprised when my assistant put through a call from him."

"I was going to ask you how he got your cell phone number."

"He called the office, and when she heard who was calling, she immediately put the call through to me."

"When was this?"

"Last week. When I was wrapping up my project."

"Jansen called you last week and you're just now telling me about it?"

"Let me finish. When he called me, he told me that Tiny had mentioned to him in passing that he worked for Larrington Architecture and Design before he became the chef here. Told Jansen that you were dating the owner."

"'Dating the owner.' I like the way that sounds."

Nick laughed. "I haven't even gotten to the good part yet. Jansen said he's very familiar with the work we do and did some digging around with our other clients who are acquaintances of his to see what they thought of the company and about me personally. Apparently, he was happy with what he heard because he called to hire us for a project. A very large project."

Callie looked at Nick with mixed emotions. While she was thrilled for his success, she knew that a large project would mean more time apart. Not wanting to be selfish, she chose to lean into the happier aspects of his big news.

"That's amazing, Nick! Congratulations!"

"There's more. And this is the really good part. Do you know that mall that closed down? The one on the south end of the lake?"

Callie nodded, her curiosity piqued.

"Jansen just closed on the purchase of it and another property. He's converting all of it into a state-of-the-art cancer treatment facility. And remember that boutique hotel I was telling you about? He bought that too and is turning it into a short-term residential property that will be free for patients' families. It's all part of an expansion of the university campus project he's been working on in honor of his late wife."

Callie's eyes grew wide. She had put the new hotel out of her mind soon after Nick had first told her about it, knowing there was nothing she could do to stop it. "I always knew Jansen was generous, but this is incredible. This will be life-changing for so many. Think about all the people he'll be able to help and all the jobs he'll create."

Nick looked at Callie with a quizzical expression. "Callie, do you realize what this means?" Without waiting for an answer, he added, "This means I don't have to go back to New York.

This means I get to stay in Seneca Springs! No more visits relegated to weekends only!"

Callie quickly realized her faux pas. "Yes! And that, too!" Wanting to be helpful, she added, "We'll have to start looking around for a rental property for you."

Nick stared at her for a moment and then took a deep breath, knowing it was now or never. "I was thinking I could stay with you. Move in here."

"Stay with me?" Callie repeated dumbly. "Move in here?"

The prick of annoyance mixed with hurt started eating at Nick's confidence. "Yes. The project site is less than a thirty-minute drive. I thought it would be the perfect chance for us to live together before taking the next step."

As the full weight of what Nick was saying sank in, Callie could feel the old insecurities start to rise.

"This is where you say something," Nick prompted, hopefully adding, "Something like, 'That's a great idea!'"

"Oh, now you're going to tell me what to say?" Callie snapped. She regretted her tone immediately, but she couldn't help it. It just came out that way.

"What's that supposed to mean?"

"Nothing. Look, it's been a long day, can we talk about this in the morning?" Callie asked, desperate for a way out of a conversation she was not at all ready to have.

But Nick wasn't willing to let it go. He needed answers, he needed to know where things were heading between the two of them. Because so far, this conversation made him doubt that they were on the same path.

"No. I'm sorry. We need to talk about this now. I thought this would make you happy."

"Why would you think that? Did you even ask me?"

"I thought that's what I'm doing now. Asking you." Nick could feel his voice rising with frustration, and he was no longer willing to fight it. "What is it that you think we're doing here, Callie?"

"What?" Callie asked. She knew exactly what he meant, but she was desperate to buy some time. To avoid this conversation altogether.

"What exactly do you think we're doing here?" Nick repeated, his words clipped into a staccato beat.

"I don't know!" Callie felt her back up against an imaginary wall and struggled for an answer that would satisfy him. "Spending time together? Having fun?"

"'Spending time together? Having fun?' I could get that without having to drive this far! Are you kidding me?"

Callie shook her head, feeling the stinging of tears at the back of her eyes.

"I am in love with you. Do you understand that? And I am fairly certain you feel the same way about me. I'm ready to take the next step. To build a life with you. And I need to know that you want the same thing."

"If you know that I love you, why are you pressuring me for more right now? You know what I went through with David."

Hearing that name was the last straw for Nick, and all his attempts at controlling his emotions flew out the window. "Stop using him as an excuse! I'm sick of it. It was years ago, and you are a different person now. You use him as a wedge to maintain the distance between us, and you don't have to! I'm nothing like him, and if you don't know that about me by now, then maybe you never will."

Callie didn't know what to say. How could she convince Nick that she did know that about him, but she just needed some more time to...to what?

Misreading her silence, Nick stared at Callie for a moment before quietly standing up. When she still didn't say anything, didn't ask him to sit back down to keep talking, he went to her bedroom, grabbed his keys and wallet, and walked to the door.

"Where are you going?"

Still, he thought, she didn't ask him to stay. Maybe he had his answer after all. "I'll be by to get the rest of my things tomorrow."

Nick walked out the door and gently closed it behind him. Silence enveloped The Summer Breeze, and all that could be heard was the soft sobs of its owner.

Misery Loves Company

Tiny glanced at Callie as she sat at the kitchen table, staring blankly out the window. He knew she was hurting, even though she was going through all the motions of being a gracious hostess. She smiled and mingled with her guests, went over the financials with Lynette, and tended to her garden as she always did, but there was no real joy in it.

Ever the gentleman, Nick had always been restrained in sharing details about his relationship, even with his good friend. This time, though, he had called Tiny to let him know he and Callie were taking a break to figure some things out.

Tiny hadn't pried.

"I'm going to visit my family for a bit and then head back to New York for a couple of weeks. Then I'll be back in your area."

"Oh?" Tiny asked, surprised.

"Ironic, right? I already accepted a project for Jansen Smith, and I can't go back on my word now."

"A project in Seneca Springs?"

"Not exactly *in* Seneca Springs, but close enough. Not sure if the news is public yet, but he's purchased the old mall and a hotel down at the south end of Cayuga Lake. He's going to build it all out as a cancer treatment center and residential facility for families."

Tiny had let out a low whistle.

"Generous, I know."

Callie sighed, stood up from the table, and was about to wander out to the garden when she noticed Tiny staring at her with a concerned look.

"What?"

"Nothing. Just thinking."

"I'm fine. I told you," Callie snapped without meaning to.

Tiny held up his hands in a gesture of surrender. "Okay, okay."

"Look, I don't know what Nick told you, but maybe this is for the best."

"What is?" Alexis asked as she walked into the kitchen, catching the tail end of Callie's response.

Callie turned to look at Alexis and was about to respond when Alexis' appearance stopped the words from forming in her mouth. Her new sous chef, who had asked for a couple of days off because she hadn't been feeling well and then for a few more, looked like a faded version of her former self. She was still dressed in head-to-toe black with her hair pulled into a tight, high ponytail, but there were dark circles around her eyes. While she had the drawn expression of someone who had just gotten over the flu, there was something else there that Callie couldn't quite put her finger on. Something that made Callie want to offer her comfort.

Seeing the worried expression in Callie's eyes, Alexis repeated her question, trying to put off what she had come to do for just another few seconds. And to stave off the tears that were starting to threaten. "What's for the best?" she asked softly.

Callie didn't respond and was about to ask her own question, when Tiny asked tactlessly, "You okay, Alexis? You don't look so good."

Alexis let out a rueful sound that was half laugh, half sob. "You won't look so good either when I tell you what I have to say."

"Please don't tell me you're leaving!"

Alexis shook her head. "If I'm leaving, it won't be by my choice." She looked at her watch, knowing full well that she had given herself plenty of time before the lunch prep, and asked timidly, "Look, can we talk for a few minutes? Is Lynette around?"

Callie had watched their conversation like an onlooker at a tennis match, growing more nervous by the moment. The last thing she wanted, the last thing she could handle, was more upheaval in her life. Things at The Summer Breeze had been sailing along so smoothly for the past few months, and she wanted to keep it that way.

Wanting to take a moment to steady her nerves, she said, "Lynette's doing a walkthrough of the rooms. I'll go get her. Tiny, could you make some coffee for everyone?"

"It's okay, Tiny. You sit down, I'll make the coffee," Alexis said, desperate for something to do to calm her shaking hands.

Callie walked out of the kitchen and was about to make her way upstairs when Lynette came down.

"Lynette, got a minute?"

Lynette looked at her friend and hoped that she was finally ready to talk about whatever had happened between her and Nick. She had given her a wide berth the first few days after hearing from Tiny that Nick had left town, but she had been growing worried about Callie keeping things bottled up inside.

"Yup, I was about to send some follow up emails to guests, but it can wait." She followed Callie back to the kitchen and was surprised to see both Tiny and Alexis there.

"Alexis! We've missed you! Glad to see you're feeling be—" The words caught in her throat when she saw the expression on Alexis' face.

"It's a long story. Sit down, I've made coffee."

Lynette looked longingly at the cup. She had already had a cup of coffee that morning and wanted to heed her doctor's advice. "I'll pass, thanks."

Both Tiny and Alexis looked at her with surprise. Lynette, who never said no to a cup of hot coffee, hoped they wouldn't figure things out as quickly as Callie had. She wanted to share her good news with them, but she wanted to wait a few more weeks.

Thankfully, Callie came to her rescue. "Lynette and Mr. W are doing some sort of coffee detox." Callie sat down at the table and asked, "What did you want to talk to us about, Alexis?"

It took a few moments for everyone to settle in. Alexis served the coffee while Tiny loaded a plate with generous slices of banana bread he had made earlier that morning.

Even though Callie was going through a difficult time, and even though she knew that whatever Alexis wanted to talk about was going to be difficult to hear, she couldn't help but take a great deal of solace in sitting around the table with her friends.

"I'm grateful for all of you. I hope you know that," Callie said on a whim, meaning it with all her heart.

It was all Alexis needed to hear to break her resolve not to cry. First one tear, and then another dripped from her eyes, and she wiped them away. Something she had been doing a great deal of over the past few days.

"I need to tell you all something. It's bad. And I'm so sorry." She looked at the three faces staring back at her with concern, and knew it was best to keep things short and simple. "Jorgan and I broke up. But that's not why I'm this upset. I found out that it's his family business that bought the hotel down at the south end of the lake. They're renovating it, and they're going to try to steal your customers and employees, including Tiny and me."

Once the words were out of her mouth, Alexis somehow felt lighter and stronger at the same time. She had said what she had come to say, and now there was nothing more to do but deal with the consequences. She wiped her eyes for what she hoped would be the last time and took a defiant bite of her banana bread. "But I'm not going anywhere. And neither is Tiny."

As Alexis' words sunk in, Lynette felt vindicated to a degree. Unable to stop herself, she said, "I knew it! I knew all his questions weren't just innocent attempts at starting conversations! Tell me I didn't tell you so?"

Callie looked from Lynette to Alexis and then settled her gaze on Tiny. "Did Nick mention the new project he's going to be working on to you?"

Tiny nodded once, not quite sure he understood what was going on, as Lynette and Alexis looked on, confused by Callie's sudden change of subject.

Callie turned her attention back to Alexis. "Is that why you and Jorgan broke up? Did he tell you all of this?"

Alexis shook her head. She didn't want to bring up the one person she knew everyone at the table despised, but she felt she had no choice. "Evie told me."

"Evie!" Lynette exclaimed with ill-concealed spite. "You know her?"

"No. I've never met her before. But she stopped me on the street when I was coming out of Paolina's a few days ago and told me all of it. And when I confronted Jorgan, he didn't deny it."

Callie reached out and put her hand on Alexis'. "Listen, I think there's more to this story. I'm pretty sure that the hotel you're talking about is the same project that Nick is going to be working on. But it's not owned by Jorgan. At least not anymore. It's owned by Jansen Smith, and he's converting it and the old mall into some sort of treatment and residential facility for cancer patients and their families."

Alexis' eyes grew wide as Callie's words sunk in. "Are you sure?"

"I'm sure about the project that Nick and Jansen are involved with. And I'm fairly certain it's the only hotel down in that area that was up for sale a few months ago."

Without a word, Alexis turned and pulled her purse towards her. She rummaged inside for a second before pulling out a thick, letter sized envelope. "This is from Jorgan. It came in the mail yesterday, but I was too upset to open it." She took a deep breath, slid her finger under the flap and pulled out a thin stack of papers with a dollar bill attached to them by a paperclip. Stuck to the top of the first sheet was a yellow sticky note.

"'For you, my love.'" Alexis read the words out loud. "I don't understand. What is this? It looks like some sort of legal document."

Lynette leaned over and skimmed the first page. "It's some sort of purchase agreement. May I?"

Alexis handed the papers to Lynette and waited nervously as Lynette flipped through the pages. As she got to the end, she gasped aloud. "Oh my...."

"What? What is it?"

Lynette handed the papers back to Alexis. "That, dear girl, is the agreement Jansen signed when he purchased the hotel from Jorgan. And that," here Lynette paused and pointed at the dollar bill, "Is the price Jansen paid for it."

"What? When?" Alexis asked, her voice barely audible.

Lynette reached over, flipped the agreement to the last page, and pointed.

Alexis looked at the date and whispered, "Almost a month ago."

Alexis parked her car and walked as quickly as she could without breaking out into a full run towards the only building she knew on the university campus. Jorgan had brought her and Zayne to the campus once to satisfy her son's unquenchable curiosity about what college was like. The little boy had been in awe of the ivy-covered buildings and large lecture halls.

As she approached the multiple sets of double doors, one opened and a slow stream of students began pouring out. Alexis walked in through one of the other doors and against the flow of students exiting. The building housed one large auditorium, and Alexis weaved her way through the noisy crowd to one of the side entrances. As she stepped inside, she was surprised to see quite a few students still lingering, packing up their bags and a few clustered in a small group at the front of the auditorium, near the podium. What she couldn't see was the one person she was desperate to find.

And then, as if on cue, the group in the front began scattering, and Alexis caught a glimpse of Jorgan. He was packing up his papers into a leather satchel that she loved to tease him about, and Alexis' heart pounded violently in her chest. It hadn't occurred to her in her haste, that he may not want to see her. She was debating whether to leave and call him on the phone instead when he looked up and their eyes locked. Slowly, ever so slowly, a smile spread across his face. And the beating in Alexis's chest began to calm.

A student approached Jorgan to ask a question, and Jorgan tore his gaze from her reluctantly, holding up one finger as if asking her to wait.

Alexis stood awkwardly and impatiently at the top of the stairs, hoping more students wouldn't make her have to wait. Finally, Jorgan was free, and he took the steps two at a time until he was standing only a few inches away from her.

"You got my note?"

Alexis nodded.

"And you saw the date it was signed?"

"Yes."

Jorgan paused and took a deep breath. Looking steadily into Alexis' eyes, he added, "I want you to know, that nothing, *nothing,* ever happened between me and Evie. She wanted something more, tried for something more, but I wasn't interested. She is not my type."

"She's not?"

"No. You are."

"I am." Alexis said, knowing in her heart that Jorgan was telling her the truth.

"You're not mad at me anymore?" It was more a statement than a question.

"No."

Jorgan's smile grew even wider. "Can I come with you to pick up Zayne?"

Alexis nodded and whispered, "Yes."

Leaning towards her, he gave her a light peck on the cheek and took her hand in his as if nothing had happened. As they walked towards the auditorium door, he asked, "I know it's a school day, but I was thinking, maybe we can stop by Grace's and pick up some cupcakes for him."

Alexis looked around the room to make sure they were alone and let out the sob of emotion she had been holding in ever since she had parked her car. Pulling Jorgan back inside, she cupped his face in her hands, and kissed him, leaving absolutely no doubt how she felt about him.

Where There's Smoke...

Callie sat on the garden swing nestled in the trees at the back of her parents' backyard, swaying gently back and forth. The sun had just begun to set, and the breeze had cooled enough to make it light sweater weather. She tilted her head back, looked up at the canopy of leaves that were just starting to change colors, and breathed in deeply. This was easily one of her favorite spots in the world, filled with happy memories and laughter. She had been sitting in this exact place when the idea of opening The Summer Breeze had come to her.

Callie was glad she had let Lynette convince her to take a few days off. Things were running smoothly at the B&B thanks in large part to Alexis being back in the kitchen and Jorgan being back, on an almost daily basis, as a guest. Reservations for both The Summer Breeze and The Terrace were booked solid for the foreseeable future, and Callie knew she had left her business in the best of hands while she took some time for herself.

It had been almost three weeks since Nick had walked out of her life. For the first few miserable days, she had almost expected him to call her and pick up as if nothing had happened. But as the days ticked by, she began to realize that he wasn't going to take that first step. He had told her in the simplest terms how he felt about her and what he wanted. And she hadn't reciprocated any of it. After all this time together, hours spent talking and spending time with each other, laughing and loving, she still hadn't reciprocated any of it.

Callie felt as though she had been on a roller coaster ride of emotions ever since Nick had quietly closed the door behind him. At first, she had been angry with him for unexpectedly asking her to take the next step. Then she had started missing him, holding out hope that he would come back to her. And that feeling had slowly been replaced by a loneliness that had become all encompassing. He wasn't going to come back. And if she wanted to see him again, she was going to have to figure out how she truly felt about him and what she wanted in life, because she was going to need to take the first step. These questions weighed heavily on her, and even though she had tried to put on a happy face for the sake of her guests and her employees, her friends had seen right through it.

A gentle rustling in the leaves brought Callie back from her sad musings, and she squinted through the gathering darkness to see her sister walking towards her carrying a bottle of wine and two glasses. Callie smiled, happy for the company of her best friend.

"Did he go to sleep?"

"Nope. Staying awake is his new favorite activity. But Jack will figure it out. I'm guessing I'll find the two of them fast asleep in our bed when I go back inside." Nica handed a glass to Callie and poured the wine. She held the bottle out so that Callie could see the label. Even though it was too dark to read the writing, Callie recognized the logo immediately.

"Ooooh, my favorite! What's the occasion?"

Ignoring Callie's question, Nica said, "I had a feeling I'd find you out here. I opened the cork as soon as we were done with dinner and left the bottle on my counter to let it breathe while I tried to put your nephew down for bed."

Callie took a sip of the pinot noir and let the flavor settle in her mouth before she swallowed it. As the liquid flowed through her, she immediately felt the warmth of it. "It's perfect."

Nica smiled. She had known almost to the word what her sister's reaction would be. In so many ways, Callie was like an open book to her, but when it came to men, she was a complete mystery. Nica had never been able to understand how Callie had let things go so far with David. When she had first told Nica about him, Nica had gotten caught up in all the romance surrounding their budding relationship. But as time went by and Callie told her about some of the things that were happening between them and then making excuses for David's behavior, Nica had wondered why her sister chose to stay with him. When Callie had announced their engagement, Nica had been shocked. But it wasn't until she had noticed how withdrawn her sister had become that she had put her foot down and dragged her to the B&B on Long Island for an honest, heart to heart conversation.

And now, Nica was hoping to have another heart to heart with Callie, because her reaction to Nick walking out of her life was an even bigger mystery to Nica.

Nica took a big sip of her wine for courage and decided to dive in headfirst. "Have you spoken to Nick yet?"

"Nica…" Callie said with equal parts warning and fatigue. "Do we have to talk about this right now? It's such a beautiful night. Let's just enjoy life."

"Is that what you call what you're doing right now? 'Enjoying life?' Because it looks to me like you're *avoiding* life. You're just going through the motions."

Nica had hit the proverbial nail right on the head, and Callie sighed. "Look, I'm not going to deny that I miss him, but he made his choice."

"He made his choice. But did *you* make *your* choice?"

"That doesn't even make sense. Of course, I made my choice. Who else would have made it for me?"

"David."

"What? Don't be ridiculous. He wasn't even there."

"Look me right in the eye and tell me that you didn't bring up his name when you were talking to Nick."

Callie tried to meet her sister's steady gaze and then slowly looked down into her glass instead.

"I thought so."

"It's complicated. Okay?"

"It's only complicated because you're complicating it. From where I sit, it's all pretty straightforward. Nick is a great guy who is crazy about you. And more importantly, he is perfect for you."

"I feel like you're giving me a sales pitch," Callie snapped.

"A sales pitch? Tell me, Cal, what am I trying to sell you?"

"Nick."

"You're the dumbest smart person I know, you know that?"

"What's that supposed to mean?"

"I'm not trying to sell you on Nick. I'm trying to sell you on yourself! I don't care whether you stay with him or not. What I do care about is that you not sell yourself short. You're letting the one mistake you made with David cloud your judgement. Just because you didn't put an end to things with him earlier, doesn't mean you have to put an end to your happiness with Nick. Tell me something. Does he pick out your clothes for you? Decide what you're going to order at a restaurant? Plan out every moment of every day of your life?"

Callie stared into her wine glass and swirled it around.

"Does he listen to you? I mean really listen? Does he value your opinion? Take genuine joy in your accomplishments?"

Callie took a slow sip of her wine and finally met her sister's gaze.

"Maybe it's time you trust your own judgement. Because the facts are clearly in front of you. You made a mistake once, that doesn't mean you'll repeat it. You learned from it. Let go of the past, Callie. It's time."

Tears were beginning to pool in Callie's eyes, and she took a deep breath, knowing, just as she had known before, that her sister was right. She had let her fear cloud her ability to see Nick for what he was. She had known the answers to Nica's questions without even having to think about them. Nick was nothing like David. And she was nothing like she used to be.

"I miss him," Callie whispered.

Nica put her arm gently around her sister's shoulder. "So, what do you want to do?"

"Change everything."

Nica was about to ask Callie if she wanted to call Nick when the sound of a baby cooing could be heard nearby.

Callie looked up at Nica with the smile she always had ready for Aidan and quickly wiped her eyes.

"Are you kidding me?" Nica asked, chuckling, as Jack walked through the trees carrying his very happy, and very wide-awake baby.

"Hey, Li'l Bug!" Callie handed her wine glass to her sister and held her hands out to Aidan.

"I tried. I really did, but he has zero interest in sleeping."

As if on cue, Aidan let out a loud squeal.

Nica laughed and held her glass out to Jack who took it gratefully.

"I thought I heard Aidan's voice. Shouldn't you be asleep little man?"

Callie looked up to see her parents walking towards them. "We were sitting on the back porch when we saw Jack making his way out here. Okay if we join you?"

Callie laughed with pure joy and lifted her cherubic nephew into the air. "The more the merrier."

—⁓—

The family had stayed out late into the night enjoying one another's company, long after Aidan had finally fallen asleep nestled on Callie's shoulder. They were all just sitting down for breakfast when a persistent and unexpected knocking broke the sounds of their morning routine.

"Who could that be at this hour?"

"I'll get it." Callie picked up her coffee cup and rose from her chair. As she made her way to the front door, the knocking got louder, and turned into pounding. Without looking through the peep hole, Callie opened the door and was shocked to find Lynette standing on her front porch, looking exhausted and frantic.

"Lynette! What's happened? Are you okay? Is Mr. W okay?" Callie's heart was pounding in her chest.

"We're both fine, Callie," Mr. W said calmly as he came up the walkway and joined Lynette on the front porch. "But we need to talk to you. Can we come inside?"

Realizing she was blocking the doorway, Callie stepped aside, "Yes, yes, of course. Did you just drive here from Seneca Springs?"

Hearing the alarm in Callie's voice, her parents came into the hallway and were equally surprised at who they found standing with Callie.

"Lynette! James! Is everything okay?" Her father's tone mirrored Callie's.

Callie's mother, ever the voice of calm in their house, took in the situation and said, "Why don't we go into the kitchen and sit down. I'm sure Lynette and James must be tired from the drive."

Callie looked at Lynette, desperate for a clue. But Lynette wouldn't meet her gaze, and, Callie realized, hadn't said a word since she'd opened the door.

Quietly, they walked into the kitchen and took the open seats around the table. Callie helped her mom get extra coffee mugs and plates, and as everyone got settled, it was all Callie could do to stop from screaming in frustration.

"Callie, something's happened at the b and b," James said gently.

Callie's breath caught in her throat, and she felt a hollow pit form in her stomach.

Lynette who had been staring despondently at her plate without a sound, finally looked up at Callie. "I think I should be the one to tell her."

James put his arm around his wife to give her comfort and strength for what she was about to do.

Lynette took a deep breath and told Callie something she was completely unprepared to hear.

"Callie, there was a fire at The Summer Breeze."

...There's Fire

It had been a typically busy evening at The Summer Breeze, and Lynette had been ready to call it a night. Having the extra task of checking all the appliances, doors, and windows had added to her checklist, but she had been happy to do it since it meant allowing Callie some much needed time off. By the time she had gotten home and changed into her pajamas, she was ready to call it a night. Hoping she would be able to sleep through the night without having to get up to go to the bathroom or grab a snack, Lynette laid down. She fell asleep as soon as her head hit the pillow.

When Lynette opened her eyes, she knew from the darkened windows that she had hoped in vain for a full night of sleep. Sighing and knowing full well that she wouldn't be able to fall back asleep, she got up and shuffled to the bathroom. Once she was up and moving around, her stomach decided that it needed to be tended to and let out a low growl.

Quietly, so as not to wake her sleeping husband, Lynette made her way to the kitchen for her wee-hours-of-the-morning snack. She had been trying to find a balance between eating healthy and satisfying her cravings and had found that a banana and a glass of chocolate milk did the trick. She finished eating, let out an unladylike burp, and was about to go back to her bedroom when an eerie light filtering through her kitchen window caught her attention.

Lynette walked to the window for a closer look and stared in confusion for a moment. A flickering, yellowish light was just noticeable coming from across the street. She rested her forehead against the window and squinted to get a better look. It took a few seconds for realization to dawn that the light was coming from behind The Summer Breeze. With her heart beating faster, Lynette walked to the front door and stepped out onto her porch. The unmistakable smell of smoke was in the air.

Running into the house, she screamed for her husband to call 911.

By the time the fire department had shown up, the flames had intensified, and the sound of destruction had been added to the smell of smoke.

Callie, who had listened to Lynette's words with growing dread, took a deep, quivering breath. Her parents both had tears in their eyes, and Lynette was crying openly.

"Was anyone hurt?" Callie asked, her voice surprisingly calm.

"No. The smoke alarm must have gone off around the same time that we called 911. All the guests were outside by the time the first fire truck pulled up."

Callie nodded with immense relief. "Where are they now?"

"Those who live close enough decided to drive home. Tiny drove one couple to a motel and is helping to get them settled," James responded. Wanting to prepare Callie, he continued, "Callie, the damage is quite—"

But before he could finish, Callie, who was surprised to find herself dry-eyed and feeling very rational, cut him off. "The damage doesn't matter. As long as no one was hurt." She rose from the table and said, "I'm driving there now."

Her father and James both stood up. Knowing they were planning to come with her, Callie said with firm resolve, "Alone. Lynette, you and James rest up before the drive back. Get something to eat. Mom and Dad, please give me some time. Let Nica know what's happened, and then you can meet me in Seneca Springs. What's done is done and there's no point in rushing."

—⁓—

The drive to Seneca Springs went by faster than Callie had expected. She had left the radio off and focused on the road, the passing scenery, and her own, steady breathing. Every so often, a memory from the past year and a half popped unbidden into her mind, and Callie allowed it to stay for just a moment, savoring it before letting it go. The only thing she wanted to think about now was the future. With one intention resounding throughout her body. Rebuild. Restart. Renew.

Callie took the exit for Seneca Springs and drove the final few miles in a state of calm determination. Somehow, she knew she was strong enough to handle whatever she would find. With her family and her friends at her side, surrounded by her community of neighbors, she would be able to face anything.

As she pulled onto Oak Trail and drove towards her home, she saw several firefighters loading gear back onto their truck. She parked behind them and got out of her car. The sky was a clear blue, but the smell of smoke still lingered in the air.

"Excuse me? I'm Callie, I own The Summer Breeze. Do you know what happened here?" Callie called out.

The firefighter closest to her turned and removed her helmet. Her jacket was covered in wet ash, but her face looked unscathed. "You're the owner?" she asked, sounding surprised at how calm Callie appeared.

Callie nodded. "I was at my family's home about two hours away and drove here as soon as I heard the news."

The firefighter looked from Callie to her car and then back at Callie, clearly impressed that she had driven alone after receiving such upsetting news. Finally answering Callie's question, she said, "Thankfully no one was hurt, and we were able to put out the fire before it destroyed the entire house. Hold on a sec, let me get the chief for you, and he'll give you some more information."

Callie watched as the firefighter leaned towards her right shoulder, pushed a button on the small walkie-talkie mounted there, and mumbled a few words. "Please wait right here, he's just finishing up out back and will come talk to you."

Callie stood looking up the gentle incline at the house that had become her home. From the front, The Summer Breeze appeared unscathed, but Callie knew she should brace herself for what she would find in the back. A stream of muddy water was slowly rolling down the driveway, and Callie could see that the grass along one side of it was trampled, as though many people had rushed to one location simultaneously.

The door of a fire department pickup truck that had been parked in the driveway opened, and a man stepped out. Unlike the other firefighters, who were all dressed in heavy duty yellow gear and were covered with ash and water, this man wore dark blue field apparel with reflective stripes. Callie surmised that he was the fire chief and walked to the end of her driveway to meet with him. She took a deep breath and prepared herself for whatever was to come, knowing full well that the hardest news was already behind her.

"Callie Williams?" the man called out as he got closer.

Callie nodded and held out her hand. "Thank you for saving my home. I understand that the damage was contained to the back of the house, Chief...?" The sentence hung in the air as Callie waited for the man to give her his name.

Shaking her hand, he responded, "Bronson. Chief Bronson. You can thank that neighbor across the street from you. She's the one that called us and made sure we got here in time. You can also thank whoever is in charge of making sure the batteries in your smoke detectors are working because every single one of the alarms in the house went off in time to get everyone out safely."

Callie smiled. What Chief Bronson didn't know was that the person who saved her house and the person who saved all those lives was one and the same. Lynette.

"Can you tell me what happened?"

"We're still looking into that but hope to have some answers in a couple of hours."

"Was it an electrical fire?"

"Ma'am, I'd prefer not to speculate. Better to have all the facts."

"I understand. May I see the damage?"

Chief Bronson nodded somberly, and, catching the eye of the firefighter whom Callie had first spoken with, waved her over.

"We'll walk you up there. Please watch your step, lots of mud and water."

The female firefighter handed Callie a helmet she had brought along with her, and the threesome walked up the driveway in silence. The smell of smoke got thicker, and Callie noticed streaks of ash on the side of her home.

"The other building there," the Chief gestured at the spa, "wasn't damaged at all."

Callie looked up at the building that had once been her temporary home during the renovation and now hosted the spa and gym. It looked exactly as it did on every other day. Another thing to be grateful for, Callie thought to herself before turning and catching her first glimpse of the backyard. She raised her hand to her mouth in shock and took a deep, quivering breath.

The grass and vegetable beds were completely destroyed. Charred, trampled, and muddy. The outdoor dining tables and chairs were burned and almost unrecognizable in their blackened and disfigured state. The arched gates and fence were damaged and scorched but appeared to have held up better than the furniture.

Slowly, Callie turned to face the back of the house. The hot stinging of tears threatened her eyes, and she took another calming breath.

"Oh no...." she lamented in a quiet whisper.

Chief Bronson and the firefighter who had accompanied him prepared themselves to offer support in case Callie needed it.

"The restaurant is completely destroyed?" she asked rhetorically. It was clear that The Terrace had been devastated by the fire. Without waiting for an answer, she gathered her strength and continued, "What about the kitchen?"

"Partially damaged."

Those words were like music to Callie's ears.

"The wall of the kitchen adjoining the restaurant is ruined. Some damage to the ceiling and some of the cabinetry is burned. And it's a mess in there. Ash, water, mud everywhere. Mostly from us doing our job, but with time and elbow grease, it can be cleaned."

Callie let out a mirthless chuckle. "Those are two things I have in abundance now." She turned towards the chief and held out her hand first to him and then to the woman with him. "Thank you both so much for your hard work and service. I'd like to go see the damage inside with my own eyes. Alone, if I might?"

Chief Bronson looked first at his colleague, who shrugged her shoulders as if to say that it was his call, and then at Callie. "You'll be okay by yourself?"

Callie nodded once, and although the chief appeared concerned, he was convinced. "There's a plank of wood we laid over the stairs. You can use that to get inside. Put your helmet on and keep it on."

Callie took her hair out of its ponytail, slid the rubber band onto her wrist, and put on the helmet she had been carrying.

"We'll be finishing up out here if you need anything."

Turning towards her home, Callie took a deep breath and started making her way gingerly to what was left of the back steps leading up to the house. By the time she arrived at the sturdy looking plank laid atop the damaged stairs, her boots were covered in slick mud. Slowly and carefully, she placed one foot in front of the other and waited to get her balance before moving forward. A climb that normally took just seconds took several minutes as Callie struggled to stay upright.

Finally, she reached the top step where she found a series of planks laid in a haphazard path to the back door. Callie slowly made her way across the walkway and took in the devastation all around her. The Terrace was an almost unrecognizable heap of burned furniture and fixtures. Callie's heart broke as she wondered if she'd ever hear the happy sounds of her guests laughing and talking over a meal. Shaking her head to fight off the tears that were beginning to threaten again, Callie repeated her mantra. Rebuild. Restart. Renew.

The sound of scraping coming from inside the house brought Callie back to the present, and she stepped through the door into the kitchen, expecting to see some firefighters finishing up their work.

Surprised to see a man in civilian clothes working with a shovel and with his back turned to her, Callie called out, "Hello?" His boots and the bottoms of his jeans were covered in mud and ash and there were stains on his t-shirt as if he had been working on the site for some time.

The man appeared not to have heard her over the sound of the shovel scraping, and Callie said, a little louder, "Hello?"

The man turned around in alarm as he recognized the voice calling out to him. He looked at the woman standing in front of him and wondered for the millionth time how he could have ever walked out on her. Her clothes were starting to look almost as filthy as his, and she was wearing a firefighter's helmet that was too big for her head. And all Nick could think about was how much he loved her.

"Nick," Callie whispered, feeling a tear slowly trickle down her face.

"I came over as soon as I heard."

Callie nodded, not trusting her own voice to speak without breaking down in sobs.

"Listen to me. This can all be rebuilt. I can rebuild all of this for you. I *will* rebuild all of this for you."

In an instant, Callie's brain became convinced of what her heart had always known. She took off the hair rubber band she had placed on her wrist only a few moments earlier and walked towards Nick. As she closed the distance between them, the sting of tears was replaced by a feeling of serenity and contentment.

When she reached him, Callie slowly dropped to one knee and held out her hand. "Will you marry me?"

Nick looked at her in shock and reached down to help her up, trying to process her words. "The floor is filthy, what are you doing?"

"What I should have let you do a long time ago." Callie grabbed one of his hands and dangled the rubber band in front of him. "Well? Are you going to make me ask you again?"

"No."

"No, you don't want to marry me?"

"No," Nick laughed, fighting back tears of his own. "I mean no, I won't make you ask me again."

Callie took the rubber band off her wrist, twisted it in two, and slipped it around Nick's ring finger. She beamed up at him.

"Does this mean I can finally give you the ring that I've been hiding all this time?" Nick asked, the mischievousness Callie loved returning to his eyes.

"You already bought me a ring?" Callie laughed.

"What can I say? You've turned me into a planner. Come on, get up now. I want to kiss you."

Callie stood up, threw her arms around Nick's neck, wrapped her legs around his waist, and gave him exactly what he wanted.

"I love you, Nick."

"I'm just glad you finally realized it."

Callie laughed again as he gently placed her down. Looking around, Callie asked, "Can you really rebuild it?"

"Yes. Every last inch. Exactly how you want."

"You know what that means."

Nick nodded and smiled at her, "I do. Bring on all your lists. I'm ready."

A Gathering of Friends

With a curious combination of excitement at what lay ahead for them and sadness in the face of the devastation from the fire, Callie and Nick surveyed what remained of the kitchen, The Terrace, and the backyard. It would take months to rebuild, but Nick was insistent that if they set their minds to it, they could have everything done in less than six weeks. Just in time to celebrate Thanksgiving together, much as they had the year before. Callie, however, remembered how long the original renovation had taken and was doubtful they would get everything done before the winter freeze set in.

"Callie, just think about it. You already have experience with a major reno. You already know where to source everything and which vendors you prefer to work with." Nick counted off his points on his fingers. "Tiny and I have enough combined experience in design and construction to get you over the finish line. I'm assuming most of the tradespeople you worked with are still around. And you have your family and Lynette. What more could you want?"

"Maybe..." Callie said, allowing herself to feel hopeful for the first time. "Speaking of family, I wonder where they are."

"I'm sure they're on their way. Why don't we go over to Lynette's and get cleaned up, grab some coffee."

"She's probably not back yet either. If she were, she would have come straight here."

"You have an extra set of keys, right? I'm sure they wouldn't mind."

Callie was equally certain that Lynette would be fine with it, but she still wanted to check in. "I left my phone in the car. Let me give my parents a quick call and then talk to Lynette." She was about to head towards the back door, but seeing the planks, thought better of it. "Maybe we'll just go out the front."

Hand in hand, she and Nick walked down the hallway, thrilled to see that, apart from the smell of smoke, the rest of the home appeared to be unscathed. As they approached the door, the faint sounds of people talking outside drifted in.

"The firefighters are still here?" Callie asked Nick over her shoulder as she opened the front door.

"Take a look for yourself." Nick pointed towards the front yard, and Callie turned to look outside. It took a moment for the scene in front of her to sink in. The firetrucks and the firefighters were all gone. But there, under a myriad of mismatched pop-up canopies, was a large gathering of her friends and family setting up chairs around tables that were already piled high with food and beverages.

Callie slowly stepped onto the front porch and watched quietly as they all went about their business, not noticing that she had seen them. Her family must have just arrived. She saw Jack carrying Aiden and the diaper bag while Nica was trying to unfold the stroller. She saw Lynette and Mr. W, Tiny and Grace, Kirsten and Chad, Alexis, Zayne, and Jorgan. Several of the wait staff and the entire cleaning crew were also there, talking in small groups with looks of shock on their faces. Callie watched as Paolina and her husband pulled up and handed several large pizza boxes to Tiny before waving to everyone and driving off again.

Nick, sensing how emotional Callie must be feeling, came up behind her and put his arm around her shoulders. "Ready?"

Callie reached up and placed her hand on his. "Ready."

Callie looked at the faces gathered around her and thought for the hundredth time how fortunate she was. On one of the most difficult days of her life, she was surrounded by those who loved and supported her. Her heart overflowed as she listened to the conversation, and she felt joy as she heard the sounds of people laughing and talking over a meal. The sounds may not have been coming from The Terrace, but they were still alive and well at The Summer Breeze.

Callie was about to reach for another slice of pizza when she heard the low rumble of a car coming down the street. She turned to see Chief Bronson's truck pull up and park behind her parents' car. Not expecting to see him quite so soon, she wondered if he had some news to share. As she stood up from the table, Nick asked if she wanted him to join her.

"No, you keep eating. I'm sure it's just a formality. I'll be right back."

Callie crossed the yard and met Chief Bronson by his truck. "Chief, can I offer you something to eat?"

"Thanks, but I'm all set. Paolina dropped off a bunch of pizzas for us."

"That's very thoughtful of her."

"I see she's been by here, too," the Chief said gesturing towards the pile of empty boxes on one of the tables.

"She has. I'm grateful."

"I have some news for you, Callie," Chief Bronson said cutting to the chase, his tone suddenly serious. "Would you like to find somewhere to sit down?"

"No, that's okay. Please tell me what you've learned."

"There's no easy way for me to tell you this except to just come out and say it."

Callie's heart skipped a beat as she wondered what the Chief could possibly have to say that was any worse than what she had already heard that day.

"We are certain, given the unusual burn patterns, that this fire was set intentionally. That this is a case of arson."

—ele—

Nick had been watching from his chair as Callie had walked over to talk to Chief Bronson. For a few moments, the two had appeared to be making small talk, but when Callie had suddenly bent over with her hands on her knees, Nick knew he needed to be by her side.

"What happened?" he demanded as he approached the pair.

Callie straightened up and took a deep breath. "Chief Bronson says he knows what happened here. What caused the fire, Nick. He says it was arson. Someone did this to me. Intentionally." Callie's voice shook with emotion as she said the words.

Nick reached out and took Callie's hand in his and gave it a tight squeeze. "Based on what evidence, chief?"

Chief Bronson reached into his car and pulled out a tablet. He turned it on and appeared to be swiping through some photos before stopping on one and showing it to Callie and Nick.

"These are photos from the tables in the backyard." Chief Bronson swiped through three photos that all appeared to have a similar pattern on them which radiated out from the center. "These are three different tables. All with the same burn pattern. That was our first indication that something seemed amiss. Tell me, Callie, do you keep candles on the tables?"

"Yes, there's one at the center of each table," Callie said slowly, feeling the bile rising in her stomach again.

"We're fairly certain that someone lit the candles on these three tables and then tipped them over."

"Could it have been the wind?" Callie asked, desperate for another explanation. Desperate to escape the thought that someone would want to hurt her intentionally.

Chief Bronson shook his head. "We checked the weather records. The wind was too weak to knock anything over."

"Maybe someone forgot to snuff them out when we shut down the restaurant?" Nick asked, wanting the same thing Callie wanted.

"Given the amount of time between the restaurant closing and the 911 call coming in, that's unlikely. The fire would have been raging out of control by the time your neighbor noticed it. And there's a good chance someone could have been injured or worse. No, this is not a case of human error or bad weather. This is arson. And, I have to tell you, the chances of us ever finding the culprit are slim to none in these cases. The nature of the crime destroys much of the evidence." Chief Bronson turned off his tablet and continued, "Unless you have security cameras."

"No, I never installed them out of respect for my guests' privacy." Callie shook her head in frustration, wondering if she had made a mistake.

"Wait a second, Callie! Don't you still have the cameras we put in the backyard to find out what was happening to your garden? Maybe those captured something?"

"I haven't used them in a long time. I don't even know if they still work."

"Why wouldn't they? Do you still have the app on your phone?"

"I think so. But I haven't checked the videos in months."

"It doesn't matter, they're all saved to the cloud."

Callie pulled her phone out of her back pocket, punched in her password, and found the app tied to the security cameras. Navigating to the saved videos recorded from the motion activated cameras mounted at the back of the house, she clicked the play button for the only video that was time stamped from the wee hours of that morning.

"That video is from about thirty minutes before the 911 call came in," Chief Bronson said, his pulse quickening and his instincts abuzz.

The three of them hunched over Callie's phone screen and watched as the scene from the backyard sprung to life. Moonlight gave shape to the tables and chairs, but there was no other movement to be seen. Callie squinted at the screen until suddenly, the distinct shape of a human could be seen entering the gate and walking towards one of the tables. There was a brief flash, as if from a matchstick or a lighter, and then a slow fire spreading across one table and then another, but the person had his back to the camera, with a hood covering his head.

With their eyes glued to the screen, they watched as he turned towards the back of the house and made his way to the gate as the fire began to blaze behind him. Then, almost as if it was an afterthought, he took three steps backward and stopped at the third table. Lifting the candle in his hand, he flicked the lighter and lit the wick before smashing the candle against the table.

Callie gasped aloud while Nick stood with his mouth open in shock. The light from the candle had been just enough to make out who the person was. And it wasn't a *him*. It was a *her*. There could be no doubt that the person who had set the fire was Evie.

—⁘—

"Who would have thought that a day that started out like this one did would end in this way?" Nick asked as he raised his glass and looked around at all the familiar faces around him. The tables, still set up in the front yard, were now heaped with a wide assortment of dishes made that afternoon by Tiny and Alexis in Grace's bakery kitchen and by Callie and her family in Lynette's kitchen. Nick had been tasked with getting wine pairings from their favorite local vineyards, and Grace had secreted herself away to bake a special dessert she refused to reveal until the exact moment.

The only things different from the afternoon's gathering was that everyone was wearing clean clothes and the panoply of canopies had been taken down so that they could dine under the clear, moonlit sky.

"Here, here!" Said Jack, raising Aidan's milk bottle with one hand and his chubby little baby with the other. As if on cue, Aidan let out a loud, happy squeal.

"Speech, speech, speech!" Nica started chanting and the others quickly joined her, banging their hands against the tables.

Callie, utterly exhausted from the rollercoaster ride of emotions she had been on all day, shook her head with regret. From the moment Lynette had arrived on her parents' doorstep, Callie had been fighting off tears of one form or another. Tears of sorrow, tears of joy, tears of utter frustration. Sometimes she had won the battle, sometimes she had lost. From the shock of hearing the news of the fire, to her surprising calm as she had driven to Seneca Springs alone, repeating over and over in her mind that she would rebuild, restart, renew. Her surge of emotions at finding Nick already hard at work cleaning up after the fire and her overwhelming love for him. Her gratitude for all the love that had surrounded her that afternoon in the front yard. It had all carried her through the gut-wrenching news that someone had set the fire intentionally. And even though Evie had been adamant when she was arrested that she had never meant to cause so much damage, Callie knew it would be a long time, if ever, before she could forgive her.

Callie looked around the table at all those she loved so well and smiled. "Not this time, Nica. I'm exhausted."

Nick, who had been sitting next to Callie, stood up unexpectedly, and pushed his chair away from the table. Looking into Callie's eyes, he slowly removed the rubber band he had been wearing around his wrist all day.

"What are you do—" Callie began to ask.

But before she could finish, Nick got down on one knee. He reached into his pocket and pulled out a small box. Taking out the beautiful ring that sparkled like the stars high above, he put the box down on the table and gently took Callie's hand in his.

His words were drowned out by the screams and applause of those gathered around them. But Callie heard them in her heart and knew what her answer was. What her answer would always be.

The Summer Breeze Series by Shail Rajan

<u>The Summer Breeze: Bed & Breakfast</u>

(Book 1 in The Summer Breeze Series)

Callie Williams is in desperate need of a fresh start. But will leaving big city success for small town living bring her happiness or heartache?

Other Books by Shail Rajan

The Recipient

Small town mayor Kacie Nolan's life is thrown into turmoil by the mysterious arrival of Jett Vanders, a world-famous musician desperate to escape the limelight. When a celebrity stalker sets her daring plan into motion, a shocking revelation forces Kacie to decide whether she's willing to let go of the past and risk everything for the future.

About the Author

Shail is a women's fiction author whose heart-warming stories are character driven and embrace the role of family, friendships, and food in our everyday lives. Readers have described her books as feel-good reads with characters you'd want as friends and food you'd like to eat.

She was born in India, raised in beautiful Upstate NY, and is now settled in Northern California with her husband and three children.

For more information about Shail Rajan and her books, visit her website at www.shailrajan.com.

instagram.com/shailrajanauthor/

tiktok.com/@shailrajanauthor

Made in the USA
Las Vegas, NV
31 May 2023

72767766R00236